THE LONG LOST

A NOVEL BY TOM NIXON

Dedicated in memoriam to Robert Burke Kennedy,
who inspired me to write...and challenged me to write better.

We will never forget you.

CHAPTER 1

THE CALL

EVERYBODY knows someone like Joel Thomas.

I once heard someone describe him as the man who was friendly with everyone...but friends with no one. Which isn't exactly true. It's not that he was particularly at odds with any one person, or even that he was standoffish. It's just that, when it came to having meaningful, deep friendships or relationships, there was nobody you could point to and say, "Those two are very close."

But yet, there he was. Joel was at every party...every night out...every group outing. He seemed to like sports, the arts, movies, TV, pop culture. He knew a little bit about everything, so he always seemed to fit in, no matter what the occasion. But you were hard-pressed to say why, if asked.

Joel was married for a little more than 16 years to Mary, a woman he met in college during his study abroad program. They never had kids, but they did acquire the obligatory dog and 2,500-square-foot ranch in the suburbs. It was a normal life, if unspectacular. But that was Joel. Normal, sure. But unspectacular. A man that was seemingly liked by all...but loved by nobody in particular.

It would be a shock, then, when Joel suddenly disappeared.

I got the call around 7:30 that night. Mary seemed put off, but not frantic. I can't tell you why I remember her demeanor in that way, only that it seemed significant at the time. Was I expecting the reaction an actress might have on a bad primetime cop show? I don't know. Then again, Mary was Joel's mirror image in some ways, so a subdued (though, certainly distraught) state of mind wasn't entirely out of character. Still, it just seemed...*different.* Different than what I'd suspect, but I wasn't sure if it was meaningfully different, or just different.

And I can't claim to have been in the proper state of mind to be a judge of such things. Not that night. It's a strange thing when you get "the call." Or, in the movies, it's the knock on the door. If you've never been so unfortunate, you'll know when it happens. I'll never forget watching my dad get the call when grandpa died. I'd never seen my old man cry before. It was jarring. It was a shock, to be sure...but grandpa was 84, and with a history of heart problems.

There's a part of you that expects it...one that has been waiting for such a call. There's another part of you in paralyzing shock. And there's this weird part of you that starts immediately and reflexively having the sort of reaction others might expect you to have. Like *you're* the one on the TV show. Call it, macabre exhilaration? *This is happening. It's horrible. But it's excitement, in a sick sort of way.* All of those parts of you begin an instant quarrel inside of you for supremacy, and it's not until several hours, days or weeks later that reality sets in, and you hate yourself for feeling anything other than grief.

"Jason? Hi, it's Mary. Sorry for calling so late." A long, pregnant pause. "It's Joel."

Shit. Those words rang out like a shotgun in the open prairie air. It's Joel. Whatever came next, I knew it wasn't good. I immediately hunched down into a chair at the kitchen table. I'm not sure if I said anything, let out a self-defeated groan, or just waited in stunned silence for Mary to continue.

"It's Joel. He's not answering."

2

"Not answering what?" I asked, now grasping to a lifeline of hope. Maybe I got ahead of myself with needless worry.

"Anything," Mary responded, immediately sucking the wind out of my hopeful sails. "The phone, texts, the door. Normally I wouldn't worry. We sometimes go weeks — maybe months — without talking. In fact, we usually do."

"So what's the worry?"

Mary paused. I could tell there was a "next part" that she didn't want to get to. But she gave in. "It's not normal."

"What's not?" I pressed.

"To get something in the mail."

"What something? Something in the mail? From who? What was it?"

Another long pause.

"From Joel."

"Mary, what are you saying? What the hell happened? Spit it out."

Mary started slowly and softly, building both pace and volume as she continued. "I've been trying to get ahold of Joel for a few days. We got a strange tax thing in the mail, and it didn't seem to make any sense, so I scanned it over to Joel last week. Followed up with a phone call. No answer. Then the texts. Nothing."

"Yeah…" I needed her to get to the point.

"So I stopped by a couple days ago. No answer at his place. His car was there, though. I kinda poked around a bit, peeked in some windows...nothing. So I called the office. They said he's on vacation. So I started to calm down...didn't think much of it."

"There ya go," I reassured her. "He's probably just out of the country or something. No cell service, ignoring emails and stuff."

"That's what I thought," she continued. "Then I got this in the mail."

"What?"

"A note. In a box. Like a cardboard shipping box. It looked more like a parcel at first, with no return address. But it was light...like a letter, you know? I opened the box, and there was just this note in there."

"Yeah?"

"Jason. It was Joel's handwriting."

"So? What did it say?"

And now, the longest, most silent, pause.

"Mary, what did the letter say? Read it to me."

"Read it to you?"

"Yes! Read it to me!"

"No need to read it...I have it memorized...it was only two words."

"Mary, what the hell did the letter say?"

A shorter pause. A softer voice. A slower pace. Finally, Mary got to the point.

"Tell Jason."

CHAPTER 2

30 Years Ago

FALLING leaves fill the breezy air and adorn the grassy expanse between the time-frozen, almost aristocratic buildings of Manchester College. Slate cornerstones serve as the foundation to brick and stone monarchical facades bearing hand-blown stained glass windows.

Small pods of coeds collect on the quad, some failing to master hacky sack, others sharing a frisbee, still others sitting in deep discussion about politics, or religion, or philosophy. Wispy hints of cloves and cigarettes mask the sweeter aroma of marijuana, as the crisp air forestalls the pleasantness of the sun's cast. Traces of Dave Matthews Band and Blues Traveler compete in the distance to become the score.

A couple walks arm-in-arm, pretending to embrace for warmth, but rather stealing an opportunity for intimacy. They walk almost as one, in synchronized strides, her head periodically resting upon his shoulder, in the distance now...but approaching.

"Jason, who's that?" asks one of three friends gathered under a tree, watching the couple approach.

"That's Joel, dumbass."

"No shit, Sherlock. Who's that with him?"

"I don't know. Russell, do you recognize her?"

"Recognize her, yes. Know who she is, no. I've seen her on campus, though, I think."

She has long dark hair, straight, but with a wave that frames her face as the gentle breeze blows through it. She has a slender build — a petite frame that floats on the sidewalk beside him.

"She fine."

"Ziggy, she's not your type."

"What, white?"

"No. Fine."

The couple approaches. The three men stifle their giggles and whispered commentary as they walk up to greet them.

"Hey guys," the approaching man says.

"J-T. What up?"

"Not much," the man replies, as he looks fondly at his female companion. He has short, spiky blond hair that resembles that of a military man or fraternity brother. He dresses in khakis and loafers, with an argyle sweater vest atop a light blue button-down dress shirt. "Fellas," he continues, "this is Mary."

"Nice to meet you all," Mary demures.

"Good to meet you, Mary. But what are you doing with this guy?"

More adolescent — yet overtly and intentionally macho — giggling.

"I thought I told you guys about Mary," he says, then turning to her with a smile. "We met in Spain."

"Yeah, we know who 'Mary' is. We just didn't think she was real!"

"Hah. And now that we see her, we're still not so sure."

"Russell, enough. Cool, Joel." To Mary: "He's one of the good ones, Mary. Don't let him get away."

"Thanks, um…"

"Jason."

"Thanks, Jason."

"Hi, I'm Ziggy. Don't listen to Russ. He just don't get no chances to talk to pretty girls."

"Um —" Russell interrupts, then stands to extend a welcoming handshake to Mary. "Hi. It's Russell. Nice to meet you, Mary. And, yes...I do get to talk to pretty girls. Most of my friends are pretty girls."

"For real, Russ? C'mon, man."

"You guys. Can we just let the happy couple have a normal introduction?" Jason insists. "Sorry, Mary. You can tell we make a great first impression."

"No worries. Joel told me all about you guys."

"I didn't tell her any of the really bad stuff, guys," Joel chuckles. "Wouldn't want to break The Bro Code, right? But, yeah...she knows which ones of you to watch out for. Told her just enough to be forewarned."

"Well, sit down. Russ and Zig and I were just shooting the shit." Jason points down at a blanket lying on the grass, resisting the disturbance of the determined breeze. "We're hitting Manny's later for a pint, if you guys wanna join. Game's on."

"We might. Mary, you got a few minutes before class?"

"Yup."

"Cop a squat, then, guys."

"Um, thanks, gentlemen," Mary smirks shyly, using her hand to pull the hair from her face and secure it behind an ear, as she begins to take her place on the blanket. "Though I can tell I'm gonna regret this."

CHAPTER 3

FINDING THE WILL TO GO ON

"TELL Jason *what!?*"

"Hell if I know. That's why I'm calling *you*."

"Mary, hold on. Back up. What else was in the box?"

"I told you. Nothing. Just that note...with Joel's handwriting. *Tell Jason.*" She waited. "Jason, what is going on?"

"I have no idea."

We both sat in silence for what seemed like 30 seconds, but looking back, I bet it was no more than three. As we both raced through our thoughts looking for answers and explanations, but drawing no conclusions, it was as if we each knew the other one was frantically processing what little we knew. Neither of us wanted the other to hang up, but neither knew what to say.

I finally broke the silence. "Mary. Why don't I come over? We can try to get ahold of Joel. Or figure out what's going on. I'm sure it's nothing. Here, I'll text him...or call him. Just sit tight for a bit and I'll be by. You got anything going on right now?"

"Uh, not exactly," she replied, both crying and laughing at once.

"Okay, give me an hour," I said, in what I attempted to be the most reassuring voice I could muster. "I'll be by in an hour. By then, I will have talked to Joel, and we can figure out what the hell that mail is all about."

"Fine."

We both hung up. I don't think either of us said goodbye, as we were already both on to drawing the next conclusion, or piecing everything together.

When I arrived at Mary's house, I waited in the driveway until I could put myself in the proper state of presentment. I didn't want to freak her out by being just as worried as she was, but I didn't want to come across as overly dismissive, either. I'm not good at this sort of thing — being the rock. I hate to be the one who "keeps up appearances" in the face of drama, tragedy or loss. But I wasn't about to let Mary fall apart before all of the facts were in. I'd be strong. Comforting, for sure. But no condolences. Not yet. There was still reason to hope.

You hear plenty of stories about this person or that person "disappearing," only to come to find out they were just temporarily hiding. Maybe slinking off to some dark hole in the wall for a much-needed, if altogether ill-timed, stiff cold one to mask the discomforts of reality. Or the guy who coincidentally "disappears" to the same exact sleazy motel to which his mistress disappeared that very night. Or the desperate man, unemployed and out of options, who "disappears" to pick up a quick pack of smokes, only to re-emerge decades later when the children are grown.

But Joel wasn't much of a drinker. At least, I didn't know him to be. Not to excess, anyway. And he and Mary were no longer together, so no need to slink away with a floozy. But that's usually how these things end up. Just a big misunderstanding is all.

Of course, some people aren't so lucky. There was that story on the news about the teenager who they thought had run away, only to find out she was abducted at knifepoint and held captive in some creep's basement for three days. But those are more the exception than the rule. Those are the stories that make the evening news. The "hey, it turns out old Mister Mister was just getting a piece on the side" stories don't make headlines anymore.

Still, there was no reason to get ahead of ourselves. A divorced man with no close connections sometimes just goes missing every now and again. Not because of any foul play, but because fair's fair, and nobody's stopping him. I wanted Mary to hope for the best, despite what my worst fears were, so we were going with that line of hypothesis until something proved us wrong. He's just...away.

But there was that letter. What the hell was that? Who sends a letter in a shipping box? And why, of all people, would Joel send something like that to Mary? It made no sense. If it weren't for the fact that Mary said she'd recognized his handwriting, I'd think someone was just messing with her. Or, more to the point, *me*.

Tell Jason. Tell Jason *what?!* And who the hell *are* you?

"Hey, Jays," she welcomed me in her doorway as I waited on her front porch. "Come on in." Mary stepped aside to let me in.

"Mary. How ya holding up?"

"Um, fine. I guess. Did you hear from Joel?"

Dejectedly, "No. Sorry."

"Nothing?"

"I called his cellphone, but it went straight to voicemail. No rings, even. Sent him a text...nothing. I don't get it. Unless he really is out of town. Out of the country, maybe. Don't cellphones not work over there? In Europe, or wherever?"

"Well, they can work," Mary seemed to know. "But most people don't go through the trouble and expense of making them work. Especially if you're on vacation. Good excuse to disconnect from it all, you know?"

"Guess so," I conceded.

"You want a cup of coffee or something?"

"No, I'm fine."

We both looked around the living room before taking a seat — her on the loveseat, me in the recliner. We were searching more for words than next steps, as it had been a while.

"How ya been?" Small talk was not Mary's strong suit.

"Uh, good. Good, I guess. Can't complain."

"Anything new on the home front?"

"Nope. Nope. Still just me. Living the vaunted single life."

"I'm sorry."

"Don't be! No...I'm fine. I really don't mind it. I don't think I was ever the marrying type. Or the dating type...or..."

Mary quickly wanted to change the subject, or at least it seemed so. "What the hell is going on, Jason?" Things suddenly took on a serious, more urgent, tone once again.

"I have no idea, Mary."

"I just feel so hopeless!"

"I know. I know. But look, we don't know anything yet," I reminded her. "I'm sure there's nothing to all this. Or at least not as much to be worried about as we are. Why don't we just track down Joel and tell him he's gotta start responding to texts and phone calls from now on, so the rest of us don't lose our shit when we can't get ahold of him?"

"You're right. You're right...you're right...you're right," Mary repeated in earnest, bucking up like a true camper. She brushed off her lap — literally, but perhaps symbolically, more to the point — and stood up. "What do we do?"

"Let's head over to his house," I offered as a potential first step. "Maybe he's there. Knowing Joel, he's locked in the basement in the throes of some epic stint on Call of Duty with a bunch of other grown nerds wearing nothing but boxer briefs and headsets."

Mary chuckled as she sniffed in the faint beginnings of tears.

"Hey, I still have a key," I pointed out, "from when I was dog-sitting Max. If he doesn't answer, we'll just let ourselves in and see what's going on. Sound good?"

"Yep," she answered, now showing the slightest hint of hope since the first moment we'd reconnected. "Sounds like a plan. I'll grab my stuff."

As Mary collected her things, I ambled around the living room, taking in the scenery. Mary had carved out a pretty decent life for herself. She kept the 2,500-square-foot ranch in the suburbs, and adorned it with what seemed like the entire Pottery Barn catalogue. The mantle still featured on display numerous photos of her and Joel, taken when they were still the happy couple that just about anyone in their right mind would envy. That was a long time ago. She kept the house...and the memories. Joel got the obligatory dog.

"I'm ready," she announced, as she returned to the living room with her purse and coat.

"Let's go."

The drive over to Joel's place was more silent than what you'd might expect. There was a lot of catching up to do, but right then seemed neither the time nor the place. Perhaps we were both still frantically searching our vacuous mind holes for some answers, even knowing that none would be forthcoming. There was just too much not to know. Nothing made sense.

We slinked up the driveway to approach his house as though we were two private detectives looking to make our mark. Why the surreptitiousness, I can't tell you. We certainly weren't sneaking up on anybody. But I think neither one of us was overly eager to see what was inside.

We banged on the front door in unison, intermittently ringing the doorbell like we were playing the "challenging stage" in Galaga. "Joel! Open up! It's Jason and Mary!"

No answer.

"Joel!" I repeated, a little louder this time.

"Try his phone again," Mary directed.

Instead of heeding her request, I pulled out Joel's key from the back pocket of my jeans and ceremonially presented it to her. "Let's just go in," I said with confidence.

I unlocked the front door and opened it slowly, not sure what I was afraid of. Mary slowly stepped in beside me.

"Joel?" she beckoned. "Joel, you here?"

No answer.

Mary stopped. "Jason. Where's Max?"

"What?"

"Shouldn't Max be attacking us by now? We're intruders, aren't we?"

I paused. If I was hunching over as I crept in, I stood straight up, I'm sure. I turned to Mary. Again...looks like I have the unfortunate burden of being the rock.

"He didn't tell you?" I innocently asked her.

"Tell me what?"

"Max passed away," I solemnly responded.

"Oh, God, no. When? Why?"

"I just assumed you knew. I'm so sorry."

"God damn it." And now the tears would come.

"I'm so sorry, Mary."

"What the fuck, Joel?!" Mary scolded, into the open air.

"Mary. I'm sorry. I guess I thought he would've told you. You, of all people."

"When? How?" she asked, with a more steely resolve, perhaps.

"I'm not sure when, exactly. Within the last year. Maybe the last few months."

No answer.

"He'd been sick," I cautiously continued. "They weren't sure if it was cancer or what. He just got real sick, real fast. And he didn't make it. I'm so sorry."

No answer.

"Sorry you have to find out like this. Now. Of all times."

She let out one final sigh. Well, final for now, it would appear.

There were more pressing matters at hand. Even more pressing than losing the dog you raised as a puppy, to a man you fell out of love with, and eventually, now, to dog heaven...without so much as a text or a phone call.

"It's okay," she exhaled, summoning the fortitude to put it past her, if only for the moment. She looked again around the emptiness of Joel's house, calling out once again, "Joel?"

No answer. Only more silence.

A thought occurred to me. Reflexively, "I'll check the basement," I said.

That was no preferred detail, I can assure you. In my experience, the basement is where bad things turn up, if bad things are going to turn up. But I was the man. (Is that still a thing?) And if anyone was going to go down there, it was going to be me. It was my fleeting thought, however morbid it might have been, and I was going to be the one to volunteer to investigate it — not Mary. I walked over, flipped on the lights, and made my way intrepidly down the stairway, firmly grasping the handrail, more for emotional support than physical.

I didn't get halfway down the stairs before I was mercifully relieved of basement duty, if only for the moment.

"Jason? Jason?" Mary called anxiously from upstairs. "Come here. You're gonna wanna see this."

I stopped in my tracks and started hurriedly back up the basement stairs. "What is it?" I hollered back to her as I rejoined her in the living room. There I found Mary standing straight up in awed silence, staring at an illuminated computer screen that sit atop a work desk in the corner of the room.

I hesitantly inquired, "What is it, Mary?"

"This."

She pointed at the screen as I walked over see to what had caught her attention and despair. It was a mostly blank page — a document

— with only four words splashed across what looked to be the title page.

Last Will and Testament.

"Mary, what the hell is this?" I begged of her in both disbelief and confusion. "Was something going on? Did you know he was doing this?"

No answer.

"Mary," I repeated, attempting to awake her from her stunned paralysis. "Mary. What was that 'tax thing' you got in the mail? What did you scan over to Joel the other day? Mary…"

No answer.

CHAPTER 4

30 Years Ago

A GIRL wearing an intentionally ironic beret sits on a barstool in the corner of Manny's, playing old Simon and Garfunkel cover songs on a road-weary acoustic guitar, her set intermixed with Indigo Girls and Melissa Etheridge. The football game monopolizes the screens of most of the tavern's TVs, but only a few at the bar are paying any real close attention. Cigarette smoke and the haughty aroma of stale spilled beer seeping into old mahogany benches do their best to defeat the olfactory offense of incense-infused colognes and perfumes.

A young black man of athletic build and a well-dressed, well-coiffed male companion spread themselves amply across one side of a booth, opposite a young couple with arms entwined sitting next to another male coed. Half empty mason jars of imported drafts that litter the table appear too flat to fully enjoy, but "A dollar draft is a dollar draft," this proverbial third wheel observes, as he returns his emptying mug to the table.

"Ziggy," she says, with a reflective, observant tone. "That's a cool name. Your dad a Bob Marley fan?"

"No," he coldly retorts, maintaining his eye contact only upon the beer in front of him. "Asshole, actually."

"Sorry."

"Don't be."

"Ziggy's mom liked the old comic strip," her escort clarifies for his girlfriend. "Thought it was funny, right Zig?"

"Guess so," Ziggy assents, pulling out his wallet to display for

Mary his ID, suspiciously counterfeited to grant him access to engage in some illegal under-aged drinking at the college bars that pretend to serve only patrons of age. The name on the ID reads *Ziggy Aurelius Walton.*

"Um," Third Wheel interjects, "Ziggy doesn't like to talk about home, Mary. He doesn't mean to be rude."

"I get it, Jason," she absolves. "Neither do I."

"Everyone's got their own crosses to bear, right fellas?" Her boyfriend attempts to re-lighten the mood in jest, "Mary lived in Detroit for a bit."

"Ouch," the well-dressed young man seated next to Ziggy sarcastically intones. "Well, Ziggy's got home. Mary's got Detroit. Jason's got...whatever, and Joel's got...absolutely nothing, actually."

"What about you, Russell?" Joel shoots back defensively. "You think your backstory's so damn interesting?"

"Hardly. Dad and I...let's just say Dad and I never saw eye-to-eye, if that's a thing."

Ziggy scoffs. "Bullshit."

"Beg your pardon, Ziggy?" Russell responds, obviously a bit taken aback at the accusatory tone of the expletive-laden commentary.

"Bullshit," he repeats. "White rich guy grows up in Happytown and Daddy buys him the wrong-colored Porsche? That about it, Russ?"

They laugh. Uncomfortably. To ease the attention, it would appear.

"Whatever, Zig. Not all of us grew up as the villain in a made-for-TV after-school special."

"Russ. What the hell you know about my after-school special?"

"Okay, boys. Let's not go there," Mary intercedes, attempting to restore the levity. "Sorry I brought it up."

They drink. Nervously. Joel finishes first and beckons to the bartender for another round.

"We cool," Ziggy insists, trying to ease her obvious discomfort. "Just messing around. Russ and I are boys."

"You all meet at Manchester?" she casually inquires, seizing the opportunity to make lighter conversation.

"We did. What about you and Joel? How did you kids meet?"

"Well, as you know, I met Mary in Spain, of all places," Joel speaks up for her. "Here we are, sitting for half of a semester in the same class, and we never even say so much as *hi* to one another. Then we go to Spain for six weeks, and before you know it, we're a...*thing*, I guess. Right, honey?"

"Crazy, right?"

"Crazy little thing called love!" Russell jokes.

"Russell, really?"

The second round is delivered by the overly pierced bartender baring more midriff than is appropriate for early afternoon.

"Well, Joel really has told me a lot about you boys."

"Ain't much to know about some of us. Nothing good, anyhow."

"You'll have to forgive Ziggy." Russell places a hand playfully on Ziggy's forearm. "He can be a drama queen sometimes."

"Russ, enough, okay?" Jason scolds.

"No apology necessary, Ziggy," Mary preemptively responds to Russell.

"Wasn't giving one."

Awkward silence.

"So. Mary's from Hawthorne" Joel blurts out, quickly changing the subject. "Cross-town rivals, huh, Jason?"

"Yup. Small world!"

"Where are you from, Jason?" she asks.

"Calhoune. Same as Joel."

"Oh my God, no way! We kicked your asses at homecoming last year!"

"Don't rub it in."

"Sorry."

"Hey! I gotta use the facilities," Jason announces. "I think I've rented the first round long enough. Who's with me? Russ?"

"Yup. I'll head in with you. Anyone else? We'll make it a gentlemen's soiree...?"

"You guys go ahead," Ziggy declines. "I'll make sure Joel and Mary don't do no PDA."

"K, Zig."

Russell and Jason head to the back of the pub, past the faux Indigo Girl and beyond the un-played dart boards.

Mary does her best to break the silence with small talk. "So..."

"So."

"Joel tells me you guys rushed the same frat."

"We did. We did."

"And you both got...*uninvited*."

"We did. I thought Joel might get in. But not me."

"Ziggy, come on," Joel admonishes.

"What? You think that rich-boy frat wanna let everyone in? Some people just ain't the right mix, ya know?"

"Well. Their loss, Ziggy. You too, Joel."

One more collective sip of beer. To fill the silence, if nothing else.

"And, sorry your dad was an asshole," she appends.

"Not your fault. Not my problem."

"Still. That sucks."

"Not no more."

"Ziggy doesn't talk much about his parents, Mary. It's the only time he's like this, to be honest. Right, Zig?"

"Whatever."

"Well, we all have our stories growing up. They don't all have happy endings."

"They all have this?" Ziggy pulls back the sleeve of his flannel shirt. Mary is taken by surprise at the sight of it. Joel looks away, as if he's seen it all too many times before. Cigarette burns pepper Ziggy's disclothed arm from the wrist to the elbow.

"Oh, God. Did he do that?" she asks, a hand placed gently over her trembling mouth.

"Wutchoo think?"

"Asshole!" Mary recites for emphasis. She forces herself to take another awkward sip of beer. "So, I'm guessing you're not exactly on speaking terms with your dad anymore, huh?"

"He ain't on speaking terms with nobody."

"What do you mean?"

Joel gets up. He crawls over Mary to exit the booth. "I'm gonna go join the fellas for that pissing soiree."

Ziggy looks down at his near-empty beer and continues stoically, "I mean, he ain't in a very talkative mood no more."

"Oh no?"

He takes another sip of beer — more of a purposeful gulp this time — and turns to stare out the window to his left. "Let's just say the Manchester dorms ain't the first small room I had to lay my head down in for a few months."

CHAPTER 5

GET TO WORK

THE CAR ride the following morning was a bit tense. The search at Joel's house didn't turn up much...certainly not Joel. There was, of course, the creepiness of seeing a draft of Joel's "Last Will and Testament" on his computer. But aside from being hair-raisingly ill-timed, there was nothing that peculiar about what was in it. There was no suicide note, for example. Nothing to portend a man's imminent demise, or his fear thereof. It all seemed rather typical — mechanical, even. It felt like Joel, in other words.

It must have been strange for Mary to read through it. Joel was leaving everything to her. (Who else was there?) True, there wasn't a whole lot to leave: the house (or rather, the mortgage), his savings, the 401(k). As she scanned over the document in haste, mouth agape, I detected what appeared to be a slightly guilty conscience washing across Mary's face. Did she feel bad that Joel would leave everything to her, having never found another to be his rightful heir? It wasn't her fault, I tried to assure her. You can't feel guilty that your ex-husband hadn't moved on. Nor can you take blame for the fact that he felt the need to suddenly get his affairs in order at the age of 47. That, after all, was the wise thing to do, regardless of one's life station. And Joel was all about getting the practical done. Everything in its place, nice and tidy like. But when your ex-husband hasn't been heard from, and you have only one cryptic two-word note to go on, then suddenly you see your name in the missing man's will, I guess it can be off-putting, to say the least.

"I thought a lot about Max last night," Mary started, finally breaking a good two miles' worth of silence. "Is that weird?"

"No," I replied in a comforting, reassuring tone.

"Seems weird to me."

"Weird? Weird how?"

She paused for a moment. "Well, here we are trying to track down Joel, after who-knows-what has happened to him, and all I can think about is missing my dead dog. Not Joel. Max." She sat there in silence contemplating what she had just admitted to. "I dunno. Just seems weird."

"Yup. I guess." I didn't really know what else to say.

"Can I ask you a question, and you'll promise not to get upset?"

"Sure, Mary. Shoot."

"At what point do we call the police?"

"The police?" I shot back, with perhaps a hint of intentional indignation. "Why would we call the police?"

"Jason, Joel's been missing for God-knows-how-long. At what point does this become a missing person case? Or worse. An investigation? On TV they always say you have to wait 24 hours before reporting a missing person. Well, I'm sure it's been at least 24 hours."

"Hold on, Mary." I tried to talk more slowly, if only to inject some calm, measured tranquility into the conversation. "We still don't know that Joel's missing. Or anything, really. All we know is that he hasn't responded to our texts and phone calls. He's not home, but his car is there. And you said yourself that work told you he's on vacation."

"I know, I know," she acquiesced.

"So," I started to put the pieces together with a reasoned, measured approach. "Joel takes an Uber to the airport, flies to Spain

— which we all know he fell in love with...right about the time he fell in love with you, I might add — and he goes away for a much-needed, soul-cleansing, peaceful vacation. We'll get ahold of him as soon as he gets back into the country. Or when he pays the data roaming fee to get reconnected to the real world on vacation. Knowing Joel, that'll be any minute, as you and I both know he can't go more than a day knowing he might be missing out on something."

"You're right," she conceded, seemingly confidently, to my surprise somewhat. I legitimately thought she was beginning to forfeit panic for reason, if only incrementally.

"So. Let's see what work says," I continued. "Maybe they know where he was going...when he'll be back...et cetera. 'Kay?"

"You're right."

The rest of the 40-minute drive downtown to Joel's office featured a tennis match of intermittent silence and small talk. And the small talk was *extremely* small. Weather. Comments on the passing scenery. How's work. (As if Mary even knew what I did for work. Didn't matter. Not sure she even cared at that point. Just wanted to periodically break the silence. And make sure that whatever did break the silence was going to remain breezy and inconsequential.)

All I knew was that Joel worked at a company called Pennico. Damned if I knew what they even did — or what Joel did, for that matter. I knew back in the day it was pharmaceuticals, that whole ordeal with Ziggy and all. But what now, who knows. I drove him to work for a week when he had car problems about a year prior, so I knew all of the "secret shortcuts," as Joel called them, to evade rush hour traffic. We finally pulled into their parking structure in about 38 minutes' time. I remember this because Joel would always clock me against his "personal best" — 32 minutes, door to door — so I had been conditioned to keep note of the travel time.

We exited the elevator and approached the large glass doors leading to Pennico's lobby. Noting the keycard entry requirement, I walked over to the wall just beside the double-glass-doors and pressed the button on the intercom. I could see through the glass doors that the receptionist was picking up a headset to respond.

"Welcome to Pennico. State your name and business, please."

"Hi. It's Jason — um, a friend of Joel's. Joel Thomas. Do you mind if we come in? We'd like to talk to his boss...or somebody."

"Mr. Thomas is not here today," the receptionist responded, matter-of-factly.

"Oh, we know," Mary jumped in. "I'm his wife. His...*ex*-wife. We were just hoping we could ask about where Joel went. Or how long he's gone for."

The receptionist interrupted. "Please hold a moment."

We could see the receptionist had continued talking into the headset, but not to us. There was perhaps a 60-second conversation going on, before finally...

"Come on in and have a seat. Mr. Pennington will see you."

Click. The magnets to the glass door locks had been released, and we were in.

Mary and I sat in the magnificently appointed front lobby, each in our own handcrafted leather lounger, me leafing through a three-month-old copy of *Sports Illustrated*, and Mary apparently taking a *Cosmo* quiz.

Before too long, a besuited, portly man with gray remnants of what was once a young man's hairline, accentuated with an almost-matching salt-and-pepper mustache, entered the lobby to greet us.

"Mary." Mr. Pennington approached Mary to shake her hand, feigning to have recognized her. Turning to me, "And...Jason, is it?"

"Yes, nice to meet you, sir."

"Likewise. How can I help you both?"

"It's Joel," Mary started, voice trembling ever so slightly. "We're trying to get ahold of him."

Joel's boss stared blankly at Mary for a moment, then turned his head to meet my eye. "Why don't we go make ourselves comfortable?"

We retired to what I can only describe as a "power-play room." To people who are used to such things, I'm sure they just call it "the conference room," but it was clear to me that this is where influential people meet to influence one another. The artwork on the walls appeared to be artists' originals. The conference table would seat 18 to 20, comfortably. And if they weren't comfortable enough, the leather-lined chairs would seal the deal.

Mr. Pennington got right down to business as we took our seats. "So, what's this all about?"

I decided to take the floor, so Mary wouldn't. "We're just trying to get ahold of Joel is all. He's not responding to phone calls or texts, and we know he's not home, so..."

"Yup. Been on vacation," Mr. Pennington confirmed.

"That's it," Mary chimed in. "Did he say where he was going? Or for how long?"

"Not to me. But that's not my thing. I'm sure HR knows when he'll be back. You can ask them. Or I can ask around...see who Joel might've told where he's off to."

"That would be great," I said. But I had a request...one that I didn't expect to be honored...but what the hell: "Mr. Pennington, would you mind if Mary and I just took a look around Joel's office?" He stared back at me, exhibiting both skepticism and authority at once. "Maybe he left a brochure or something," I went on, "you know, like, for a cruise or something? That might help."

After contemplating it for what seemed like an eternity, Mr. Pennington replied, "Sure. I don't see why not. I'll lead the way."

Mary and I looked at each other both surprised and relieved...and perhaps a bit anxious. Maybe there *was* some sort of clue in Joel's office. Pennington led us to the door of Joel's office, then stepped aside and extended his arm inward. "Be my guest."

Mary and I both entered slowly, and if I can't tell you why, I'm sure she couldn't either. Maybe it was the surreal nature of having just searched a missing man's empty house, then searching his deserted office the following morning, that had us both feeling out of place and out of sorts. It was becoming very cloak-and-dagger, and neither one of us wanted to be the one who discovered something Earth-shattering.

To both of our relief, Joel's office looked exactly as you'd expect the office of a mid-manager at a large, faceless corporation to look like. Unremarkable. Joel's desk was neat and orderly. No surprise there. There wasn't a ton of clutter, and you could sense that whatever it was that kept Joel busy during the day, he was on top of it...maybe even one step ahead of it. Whatever *it* was.

The one exception was his computer. Lining the edges of his computer were strategically placed yellow sticky notes. A lot of them. Each one bore a simple, yet direct, reminder on it. *Get back to Waxco Monday. Call Traci. Email proposal. Close out clinical.* They framed Joel's now dormant computer like a lion's mane.

I grabbed one off the edge of the upper right. *Get new dog food.* "Well that's sad," I remarked, solemnly.

"What's that?" Mary inquired, having lifted her gaze from a cursory search through the drawers in Joel's desk.

"*Get new dog food,*" I read. "Poor guy. Probably couldn't bring himself to throw this one away. Maybe it seemed...too...too final."

"Ugh," Mary groaned. "Oh, Max...buddy. You had a good dad."

"Look at these, Mary." I pointed in a circular motion around Joel's computer screen. "His whole life was run by sticky notes."

"I know," she acknowledged, softly. "Trust me."

"At home too?"

"Yeah. Not as much at home, I guess. But some." She shook her head, as if to shake off a memory or bad-tasting dose of medicine, adding, "But yesterday was a brutal reminder."

"A brutal reminder of what?" I probed. I wasn't following.

"Of the sticky note obsession."

"The what?"

"The package from Joel," she insisted, seemingly perturbed at me for making her say it.

"What, the letter?" I asked.

"Yes, the note!" she stated with exasperated authority.

"There was a sticky note on it?" I still wasn't following.

"No, Joel. The letter *was* a sticky note."

"I thought you said there was a letter in that box."

"I don't know what I said. Note...letter. *Note*, I think." Mary continued rifling through the top drawer in Joel's desk. "Yeah, I never said *letter*...I said *note.*"

She looked up to see me staring at the sticky note still in my hand. It wasn't the message that had my breath bated, but rather the medium.

"Anyway, what's the diff?" Mary begged.

I continued to stare at the note. Slowly, the realization washed over me. It all started to make sense. What made no sense yesterday suddenly came into view, like the headlights of a car closing in on you in the rearview mirror.

"You said the letter — or, note or whatever — came in a package."

"That's right."

"Like a shipping container."

"That's right. A cardboard box," she played along.

"For, like, a box or something?"

"Yeah, so?"

"And all that was in it was this sticky note, with the two words on it, *Tell Jason?*"

I could sense Mary's tone of voice becoming increasingly tense. I was beating around the bush, or so it seemed to her. But I wasn't. I was piecing it all together. Or at least piecing together the next big conundrum.

"Jason, what is it? What are you getting at?"

I spoke measuredly, and softly, as the hypothesis was formulating at the very moment each word passed over my lips. "Joel didn't send you that note."

He didn't? Then who did?"

I continued. Still soft, and still measured. "No, Joel sent *it*, all right. It's clearly his handwriting. Look at all these things on his computer." I held the note in my hand next to the others littering the edge of his computer screen, in order to emphasize the uniformity in the handwriting. I went on, "But it wasn't a letter. At least, that's not all it was." I paused only briefly, then revealed my suspicion. "Whatever he meant to send you was removed from that package."

"What?" Now it was Mary who wasn't following.

"The sticky note was a reminder. It was meant to be attached to something. As a reminder."

"A reminder? To himself? Or to me?" Mary peppered, now with the same anxiety tingling through her every pore.

"I don't know," I conjectured, "but, whatever he meant to send to you...?" I waited for her assenting nod. "That sticky note was attached to it. And somebody took it out of that parcel...before it ever got to you!"

CHAPTER 6

30 Years Ago

JUST off campus of Manchester College sits a house, an old colonial, very large. It's night. Empty red solo cups are strewn about the front lawn. Half-drunken students amble in and out in small groupings: prancing in, some; stumbling out, others. The muffled drone of loud music barely makes its way through the windows and walls out to the front yard.

Inside, it's ear-achingly loud. Girls in batches of four to six gather, bottles in hand, in the middle of the living room to scream the lyrics they barely know and dance along as they laugh at one another's moves. The walls are draped with gaggles of boys, each with red solo cups of their own, watching the performance on display.

Two boys lean against a wall adjacent to what used to be the fireplace. A blond in preppy clothes with a Princeton haircut stands next to a man in a "casual" linen suit, with laced wingtip shoes and a matching plaid Burberry scarf. A third young man makes his way through the crowd, holding high three beer-filled solo cups, safely delivering them to his friends with only minimal spoilage.

Conversations are not conversations, but rather shouting matches, each proclamation delivered directly into the ear canal of the intended recipient.

"WHERE'S MARY?" he shouts, handing the fresh cups of beer to his expectant cohorts.

"SHE'S ON HER WAY! BE HERE LATER!"

"THANKS FOR THE REFILL, JASON!"

"NO PROBLEM, RUSSELL! HOW'S THE ACTION?"

"IF YOU LIKE DRUNKEN FLOOZIES, THIS IS YOUR PONY SHOW!"

Jason looks over and admires the dancing and pantomime stylings of one group of girls in particular. He makes eye contact with the blonde, who smiles back with an inviting grin and eye glimmer.

"I'M GOING IN!"

Jason hands his beer to Russell, who is now double-fisted, as he dances awkwardly toward the dancing ladies.

"HOW LONG ARE WE STAYING HERE, JOEL?" Russell shouts in Joel's general direction.

"I DON'T KNOW. WHY? YOU BORED, RUSS?"

"SHIT-FACED, ACTUALLY!"

"RUSS, YOU GOTTA SLOW DOWN. IT'S EARLY. PACE YOURSELF. WHERE'S ZIGGY, BY THE WAY?"

"HE'S PUSSYING OUT. HIS VAGINA HURTS."

"Whatever."

"WHAT?!"

"WHATEVER!"

"WHERE DID YOU SAY MARY IS?"

"I SAID SHE'S COMING. SHE'S MEETING US HERE! STUDYING FOR MIDTERMS!"

Russell takes another large gulp from his own solo cup, spilling a bit of beer out of the other he seems to have forgotten he's holding for his friend on the prowl. A burp forces its way out.

"I MAY HURL TONIGHT!"

"Nice." Joel pushes him back a bit, making a face to obviate his disapproval of the smell emanating from Russell's open mouth.

"MARY'S LUCKY!" Russell announces.

"WHAT?!"

"MARY'S LUCKY!"

"WHY, CUZ SHE'S NOT DRINKING PISS WARM SCHLITZ AT A HOUSE PARTY BEING OGLED BY SWEATY FRAT GUYS? DON'T WORRY, SHE'LL BE HERE SOON ENOUGH!"

"NO, SHE'S LUCKY! ...AT LIFE!"

"RUSSELL. Your breath smells like shit, bud. HOW MANY BEERS HAVE YOU HAD?"

"SHE'S LUCKY AT LIFE!" Russell almost falls forward with this attempt at emphasis for effect.

"OKAY, RUSS. SHE'S LUCKY." Looking over at Jason, and gesturing toward him with his solo cup. "I'D SAY JASON IS THE LUCKY ONE RIGHT NOW!"

Jason dances, poorly, in the middle of a circle of girls, each holding their bottles above their heads as they take turns bumping hips with the monkey in the middle.

"FLOOZY BITCHES!"

Joel pushes Russell back again as he stammers toward him, just enough to get his friend's drunken, spit-laced and slurred spewings out from under his own nose.

"All right, Russ."

"THAT'S WHY YOU'RE LUCKY TOO! YOU GOT MARY! SHE'S NO FLOOZY BITCHES!"

"Russ, what...is...up? ...RUSSELL! WHAT IS UP?"

Russell stops making his case. He erects his posture, though in a stammered manner, struggling to remain standing. He looks directly into Joel's eyes — as direct as darting, glossy eyes can look. He leans in. He closes his eyes as his face approaches Joel's.

"DUDE!" Another abrupt push away.

"I'm sorry."

"DUDE! WHAT ARE YOU DOING?"

"I'm so sorry."

Jason rejoins them, dancing his way back to their designated wall space next to the fireplace.

"WE GOTTA GO, JASON. RUSSELL'S WASTED!"

"HAD TOO MANY, RUSS?"

"I'm sorry." Now looking at the ground, swaying in place. "I'm sorry."

"Jason, I think Russell just tried...just tried to *kiss* me!"

"WHAT?!"

"I THINK RUSS JUST MADE A MOVE ON ME!"

Jason looks over at Russell, smiling in dismissive recognition. "I KNOW HE'S DRUNK. BUT THAT DOESN'T MEAN HE'S WASTED!"

"WHAT ARE YOU TALKING ABOUT? LOOK AT HIM! AND HE JUST MADE A MOVE ON ME! WHAT THE HELL, MAN?!"

Jason leans into Joel's ear opposite from where Russell is standing/swaying and places his hand on Joel's shoulder

"Dude, take the compliment," he says, just loud enough for Joel to hear, but not Russell. "And get a fucking clue."

"WHAT?!"

"If you're just figuring it out now, you gotta grab a mitt and get in the game."

"WHAT?!"

"Dude. Russell's gay."

CHAPTER 7

DISCOVERY

I GUESS heading back to Joel's house made sense — even though the first go-round turned up next to nothing. Truth is, the first time around, we weren't even really sure what we were looking for. Now we were. Or at least we had a clue.

The sticky note thing seemed to be a revelation. Though begging more questions than it answered, it seemed to explain why whoever sent Mary that note — *Tell Jason* — did so in a box, rather than a small envelope. There was supposed to be something in there. At least that made more sense than sending a box filled only with a paltry little sticky note. But what? And who sent it? Maybe it was Joel, I supposed. But even Mary said that would be out of the ordinary. What did that sticky note belong to?

"I keep thinking about Max," Mary said, her head obviously elsewhere. This car ride was considerably more conversational than the last, which was a welcome change of pace.

"I know. I'm sorry," I said, as consolingly as I could.

"No, not that," she objected. "I mean...yes, that. But not just missing him."

"What then?"

"I keep thinking about the sticky note." Maybe her head wasn't as elsewhere as I had surmised. She continued, recalling the one particular sticky note that had also caught my eye, *"Get new dog food,"* she recited. "Obviously, Max has been dead for a while now. But yet, like you said, Joel couldn't bring himself to throwing away that sticky note. *Get new dog food.*"

"Well, that was Joel, I guess." I didn't really know what I was talking about, but it seemed like a nice, comforting thing to say. Mary was clearly searching for answers.

"I wonder if that explains the will," she posited, turning her gaze through the window to the passing rural countryside.

"How so?" This made no sense to me, but I was willing to entertain it.

"Think about it, Jason. Joel doesn't really...*have* anybody. Except Max."

"Not your fault," I was quick to enter into the record.

"I know, I know," she conceded. "But he was *close* with that dog. Probably closer than he's ever been to anyone...or anything. If fact, that's all he really asked for in the divorce. 'I want the dog.' Those were his first words to me when I told him I wanted a divorce." A long, pensive pause. Than a sniff. "He loved that dog."

"He was a good man." Was that the right thing to say?

"Maybe when Max died," Mary continued, "Joel just felt alone. For the first time in a long time. He *was* alone. Maybe that gets a man to thinking, in time."

"Thinking? About what?"

"About his own mortality," Mary speculated. "About moving on. About...*what happens when I die? Who will care? Will anyone even care?*" Sniff. Pause. "*Who gets my stuff?*"

"Oh, Mary," I tried to console her. This was starting to get heavy.

"Maybe that's all there was to it," she went on, rather ignoring my comforting offering. "Max dies, he never really gets over it, and he starts to think. That would be Joel. Time to get your affairs in order. Leave nothing unattended to."

I didn't reply, but let her supposition hang in the air. I really had no idea what to say. So I kept my eyes on the road, showing no sign of either agreement nor skepticism. It wasn't my place. Let a woman cope, right?

"He was grieving. And preparing," she went on, looking back at me now. "That's what he would've done."

"Sounds like Joel." That was the best I could do. Both agreement and skepticism at once.

When we got to Joel's house, we didn't bother ringing the bell or knocking this time. Maybe it was instinct — that we knew there's no way it would be so easy as to have Joel back at home safe and sound. Rather, we just used my key and walked in.

Mary did call out once, "Joel?" but I think she knew no one would answer. It was tellingly half-hearted.

Shortly after entering, and following a quick, cursory look around to confirm the house was indeed empty, we separated and started our renewed search in earnest. Though we still weren't exactly sure as to what, specifically, we were looking for, we both knew that we were now trying to find context to a sticky note. What did Joel (or whoever) mean to send Mary? If our working theory was correct, it was smaller than a shoe box...maybe the size of a cigar box, in order to fit inside that empty parcel Mary received...and it would have to be of some significance. What makes something significant? I guess you only know when you find it.

I started in the basement, which wasn't nearly so daunting this time. Last night's search revealed nothing, despite my more fantastical fears. No body hanging from the rafters, above a kicked-out chair. No smoking gun...neither literally nor figuratively. Nothing. So, I'd rummage around a bit, looking for something about the size of a cigar box. Or anything at all.

Mary started back on the computer where she had found the draft of Joel's "Last Will and Testament" document. She would know some of his passwords, if she needed to get into some files and emails — *M@dM@x08*. Even I knew that one. It was a ceremonial homage to man's best friend...or, more specifically, his own best friend. "Mad Max," as he sometimes called him, and his "gotcha day" year — the year Mary and he brought him home from the breeder: 2008. He was nothing if not predictable. And remarkably consistent, creativity not being his forte. I walked back into the room when she was just about wrapping up on the computer. Apparently, nothing to be found.

"I'll check the bathroom again," I announced to Mary, as I returned from the basement empty-handed. "Maybe there's something in the medicine cabinet." As soon as I said it, I wanted to take it back. *Stupid Jason. Way to freak her out.* The last thing I needed to bring into this was fears of suicide. No, that didn't seem like Joel. But none of this did. But it just slipped out. I wanted to see what was left in the medicine cabinet, sure. Still. *Don't blurt it out, dumbass. Mary's going through enough right now!*

"Okay. I'll check the kitchen," she returned. She seemed unaffected by my slip of the tongue. "We're looking for something about the size of an old cigar box?" she confirmed.

"Seems so."

The search though the medicine cabinet was uneventful. Was I grateful, or disappointed? Sure, find a bottle of oxycodone, and you're lucky enough to have a clue. You're also unlucky enough to have an apparent cause of death — one you'd never dream of, not in your worst fears. There was aspirin, an asthma inhaler, an ointment for something or another. Nothing major.

Of course, I'd never fully complete the investigation. Out came the scream.

Mary had been startled. Shocked, even. Did someone walk in? Did she find something? I dropped the aspirin and ointment and ran out to the kitchen.

Mary was leaning back against the kitchen counter, her trembling hand covering her mouth. Tears of either fright or horror were forming in the corner of her eyes, and she struggled to force out the words.

"Mary! What is it?" I said, hurrying toward her.

She just stared and shook. The pantry door was open, and something inside had scared the living daylights out of her. I continued toward her more slowly, and more cautiously now, with each passing step hoping to improve my angle to see beyond the opened pantry door. I went first to embrace her, then turned back to see inside the pantry. "Mary. What is it?"

She just pointed, finger extended and shaking toward the bottom of the pantry. My eyes followed the trajectory of the point. She was pointing at a large bag of opened dog food.

"Son of a bitch." Fleeting relief set in. She had been jarred by the sight of Max's old dog food. Just yet another memory Joel couldn't bring himself to throw away. I gathered myself, and prepared to be the comforting rock once again. "I'm sorry, Mary."

"Jason," she trembled.

"Yes, Mary?"

"It's Max's food."

"I know, Mary. I'm sorry. I'll throw it away."

I started toward the bag of dog food, but Mary stopped me. "No. Don't."

"What is it, Mary? Let me just take it outside. I'll get rid of it for you. I know how hard this is."

"No, Jason. Don't." I stopped halfway over and just looked back at her. She collected herself, somewhat. "Look inside."

Now I started to freak out. Look inside? This is the part of the horror movie when you find the severed head, right? I didn't ask any further, but slowly walked over to the bag of dog food. The top had been unrolled, by Mary obviously. I gently grabbed the sides of the bag, slowly pulled them apart, and peered inside.

No severed head. Thank God. But I could see why Mary screamed. Inside were the corpses of three dead rats. Disgusting. I crumpled up the bag again and stepped back, forcing down a regurgitation of my breakfast.

"Rats, Jason."

"Yup."

"Dead rats."

"Yup."

"Why would there be dead rats in Max's dog food, Jason?"

"I have no idea, Mary." Instinct and reflex had me walking slowly back toward her, pulling her into a comforting embrace. She didn't resist, and cautiously returned a half-hearted and distraught-filled hug. I repeated my words of comfort, "I have no idea."

"What would kill rats like that?"

"What do you mean?" I asked.

"Why would there be dead rats in Max's food?"

"Who knows," I answered, with no explanations of my own. But I tried. "Maybe since Joel's been gone, the rats came out and had a feast. He's probably always had them. They just came out of the woodwork, now that he's gone."

"But dead."

"Yeah, they saw the smorgasbord in Max's dog food and dove in."

"But dead."

"Yeah. I saw."

Mary asked again. "Why would there be dead rats in Max's dog food? What kills rats?"

"Well," I tried to posit, "I wouldn't think they'd die from eating dog food. Rats eat just about everything, don't they? They're scavengers."

"That's what I mean," Mary said, finally starting to compose herself in earnest. "There's only one thing I know that kills rats."

"What's that?"

She looked directly into my eyes. "Rat poison."

I wasn't really sure what to make of her line of reasoning. She was distraught. She was question-begging. Flailing for answers. But what she said next revealed where she was going with this. And it was a conclusion I had feared more than anything.

"Jason? I think it's time to call the police."

CHAPTER 8

29 Years Ago

THE TOMAHAWK River runs north of Calhoune and Hawthorne, beyond the urban core and its suburban outer rim, approaching the hills that give way to the mountainside. In the midsummer evening, the sun manages to peek through the limbs of mature evergreens, maples, oak trees and elms. The soft glimmer of a fading sun echoes off the lethargically flowing whitewater.

A jeep is parked next to a VW Beetle, just off the river bank. Canoes and kayaks lean against nearby trees, with life jackets draped about them to drip dry. Tents have been pitched, and the telltale aroma of a crackling campfire pierces the otherwise pure country air.

They gather around the campfire, not for warmth, but for ritual, drinking everything from beer to wine...to wine coolers and Schnapp's. Some brought something stiffer. She toasts a marshmallow over the crackling fire while grasping her half-empty wine cooler.

"Okay. New game. *I Never.*"

"What's that?"

"*I Never*," she repeats. "Somebody says something that they've never done. And if you've done that thing, you have to drink."

"I'm in!" he says, eagerly raising a silver flask to the air.

"Awesome, Russell," she welcomes him. "I knew you'd be up for it. What about you guys?"

"Um, no thanks. Y'all ain't play *I Never* with someone who been upstate."

"Come on, Ziggy! Just leave out all the...bad stuff."

"Hell, that's all there is."

"No no...come on," she persists. *I Never*. I'll go first."

Audible groans, collectively.

She removes the marshmallow from the stick and takes a bite, reaching down with her free hand to the ground beside her to grab her drink. "Okay, I'm starting. And you're all playing. Drink if you've done this, right? Okay, let's see...I never...Oh! I got it! I never kissed a boy on the first date."

Russell raises his flask. "Drink!" he confesses jubilantly, and takes a good hearty swig.

"Might've known," the man next to him laughs.

"You know it, Jays," Russell laughs. "Just don't be jealous. You weren't the first, hate to tell ya."

Jason shakes his head dismissively and smiles.

"Okay, okay. My turn," Russell announces, taking one more swig from the flask. "I never...I never...let's see....I never cheated on a midterm by sneaking into the professor's office and stealing his answer key, only to get caught, then cry my way out of it and offer to sleep with the professor to get out of suspension."

Silence.

Then collectively, in unison: "Drink!"

Russell, in stunned amazement looks back at them with wide eyes and mouth agape. "You...bitches!"

Laughter.

"Okay," the man seated closest to Mary reluctantly chimes in. "I never tore the mattress tags off, under penalty of federal imprisonment."

"Boring!" Russell scolds. "Next!"

"Fine...drink." Jason chimes in, reluctantly raising his beer only slightly. "Okay, me. My turn, I guess."

"Here we go."

"No, no, Mary," Jason says, waving the suggestion off with one hand. "I got one. Let's see. I never….I never…"

"C'mon, man! You ain't never done nothing?"

"Hold on, Zig. Hold on...I'm thinking. I never...I never…."

"Okay, while you *never* never with your boys here," Mary interrupts as she stands, "I'm hitting the ladies room. Be right back."

Mary walks over to the mercifully situated porta-potty just beyond the tree line. It reeks inside. She allows the door to slam behind her as she enters, then proceeds to relieve herself, managing to do so without ever touching cheek to seat. *The power squat,* she thinks to herself, as she hurries about her business. *A merit badge that any camping woman needs to earn. It's a race against time. If the darkness doesn't creep you out, the stale, dank air, filled with an aromatic bouquet of urine, feces and disinfectant will choke the breath out of you.*

She emerges. The sunlight has fallen below the tree line, as darkness just begins to set in. It is not yet dim enough to affect one's eyesight, but enough to make the glow of the campfire apparent. The glow of an *abandoned* campfire. *Where is everyone? Where'd they go?* she wonders.

"Joel? Jason?"

She walks slowly and trepidatiously back toward the campfire. The jeep and the VW are still parked; the canoes and kayaks remain untouched.

"Guys? Joel?"

Silence. The campfire continues to crackle.

"Come on, boys. Not funny. Joel? Jason?"

Nothing.

"Ziggy? Russell?"

Nothing.

"Come on, guys. Enough. I'm not playing around."

The scenery begins to swirl around her, as her head darts back and forth, over her shoulders, then back...under the cars, down by the river...back to the empty chairs by the campfire, back to the porta-potty. Back in front of her.

"Guys!" She takes a deep breath. "GUYS!!!"

Silence.

Finally, a muffled snicker.

Mary lowers the tension out of her shoulders and exhales. "God damn it, guys."

Ziggy emerges from behind the jeep, belly laughing and cupping his hand over his teeth-baring grin.

"Gotcha!"

Jason ducks out from behind a leaning canoe. "Campfire ditch!"

"Hardy-har-har, boys."

"Sorry, sweetie." Russell emerges from the thick of the forest.

"Very funny, guys."

They all re-gather by the campfire, and take their seats.

"Boy, what would a girl do without funny fucks like you guys?"

"Hey," Jason turns serious for a moment, looking around his immediate surroundings. "Where's Joel?"

"Joel!"

"What the hell, man? Where he go? He think this a contest, or something?"

"Joel! Enough, babe," Mary calls out into the darkening wilderness. "Come on out. Campfire ditch is over. I was very amused."

Silence.

"Joel? Not funny. The boys already had their fun, you can come out now."

Silence.

"JOEL!!!!"

"He's in the tree." Russell sips his flask calmly and collectively, with the knowing confidence of the private detective who solved the whodunnit.

"What tree?"

"That one." Russell points to a tree hanging over the parked VW, upon which a kayak had been resting.

They look up — almost directly up. Joel is perched high on a branch, and begins to laugh.

"Attention whore." Russell takes another sip from his flask.

"Get your shit down here, dog."

"Come on down, babe. Very, very VERY funny! You win the award for biggest douche of the ditch."

"Heheheh. Thank you, thank you, thank you." Descending from the tree, "How'd you know I was up there, Russ?"

"'Cuz I know you crave attention, and you constantly gotta pull shit like this."

"Geez, Russ. Lighten up."

"Sorry, Jays. But he loves being the center of attention. I'm sorry, he does. Besides. All of the moss was scuffed off of that tree trunk. It was there before when we got here. Now it's not. Voila. Douche of the ditch is in the tree, getting all the attention he so desperately craves."

"Wow, perceptive," Mary marvels.

"Yeah, dog. You like Sherlock Fucking Holmes, man!"

"Yeah, Russell. Impressive."

"Thank you, Jays."

"You really paid attention to all that?"

"Yup."

"Why?"

"Why what?"

"Why notice the moss on that tree trunk to begin with? Who in their right mind would give a shit about something so trivial, let alone notice it?"

Pause. Another sip of his flask.

"I notice everything."

CHAPTER 9

OUT OF THE BOX

"THE police?"

"Yes," she insisted. "The police."

"Hold on, Mary. Calm down."

"Well we can't just sit here and do nothing!"

"We're not doing nothing. We're trying to get to the bottom of this."

"That's the police's job!"

"Not yet it's not."

"But we need to tell them *something!*"

"Tell them what, exactly, Mary? *Hi, officer? I'd like to report a vacationing person. His dog died a few months ago, and now we have three dead bodies. Sure, they're rats, but —*"

"Jason. I'm freaking out right now."

"I am too," I said, de-escalating the charge that was building in the air. I approached her again to offer another comforting embrace, but she paced right past me this time.

"We have this dog food. That's a clue," she began.

"A clue to what?"

"I don't know. Something. Don't you find it odd?"

"Dead rats? Not really."

"But in Max's dog food. Food that he was eating?"

"Yeah, so?"

65

"Maybe Joel wasn't simply contemplating his own mortality. Maybe that's not why he was writing his will at all."

"What are you getting at, Mary?"

"Maybe he thought something was happening." She paused, and reflected on her own morbid thoughts a bit. As crazy as it must have sounded in her head, it sounded even crazier coming out. "Maybe he thought someone was catching up to him. Maybe that's why he was putting all of his affairs in order. Writing the will…"

"That's crazy," I injected.

"And now Max is dead. Maybe poisoned! If they could poison a dog, who's to say they couldn't…"

"Mary, listen to yourself."

I paused a moment, in hopes that cooler heads could prevail. Maybe the more she processed her own words the more she would see that she was grasping at straws. I continued, before she had the chance to jump down my throat again.

"Listen. There was this dog food from China a few years back. Remember that? It was killing dogs left and right. They finally pinpointed the manufacturer and recalled it all. Terribly sad, especially if yours was one of the dogs infected. But it wasn't anything more than that."

"You think that killed Max? Bad food?"

"I don't know," I said. "But I know if it could take down a dog, it could certainly take down a couple of scrounging rats."

Mary finally seemed to be calming down. I took that as an opportunity to continue to explore the route of reasoned rationale.

"Why don't we at least check the recall lists, and see if Max's food was on it? Then we'll know. Or we'll know more. If his food was being recalled, maybe that's what killed him. And that's definitely what killed these three blind mice here."

"Fine." Mary finally exhaled. "But I still think we should call the police."

"Maybe," I was willing to concede. "But not yet."

"When?"

"Well...for starters...first you need to be completely straight with me."

"Straight with you? About what?"

"About what you scanned over to Joel," I said, for a moment no longer wary of making the suggestion, or how she might react to it. "That tax *thingy*? What was that?"

"I told you," she replied with a bit of obstinance. "It was some tax form. I didn't think anything of it. It looked like they were assessing back taxes on the cabin or something. Something from when we were married. We sold the cabin, so I didn't know what to do about it. So I sent it to Joel to let him handle it."

"That's it?" I asked, opening the window of opportunity for her to provide an addendum or further explanation.

"That's it. Why the third degree?"

I took her by the hand and escorted her over to the kitchen table, where we both calmly took a seat.

"Well, all this talk about calling the police. I just think we need to get our stories straight. Level with each other."

"Stories straight?" she started abruptly. "Level with each other? What are you talking about, Jason?"

"Nothing, nothing." I could tell I went there too soon. But she needed to know what kind of scrutiny she was inviting upon herself. I started to explain, as calmly as I could, and in a tone that established beyond doubt that I was her ally in all of this. "It's just, you start reporting a missing person to the police, with suggestions of foul play and rat poison and everything, and —"

"And what?" she interrupted.

"And they start poking around in everything," I finished, authoritatively. "And guess who becomes the chief suspect in a missing person's investigation?"

She bowed her head in defeated recognition of the grim reality of the situation. "The spouse."

"The spouse. So unless we're ready to have cops digging into *tax thingies* and divorce settlements and life insurance and last wills and testaments, I suggest we take our time alerting the authorities."

She just stared back at me in deflated silence. Tears began to form again in the corners of her eyes. Her lips began to tremble again.

"Besides," I went on, "I'm still convinced this is absolutely nothing. Just a bunch of strange coincidences. Joel's on vacation, the dog food is under recall, and everything will be back to normal in no time."

"I'm sure you're right." She began to compose herself somewhat.

"Of course I'm right."

Mary stood up and pushed the chair back in. She walked over to the sink and ran the water over her hands, splashing a bit on her face. As she grabbed for a hand towel, she muttered, almost under her breath. "Then you gotta level with me, too."

What the hell was she talking about? "Me? Level with you?" I objected. "About what?" I made it obvious that I didn't appreciate — or understand — her tone.

"About the will."

"The will? What about it?" I couldn't understand why I was suddenly the center of conversation. "You said there was nothing to the will," I reminded her. "Weren't you basically the solely named party in it?"

"Pretty much. Pretty much."

"Except...?"

Mary held her thought, and walked into the living room to wake up the computer once again. I followed her in, cautiously. What was this all about?

She hunched over the desk and started working the mouse at a fevered pace. Suddenly, there was a focused mission at hand. How this related to me, I had no idea. But I'd be lying if I said I wasn't curious. And maybe just a little bit ill-at-ease.

"I checked it out again," she said. "The will. Gave it a more thorough read. You know...before finding the rats? When I was checking for emails, or clues, or anything at all. I looked back over the will."

"And?" I said, with both projected innocence and obvious lack of appreciation of it all.

"Here," she said, standing up and looking back at me across the room, waiting for her to reveal what she was onto. She pointed at the screen, obviously inviting me in for inspection. "Take a look. Paragraph 28."

I studied her gaze for a moment or two, then walked slowly over to the computer. What could possibly in Joel's "Last Will and Testament" that would be of any relevance to me? I stopped just before the desk, and decided to press, just a bit. "You said this was all just boilerplate. Didn't he just leave everything to you? Like you said?"

"Everything except this," she flatly responded.

I moved in closer. Standing right beside Mary, I bent over slightly to peer into the document's 28th paragraph.

"See it?" she beckoned. "Paragraph 28?"

You know the expression, *my heart stopped?* I never much related to it. How can a heart stop, and how would you know what it felt like if it did? I mean, you really wouldn't live to tell the tale, would you? But people say it all the time. "My heart stopped." I guess they take it to mean shock. Or fright. Or panic. For me, it was all of the above. And now I could relate. Right then and there? My heart sure as hell stopped, I can live to tell you. Or it leapt into my throat. Something. It was a combination of shock, fright and panic all at once. The words sat there on the screen like the revelation in a murder mystery. I read them silently to myself.

And to Jason L. Wilhelm, the contents of my registered safe deposit box at Main Street Bank & Trust, box 3473.

That was it. Nothing more. No indication as to what was in the safe deposit box. Just that one line.

"What the hell is that, Jason?" Mary said, and I could feel her staring eyeballs piercing right through me.

I truly had no idea what this was referring to. But Mary's tone was almost accusatory, and I had to reassure her of my ignorance at once. "I haven't the foggiest clue, Mary. Honestly."

"Well, why is he leaving it to you?"

"How the hell should I know? This is the first I'm hearing of it."

"Honestly?"

"Swear to God."

Mary looked back at the screen. Then back at me. Back at the screen again. "What in God's name could be in a safe deposit box that Joel would want you to have upon his passing?"

"Beats me," I assured her again.

"And why would he be doing this now?"

"No idea." I looked just as blankly upon the screen as she had the night prior.

"How do we find out?" she pressed.

"Good question."

Mary slinked abruptly into the chair that was at the computer desk, lowering her head into her hand in exasperated frustration. "Jason, what could be in there?"

"I have no idea," I repeated. "But I can tell you this."

"What's that?" She looked up to me, practically begging for a lifeline of hope.

"Whatever's in that box at the bank?..." I said, suggestively.

"Yeah?"

"It's probably about the size of a cigar box."

CHAPTER 10

29 Years Ago

SUBDUED ado clutters the hallways of the third floor of Dempsey Hall, the preferred dormitory of sophomores fulfilling their last year of mandatory student housing. It's that time of night when Saturday twilight begins to give way to Sunday morning. Many are asleep, unbothered by the remnant din of stereos left on by passing-out drunkards. There are still card games being played in this room or that, and in another, a few holdouts are determined to finish the quarter barrel, despite what their bodies and minds are telling them.

A female student is nearly passed out but sitting upright against the wall in the hallway. She opens her eyes and awkwardly lifts her head as the man steps over her legs to continue past her. "Hey, Jason," she mumbles up to him. "Long time no..." she passes back out before finishing the thought.

He laughs down at her, then back at his female companion, who giggles back in unison, before they both forge ahead together. She grabs his arm as they continue on their way.

"Whoops, don't step on her," she laughs, as she grabs his arm ever tighter for balance.

He's pretty sure where this is leading. There's a first time for everything. Her head is on his shoulder now, and he hopes it's not there to fall asleep. He's come this far, after all.

Arriving at the door, he struggles to align his key with the keyhole. Finally, success. The opening door fails to catch their fall as they spill into the room, giggling all the more. He guides her inside, closing the door behind him.

Leaving the lights off, he stumbles over to the stereo and turns it on. Mood music. Mercifully, he had left the jazz station on, and not the heavy metal station. The subtle ambience of mellow horns and piano set the tone perfectly — loud enough to obscure their clumsy movements, but not too loud to wake those asleep in neighboring dorm rooms. He brings her close to him, kissing first her neck, then gently moving toward her expectant mouth. She's not falling asleep, that much is clear.

He takes off her jacket, then his own, throwing both carelessly to the floor. She fumbles to unbutton his shirt, as he begins working on her belt and zipper. Clumsy, yes, but passionate all the same. There's a first time for everything.

Enough clothes are off now. Maybe not all. But enough. She falls backward onto his bed, and he follows her down. The passion grows, both in pace and intensity.

Moonlight pierces through the window to reveal the softness of her curves. His kisses follow the contours of whatever the moon is generous enough to reveal. She pulls his face back up from her quivering torso to meet her seductive stare. She softly embraces his mouth with both hands, then pulls it in for another kiss.

The jazz accompaniment is triumphant now. Horns blare, and the muted trumpet squeals the melody. The rhythm section matches the pace of their thrusts. Rhythmic, but disjointed. Hurried, yet patient.

Suddenly, an interruption! The sound of keys just outside. A jiggling door handle.

"Son of a bitch!" Jason throws his body up and off of her, pulling the sheets over their near-naked bodies.

The interruption enters into the darkness only slightly, the light from the hallway outside casting his unexpected silhouette from behind. He stops abruptly when he sees there's two of them. "Oh my God, I'm sorry!" the interrupting man says as he covers his eyes, frozen in the doorway. "Sorry, Jason! Sorry!"

Silence. Mercifully, he doesn't turn on the lights, but his silhouette clumsily moves about the room groping for something on the dresser. "Sorry, Jason. I'll be going."

He starts back out of the room and reaches back in to close the door behind him. Before exiting, he apologizes for his untimely intrusion. "Sorry, dude." A beat. "But aren't you supposed be hanging a sock or necktie or something on the door? Isn't that the universal do-not-disturb sign?"

Mutedly, Jason responds quietly and calmly, "Sorry, Joel," he mutters, almost under his breath, before offering in his own defense, somberly, "I thought you went home for the weekend."

Joel pauses for a moment upon his exit to look back at Jason and his companion. "Nope." He leaves, closing the door behind him.

"Son of a bitch!" Jason releases.

"Jason, go after him," she suggests.

"What, now?"

"He's your friend."

"I know. But now?"

"I think you should."

Jason stares at her in disbelief, weighing his options. The moment's passed. "Fine."

Jason leaps defeatedly out of bed. He pulls up his pants and buckles his belt. He throws his shirt back on, buttoning it as he starts toward the door.

"And, Jason," she stops him.

"Yeah?"

"Tell him I'm sorry."

His hand is on the door handle as he looks back at her, still waiting in naked disappointment under the sheets upon his bed. He sighs, before answering, "I'll try, Mary. I'll try."

CHAPTER 11

FAMOUS LAST WORDS

WALKING into Main Street Bank & Trust was a surreal experience. Main Street Bank isn't your typical "Main Street bank," not the kind you'd find in suburbia, anyway. This particular branch was on the first floor of one of downtown's high rises. It was the type of bank you'd expect to find yourself in if you were cast in a big budget action thriller. This was the bank that you'd see in the great heist films of the late 80s and 90s. Open and airy...regal and sophisticated. Echoey, even...which doesn't seem right for a bank, where customers and their personal bankers broker in discretions. Greek columns extended from the cathedral ceilings down to the marble floors, and natural light cast through tall windows that formed the street-bound facade, inviting the sunlight into the main lobby.

Mary and I walked in, I'm sure appearing about as aimless as we felt. We stood just inside the revolving glass doors and looked around, waiting for the right person to approach us for assistance. Who that right person might be, neither Mary nor I had the slightest clue. Finally, a balding, bespectacled man in a dark gray pinstripe suit stepped up from behind his desk just to our right and walked briskly toward us with a hand extended to offer a welcoming handshake.

"Good afternoon, Mr. and Mrs...?"

"Oh, we're not married," Mary was quick to correct.

"Very good," he humbly acknowledged. "I'm Mr. Stenson.

Welcome to Main Street Bank & Trust. How may we secure your financial future today?"

"We're here about a safe deposit box," I responded, matter-of-factly and almost overly abruptly. The rote delivery of the saccharin customer service tagline was a bit more than I was willing to stomach at that particular moment.

"Ah, very well," he eagerly replied, extending an arm back in the direction of his desk. "Please, have a seat."

Mary and I followed him over to his desk and helped ourselves to the two chairs opposite his perch across his well-kempt desk. He reached into a desk drawer and pulled out a form, grasping a pen in his other hand. "Let's see here. Safe deposit box. Very good. We have a generous variety of sizes and contract terms for you to consider," he continued, as he leafed through the tri-fold brochures organized neatly in a rack on the corner of his desk, pulling out just the right one.

"No, sir," I corrected. "We're not looking to take out a safe deposit box. We're here about a specific box."

"One that's already been registered," Mary added, "by a current customer of the bank."

"Oh," Mr. Stenson paused, looking at Mary over the top of his glasses that rested firmly near the bottom of his nose. "I see."

"Box 3473," I said, getting right to the point.

"Yes, sir. How may I help you?"

"It's registered to a man named Joel Thomas," Mary continued.

"That much is confidential," Mr. Stenson pushed back. "I'm sure you understand."

"Of course," Mary said, defiantly. "I'm his wife." Before *wife* had even completely passed her lips, she corrected herself. "His *ex*-wife."

"Well, what is it that I can do for you?"

"We were curious about the contents of that particular box. Or the details surrounding it," I said, retaking the floor from Mary.

Mr. Stenson appeared to take personal offense. "Sir, I'm sure you understand. We are both legally and morally bound to adhere to the highest standards of discretion and privacy."

"I'm sure," I conceded. "It's just that...I was named in the will. As the...um, beneficiary...of whatever's in that box."

"Has something happened to Mr. Thomas?" Stenson's face went blank, and his tone turned a bit more urgent.

"No, no," Mary jumped in. "Well, we don't think so. It's just that we haven't heard from him in a few days. And we're just a little worried."

I came to her assistance. "We just thought that maybe there was something in his possession here at the bank that might put our fears at rest. We thought that Mary, as his wife, and-or me, being named as the heir to the contents..."

"Sir," Mr. Stenson interjected. "If something were to happen to Mr. Thomas, I'm sure we would be notified. And, *until* something has happened to Mr. Thomas," he continued, "there's not anything I'm able — or willing — to do regarding one of our cherished client's private accounts." He pushed the eyeglasses further up to the bridge of his nose with an air of self-satisfaction, and a suggestion of finality.

Mary and I stared back at him, unsure of how to process, or reply to, this denial, even expected as it was.

Seeing that we weren't simply showing ourselves out, Mr. Stenson looked to conclude the conversation. He stood up from his chair. "So, until we have a probate order...or until you can produce some legal document acknowledging your right to the contents of Mr. Thomas's safe deposit box, I'm afraid there's nothing else I can say on this matter."

Mary and I refused to stand. We simply looked up at him, now towering over us, as both of us formulated our next move. Not knowing what further to say himself, Mr. Stenson went back to the customer service playbook. "Is there some other way that I may help to secure your financial future today?"

Mary lowered her gaze down to her lap. I looked at her, hoping she had formulated a Plan B. None was forthcoming.

"Thank you, Mr. Stenson," Mary practically whispered, as she stood in humbled despair. I stood to join her. "Thank you for your time." Mary walked right past me and didn't even pause to acknowledge Mr. Stenson with so much as a grateful glance or forced cordial half-grin. I gave him a disapproving glare, then followed Mary out of the bank.

"Well that was a big fat bust," Mary lamented, as we descended the steps from the bank back out to the bustling buzz of the busy boulevard.

"What did you expect?" I asked — not in a confrontational tone, but rather one that was intended to come off as conciliatory.

"I don't know."

I looked down at my watch. "Well. What now?"

"I don't know."

I cast my view out across the expanse of the streetscape, searching the city for guidance or inspiration. Mary simply stared off into space. "Maybe we do call the police," she said softly, perhaps to herself.

"Excuse me?" I asked. Had I heard her right?

"Aren't you starting to get just a little bit worried?" she said.

I was. "Yes, but what do we say?"

"I don't know, Jason. I don't know."

Something jarred her, and shook her from her dithering daze. A buzzing, coming from her purse. She reached into it, rifled around a bit, then extracted her cellphone.

"This is probably the office," Mary groused. "I need to tell them I'll be out for a few more days anyway. They'll have to make do without me for a while."

As I continued to survey the hustling city around me, Mary fumbled to awaken her phone. I could see out of the corner of my eye that she was now lowering the phone to her side, and slowly lifting her gaze to meet my eye. I turned toward her.

"What is it?" I asked, with just a hint of hopeful wonderment.

Her eyes lowered back to the phone, then slowly back up to meet my inquisitive glance once more. She muttered again to herself, and perhaps partially to me now as well. "Maybe we don't need to call the police after all."

I reached for the phone. "Huh?"

Mary slowly extended the phone back toward me. As I grabbed it to turn the screen toward me, a lump formed in my throat. Whatever it was, it wasn't good news. Or was it? Mary wasn't saying. She just wanted me to look for myself.

My eyes came into focus on the illuminated screen. A text message. The message was short, but not altogether sweet.

In the text field: "I'm fine. Call off the dogs."

In the *From* field: "Joel."

CHAPTER 12

28 Years Ago

DENNISON Field House, situated just outside the heart of Manchester College's central campus, is bigger than what you'd describe as a gym, but you wouldn't exactly call it an arena either. This afternoon, the windows have begun to steam over, as the risers are practically filled with vocal and enthusiastic fans, and the outside February air has everyone bundled in winter coats that they eventually shed as the game goes on and the heat inside rises. Cheerleaders flank the sidelines, ostensibly attempting to lead the crowd in coordinated cheers, but screaming fans holler right past them to the action on the court, raising their fists in jubilation, alternately shouting derisive comments at the referees.

On the court, a home-team player jukes a defender with his patented cross-over dribble, steps back behind the three-point line, and launches with confidence. Swish! The courtside public address announcer provides the punctuation over the loudspeaker. *"Walton for three!"*

"Ziggy's on fire tonight, Jason!" a fan cheers as he sits back down, having more or less completed a semi-successful high five with his buddy seated next to him. The man retakes his seated position on the riser midway up at half-court.

"Feeling it," Jason assents.

"Go Ziggy!" shouts a brown-haired woman seated next to Jason's cheering friend, her hands placed around her mouth to serve as a makeshift megaphone.

The three of them are jammed together uncomfortably, as their adjacent fellow fans bump into them in periodic and abrupt fits of celebration. A man wearing a khaki blazer seated next to Jason stands up as a whistle on court is blown. "I'm hitting concessions. Who wants something? Jays? Joel? Anyone?" He starts to make his way past them, with short, measured half-steps, as he navigates kneecaps and foot-littered risers. "Mary, you good?"

Mary looks down at her half-full bag of popcorn. "I'm fine, Russell. Thanks."

Joel stands. "I'll go with you. Russ."

"Jason, you sure? Want anything?"

"No, Russell, I'm good. Eh, maybe," he reconsiders. "What are you getting?"

"Coke."

"Just a coke?"

Russell pulls back one side of his unbuttoned coat to reveal, shoved into his belt and clung firmly to his hip, a silver-plated flask. "Unless you know of something that pairs better with Mister Jack Daniels here."

"I'm good, Russ," Jason scoffs.

Mary changes her mind. "How about a water?"

"I got it," Joel is quick to field the request.

Russell and Joel start off. Russell turns back and leans down to Mary. "If I'm not back in an hour, congratulate me in the morning."

"Huh?"

"I'm going to do some exploring."

"Exploring? Where?"

"Out on the concourse. For boys."

Jason chuckles. "Oh yeah? How you gonna know who's fair game and who's not?"

"Easy," Russell scoffs. "He's the skinny one, far too fabulously overdressed for a sporting event...and he obviously doesn't give two flying fucks about a stupid basketball game."

Mary and Jason join in a hearty chortle. Joel grabs Russell by the sleeve to pull him toward the concourse, demonstrating obvious discomfort. "Come on, Russ. Let's go."

The horn blows and the players return to the court. Mary and Jason look intently upon the court in silence as Ziggy inbounds the ball. Mary tilts her popcorn bag in Jason's direction, and he obliges by reaching in for a handful. It will be Jason that will be forced to break the silence.

"You and Joel seem to be doing good."

"Yeah, ya know? Things are good." Awkward pause. Another piece of popcorn placed onto her own waiting tongue. "How about you two? You guys were friends way before I came along. Things seem to be...okay..."

"Um...good. Things are good," he says, with a semi-forced reassuring enthusiasm — perhaps self-assuring. "I mean, not great. But good. I guess he's sticking by his promise to not let this break us. I mean, it's not like it was. But good. All things considered."

"That's good. It'll get better."

"Hope so."

"It will, Jays. Just give him time. Look at us. We're managing. I mean, it's still...there? Ya know? But if you never knew what happened...well, you'd never know it happened."

"But *you're* sleeping with him," he jokes. "What hope do I have?"

Mary forces herself to grin back at that semi-inappropriate observation.

Back on-court, Ziggy drives to the basket and lays in another basket for two points. They both clap.

He waits for the cheering to subside, then continues, "Well, I'm glad, Mary. Really, I am. Happy for you guys."

"Thanks."

"And, I'll say it again...I'm sorry."

"Don't be!" She scowls back at him. "Hey, look. We were both there that night. But nothing happened. It's done. A year later, and Joel and I have somehow managed to put it all behind us. And look. You and him can sit together at a basketball game and give each other high fives and go for beers later and...well, it's almost like nothing happened. We'll be fine. All of us. Just give it some time."

Neither speaks.

Then Mary provides an additional admonition. "But don't you dare ever take the blame for what happened that night. I won't allow it. You're done apologizing. To me, anyway." Another pause. "Just keep working on Joel. He'll come around."

A blocked shot. More cheering. People around them take to their feet in anxious exhilaration. Jason and Mary remain seated. The Manchester Marauders head in unison back down the court the other way for a fast break. The crowd erupts as the ball passes through the hoop. *"Jackson for two. Assist by Walton."*

Joel returns with Mary's water and a bag of peanuts; Russell is not with him. He hands the water to Mary, opens the peanuts, and offers Jason the first pull. Jason waves it off.

"LET'S GO, ZIG! LET'S GO, MARAUDERS" Joel yells, as he squeezes in between Mary and the heavy-set fan to her left, reclaiming his spot on the riser. He begins his task of shelling the first peanut, eventually scooping the spoils into his mouth. As he chews, and starts on the next peanut shell, he keeps his eyes fixated on the action on the court, but offers a rhetorical observation to anyone who should feel like responding. "You guys see who's here?"

"No," Mary volunteers to respond. "Who?"

"Asshole."

"Who?"

Joel scoops another helping of shelled peanuts into his mouth, then uses the same hand to point across the court at the opposite stands. "Fifth row back. All the way to the right."

Jason and Mary squint across the court to the general vicinity of Joel's gesture, working in tandem to focus in on the object of Joel's interest.

Joel helps with a description. "Big dude. Tan shirt. Black-and-gray-ish hair?"

They focus in. Jason asks first. "The black guy?"

"Yup."

"Who's that?" Mary innocently inquires.

"Asshole."

"Who?"

Joel takes another handful of shelled peanuts, and throws them eagerly into his mouth. "Leonard Walton." Quick rest. "Ziggy's dad."

CHAPTER 13

NO OTHER CHOICE

"TEXT him back!"

Mary frantically wrestled the phone back out of my hands. "And tell him what?"

"Anything!" I was just as caught off guard as Mary was, but someone needed to try to think clearly, and it obviously wasn't going to be her. "Ask him where he is!"

Mary thumb-typed as fast as she could, her hands trembling as she pecked at the screen. I could sense the final thumb thrust was done both with authority and a sense of desperation. Must've been the *Send* button. She looked up at me, breathing heavily now, with the face a woman gets right before she's either preparing to cry, or to yell at you.

I showed no emotion, wanting to neither reveal my inner panic that would only serve to exacerbate Mary's anxiety nor to demonstrate any sense of premature relief. It was too early just to assume everything would blow over. Mary was bound to be pissed. Yes, she now had reason to believe Joel was safe, but her emotions were certainly going to switch quickly to anger at Joel for allowing her to worry like this. You'd better believe that, once all of the clearing-things-up was out of the way, Joel was going to get an earful about his lack of response...not to mention the creepy parcel she'd received in the mail. Divorced or not, he still had a lot to answer for.

I simply asked, in a tone so as not to poke the proverbial bear, "What did you send?"

"*Where are you?*" she answered.

"Anything back?"

"Not yet." She gave only a cursory and reflexive glance back down at the phone, apparently not expecting to receive anything back so quickly. "What the hell, Jason?" she asked of me. I wasn't going to be able to offer much of an explanation.

I peered down at the phone, now resting at her side in a tight-fisted vice grip. "Still nothing?"

She raised the phone to her chest and stared at it intently for several seconds. I waited in silence with her. Nothing yet.

In an instant, Mary started feverishly typing again.

"What are you saying?" I curiously inquired.

"*What's going on?*"

"Any response to your first text?" I asked, pretty much knowing the answer.

"Nothing."

"Ask him if he's okay."

"He said he's fine," she snapped back.

"Okay, ask him...when he'll be back."

Mary continued typing away.

Nothing.

When she eventually ran out of both messages to type and patience to wait for the non-existent replies, Mary dejectedly returned the phone to her side, grasped firmly in a trembling hand at the end of a near-lifeless, dangling arm. We waited for what seemed like several minutes for a response, intermittently checking the phone, then meeting each other's distraught, shaking eyes, then one of us looking aimlessly across the cityscape. Back to the phone. What was taking so long?! Still...nothing.

Mary took one final look down at her cellphone. "Well, I guess that's it."

I didn't know what to say.

"He's not answering," she said.

"I'm sure there's some perfectly reasonable explanation for this, Mary. Maybe he's in a bad cell area. Maybe on a cruise, remember? Maybe he's at port, and he's having trouble getting a good signal. Good chance he never even got any of your replies." She stared off, unaffected by any of my more reasonable attempts at explanation. "Maybe he just wants his space," I tried again. "I mean, I can't tell you why, but — What are you doing?"

Mary was typing again on her cellphone, but this time she lifted the phone to her ear.

I asked, "Are you calling him?"

She didn't respond, just looked forward with a determination I hadn't seen from her in many, many years. Her hand on her hip, she sniffed in a tear that failed to make its way past Mary's newfound defiance. I swear I saw her toe tapping, but maybe I'm just remembering her overall demeanor. She meant business now.

I repeated, "Are you calling Joel?"

"Nope."

"Then what?"

"Something I should've done a long time ago." She waited for someone to answer her call.

I could sense that my attempts to calm and reassure her were starting to lose whatever battle was forming on the field in Mary's mind. My guess as to who she was calling was confirmed the moment someone answered the other end of Mary's phone call.

"Hello, this is Mary Thomas," she began. "I'd like to report a missing person."

CHAPTER 14

27 Years Ago

THE QUAD at Manchester College. A pleasant breeze whisks through the blooming trees that outline the green space and mark the walkways filled with students strolling in small groups, escorted, most of them, by their proud parents. A warm sun reflects off the windows of the 19th-century architecture onto the trees, as frantic birds playfully chase each other from limb to limb.

Under a tree, a blanket is spread, and one of five gathered friends reaches into a cooler to hand his buddy a beer.

"Careful with the brews, Russ," one warns him.

"Who gives a shit, Joel? What are they gonna do now, kick us out?"

The brown-haired woman reaches up to make sure the tassel is still on the correct side of her mortar board cap. Russell brushes some ice from the cooler off of the sleeve of his black robe. Two other men are each lying on their sides in parallel across from each other, each leaning upon a bent elbow, and each with a cap and gown matching the others'.

Sitting beside them, Joel raises his can of beer. "Well. The end of an era," he proposes.

"More like the end of an *error*," Russell quips, as he takes an ample swig of his wine cooler.

The rest raise their drinks in unison. "The end of an era," they echo. They all sip. As they lower their drinks from their respective lips, they all stare off in silent, deep, introspective thought.

The black man lying on the blanket starts to talk first, but never breaks his glassy stare. "Never thought I'd see the day." Takes another swig.

"You?" Russell scoffs. "How many professors did you have to sleep with just to make Cs?"

"Gross." Joel is un-amused. "Some of us earned our grade points."

"And some of us don't give a fuck," Russell snaps playfully. "Yet, here we are, all in our matching fancy dresses. I don't see any special merit badges on yours, sweetie."

Still staring, the black man chimes in: "Russell, you gotta get on him for every damn thing, don't you?" He delivers the line amid an observant yet satisfied chuckle.

The woman matches his chuckle, and glances over at the man lying beside the black man. "So, who's the first one of us to get a job?"

"Better yet," Joel steals her thunder, "Which one of us is the first to a million?"

"My money's on Zig," the lounging man says, taking the thunder back from Joel's attempt to emend the topic of conversation.

"Ziggy?" Joel protests.

"Yep. There's gonna be some agent. Somewhere. Wanting to take a chance on Zig. Gets him the right tryout. Boom. The next Dominique Wilkins!"

Ziggy lets out a hearty laugh. "From your lips, Jason. From your lips."

"What about you, Jason?" she says, still holding her glance upon him.

"Um. I don't know, Mary. I have a few interviews lined up. We'll see. I always kind of wanted to start my own business."

"I start my internship on Monday," Joel pipes up. "Pennico.

Anyone ever heard of them?" The overly enthusiastic question is met with brutally disinterested silence. "Pharmaceuticals. They're downtown. Had it all lined up since before spring break. They're supposed to be onto some promising breakthroughs. Exciting stuff."

In a monotone, unaffected voice, Russell interjects drolly, "Any chance you can get me some?"

"Get you some what, Russ?" responds Joel.

"Some pharmaceuticals."

"Why, something bothering you, Russ?" Joel asks enthusiastically, encouraged by Russell's sudden show of interest.

"Yes...this...ex...cruciatingly....*bor*-ing story!" Russell stands up, his punch line met with collective approval and laughter at Joel's expense. "Well, I'm off," he confidently announces.

"Where you headed, Russ? Stay." Mary tugs at the bottom of his gown.

"Love to. But it's been real. It's been fun." Pause for effect. "But not like the real fun a Thursday night at Jojo's promises." He finishes his wine cooler then places the empty bottle back in the cooler. "His name is Brad. And we're meeting for our second — yes, you heard me right — *second* date. I'm pretending not to notice the dirt under his fingernails, or that he had raccoon eyes when we got back to campus last fall. I don't care if he works construction or landscaping or whatever...he's the type of boy that goes to Jojo's on Thursdays...and that's good enough for me."

"You're too observant, Russell," Mary teases. "And so quick to conclusions. That's going to keep you single if nothing else does."

"Hey, congrats, Russell." Jason raises his beer. "But wait, before you go."

"Yeah," Mary concurs. "Stay a little while longer. After tonight, who knows when we'll all be together again?"

Against the backdrop of Mary's observation, Ziggy lowers his head and looks down at the grass in front of him. Joel takes another sip of beer and allows his eyes to wander across the distant scenes in the quad, preferring not to make eye contact with anyone. He furtively wipes away the hint of moisture forming in the corner of his eye.

"Fine," Russell acquiesces, as he grabs a beer out of the cooler. "One for the road."

"I think we should toast," Jason says, his beer still extended at arm's length.

"A toast?" Joel is able make eye contact again. "To what?"

Mary takes the floor. "Well maybe not a toast. How about a pledge? To each other. Not to lose touch."

"Fine," Jason agrees. "A pledge."

"I'll drink to that," Ziggy blurts out as he begrudgingly holds up his beer, still staring down at the grass.

Jason clears his throat. He forces the lump in his throat back down and lowers his beer. He calmly looks around the quad, hoping to summon his muse. He starts slowly and softly…

"To four of the most amazing years of my life." He pauses. "And to four of the most amazing people I've ever met in my life."

"Not a toast!" Mary reminds him. "A pledge!"

"Oh yeah. Um…yeah. A pledge. Well, let me just stay this." They're all looking at him now, listening intently. "When I got here, I had no idea what to expect. They say it's going to be the best four years of your life. And they're right. But they never prepare you for what's going to happen…or *why* they'll be the best years of your life. I certainly didn't expect to meet a great guy like Ziggy. Or have a friend like Russell. To watch my best friend fall in love." A look down, and a silent reflection. "Or to actually approve of the person he fell in love with."

They all smile, and Mary looks over at Joel. Then back to Jason.

Jason continues. "But, Ziggy. You changed the way I think about people. You taught me what it means to overcome, ya know? To not make excuses...just to get shit done. And you too, Russell. Neither one of you take shit from anybody. And if anybody ever asked you to be something that you're not? You'd tell them to go fuck themselves. I admire that. You've both been better friends than anyone could ever ask for."

Jason pauses, battling a few clumsy moments of silent searching for the next thing to say. He finally finds the means to continue.

"Some people are lucky if they have one truly great friend in their lifetimes. I have four. And I'm only 22."

Looking now at Joel, "And Joel. I finally learned what they were trying to teach me about forgiveness in Catholic school all those years. You taught me. You're a better man than I, and Mary is extremely luck to have you."

To Mary, "And you're lucky to have him." He clears his throat again. "We're all lucky."

He raises his beer one final time. "Let's not forget that. Tonight, Russell will go to Jojo's — let's wish him luck, by the way." They chuckle.

"Don't need it!" Russell takes another confident sip.

"Right, right. Silly me," Jason continues through a chuckle. "So, Russell will go to Jojo's, Ziggy's heading home in the morning. Joel, you start a big important job already on Monday. Mary, I guess we go back to being crosstown rivals, right?"

Mary smiles. "Go Hawthorne!"

"Just promise me this, guys," Jason's fleeting jocular tone turns solemn once again. "All of us. Let's all make a pledge here and now. Because, after today, life moves on...and goes and gets crazy on us. Without us even trying. We've all seen our parents, right? Things change. I don't want that for us. Not us. Let's make a pledge to be there for each other. To have each other's backs. No matter what. A pledge. No matter what."

"'Til death do us part."

Everyone turns and stares back at Russell. He shrugs his shoulders in defiance, then fires back, "What?"

"*'Til death do us part*, Russ?" Joel snickers, sarcastically.

"What?" Russell repeats himself. "All of you will get to say that some day. I won't. Just once...I'd like to be able to say that to someone. And mean it."

Ziggy and Mary laugh. Joel takes another sip of his beer. An approving grin takes over Jason's expression.

"I like that," Jason says, as he raises his beer high above his head now. "A pledge. For all of us. 'Til death do us part."

They all extend their drink-laden hands in unison, then take what they all silently understand will be their final drink together as college friends. Together, in chorus, they join in and repeat back, "'Til death do us part."

CHAPTER 15

THE BROKEN TIMELINE

THE LAST place I wanted to return was Joel's house, but that's where the police asked Mary to meet them that morning. And I'd be damned if I was going to allow Mary to go through that alone. Sure, I had expressed my opinion to Mary that calling the police was not only premature, but misguided (given all of my prior warnings about everything she was inviting upon herself), but now that there was no putting that toothpaste back in the tube, I could at least see her through this. She was going to need support, and who else was going to be around to give it to her?

The investigation, such that it was, was already a week old, and nothing was developing — at least not to the satisfaction of Mary nor me. I wasn't there when Mary entered her statement at the police station, but Mary recounted the whole ordeal to me. She had to field all sorts of questions — none of which she had the answers to — *ad nauseum* and repeatedly. "Why are they asking *me?*" she would beg of me in frustration. "If I had the answers, I wouldn't be filing the police report, assholes!"

They were only being thorough, I assured her. But I didn't have the heart to tell her that it was only going to get worse. I mean, I had warned her of that once already. I wasn't about to be the *I told you so* guy, too.

When I got to Joel's house, I pulled up to see that both Mary and at least one police car had beaten me there. Joel's car was still in the driveway, but I knew better that this meant nothing. I parked my car and showed myself in through the front door.

Two detectives were inside canvassing the house, presumably looking for clues, while Mary was sitting at the kitchen table, head in hand. As I entered the kitchen, she jumped up from the table and walked over to give me an awkward embrace. Well, awkward for me, anyway. I'm sure she was simply overwrought with competing emotions, and a friendly port in the storm had just entered the kitchen. I obliged with an equally awkward return hug, then broke the silence, "How ya holding up?" I guess something inside me felt the need to offer the cliché soap-opera dialogue, but the words just escaped my mouth before I had the chance to offer anything wiser or more calculatedly appropriate.

"I'm fine. But this is getting to be exhausting," she bemoaned.

"I know." Of course I knew. But again...no *I told you so*.

There's a reason detective shows and buddy-cop movies always portray diametrically opposed misfit partners...because, that's pretty much what you get. Detective Longfellow was the prototypical grizzled veteran; Murphy was the ambitious young junior detective. Murphy bristled with energy, moving quickly from room to room with a fervid gusto and steely determination; while Longfellow ambled casually across the living room floor, administering a studious eye to examine every visible detail with painstaking precision.

Presumably in his mid- to late-50s, Longfellow had the requisite pot belly, but wasn't necessarily out-of-shape-looking. His white mustache matched his full head of gray waves that showed not even the hints of receding. His complexion revealed that he was a smoker, or had been for much of his life, and his raspy voice was the confirmation.

Murphy was a fit, buttoned-down late-20-something. Clean-shaven and hair set with the perfect side part, aided by hair product of some kind. His jawbone was chiseled, which matched the determination in his eyes, as he poked and prodded his way through every inch of Joel's house.

"Remind us again about the text," Longfellow offered, seemingly openly into the room in general, having not yet noticed that I was even there with Mary. As he slowly turned toward me, our eyes met only briefly before Mary jumped in.

"Um," she started abruptly, "this is Jason. He and Joel are friends." She walked over to my side. "Joel, this is Detective Longfellow," and pointed over to Murphy, "and his associate Detective Murphy."

Murphy walked briskly toward me with a firm handshake extended as he walked. "Sir," he said, nodding his head in deferential respect.

I shook his hand then turned toward Longfellow. "Detective Longfellow," I greeted him. He returned the handshake, but not the greeting. He just gave me a half-hearted and half-obligatory dip of the head, if only to acknowledge my existence.

"The text?" Mary asked, returning to the matter at hand.

"Yep, the text," Longfellow said, resuming his slow, measured perusal of the surroundings in Joel's living room.

Mary responded with a seeming lack of conviction, "Um, well. It's like I showed you. That's all it said. *I'm fine. Call off the dogs.*"

"And he hasn't sent anything else since?"

"No sir," she replied.

"And nothing before?"

"No, sir. I mean, not in several days...weeks, maybe."

"How many texts did you send him before he answered?"

"I don't know...maybe a half-dozen?" Mary estimated. "Maybe more?"

"And phone calls?"

Mary looked at me, seemingly wondering where this line of

questioning was going. "Yes. A few. To his cellphone, and one to work."

"No answers, you said."

"That's right."

Longfellow paused to reflect for a moment. Then he continued the examination, "All of this seem normal to you?"

Mary looked confused, again glancing over to me before looking back at Longfellow. "No, of course not. That's why I called."

"No, ma'am. That's not what I'm asking."

Again, Mary just returned a confused glance, begging for clarification.

Longfellow continued, "Any of this seem normal?"

"What do you mean?" she begged some more.

"I dunno," Longfellow pensively pondered. "Just wondering what seems out of the ordinary, is all."

"What do you mean?" I interjected.

"Just doing my job" he replied, dismissively. "Looking for things that don't fit."

"None of it fits!" Mary scoffed.

"Well," Longfellow continued, as Murphy looked on approvingly, with his hands on his hips, standing at full attention just a few feet behind Longfellow. "See, Ma'am. We get a call from an ex-wife, about a missing ex-husband, who she doesn't really talk to all that frequently, who's on vacation by all accounts, and we have to try to piece together why the urgency."

I tried to come to her defense, if that's what was necessary at the time (I couldn't tell if Longfellow's tone had turned accusatory, inquisitive or puzzled...but it was definitely off-putting, and I wasn't even the party subject to it). I quickly inserted, "You told him about the note in the mail, right, Mary?"

"She told us, sir," Murphy quickly returned volley, apparently nonplussed at my attempt to shed additional light on recent history.

"That's right," Mary affirmed. "If it weren't for the weird note in the box, and the sudden-but-now-silent texting, I don't know that I would think anything *of* this."

"We'll come back to the box," Longfellow coldly asserted. "Back to the text. Nothing strange to you about that?"

Mary scowled. "Other than that it came out of the blue, after numerous frantic attempts to get ahold of him? Or that he now won't respond to my reply texts or phone calls?"

"Anything else?"

She thought silently for a moment or two. "No," she said softly, seemingly trying to simultaneous understand where this line of questioning was leading.

Longfellow looked like a man that was onto something. But what, I hadn't the foggiest. He finally broke a moment's awkward silence with, "He talk like that?"

Mary looked back inquisically. "Like what?"

Longfellow again responded softly, slowly and measuredly. "One text. That's all you get. He's trying to assuage your fears. Let you know everything's all right. You've been sending him texts upon texts, making call after call. I'm sure he could hear the panic in your voice when you left him those messages...see the panic in your texts."

"I would hope," she interjected.

Longfellow continued. "And all you get is one...rather cold...rather sterile text. *I'm fine. Call off the dogs.* That sound like Joel to you?"

Mary's face went blank. It didn't. Even I could tell you that. That's not Joel...at least not the Joel I knew.

"What are you saying, Detective?" Mary beckoned.

Longfellow looked back with a cold, determined look. "Not saying nothing. Just asking, is all."

I was tempted to return the favor of Mary's awkward hug right then and there, but it wasn't the time nor the place. It looked like she needed consoling, but for what, I still wasn't even sure myself.

Detective Longfellow changed the subject. "What about this dog? Max."

"What about him?" Mary asked.

"Tell me again about the dog."

"Well," she started, as she began to pace the room. "I told you about the food. With the dead rats. I told you about how he died. Um...let's see. He was our dog...me and Joel's, when we were married. When we divorced, he took the dog..."

"Mastiff," he interrupted. "That right?"

"That's right," she confirmed.

"And you said he died a few weeks ago, maybe a few months ago?"

"We think so," Mary again confirmed. "And, from the rats, we're guessing he maybe had some bad food. He — Joel — never even told me that he died. Add that to the list of things I'm going to ream him out for when he turns up."

"Maybe as much as a year ago," Longfellow sort of began leading the witness. Mary just stared back at him, conceding the floor for him to continue. "Max been gone a long time, is that right?"

Longfellow said nothing, but resumed his amble, slowly passing right between Mary and me into the kitchen. He looked over at the pantry where Mary had discovered the dead rats in Max's food bag.

"I guess it could be a year ago," Mary obliged. "Like I said, he never even told me. I mean, he was *our* dog. The one we raised as our only child, ya know, Officer? Not so much as a phone call...nothing. I had to hear about it from Jason."

Longfellow turned toward me, then.

"Yes, sir," I piped up. "Joel and I weren't all that close anymore either, sir. But we talked from time to time...off and on. He told me a while ago that Max was getting up there. Not feeling himself anymore. They thought cancer or something, I guess. Eventually, there was nothing they could do. Inoperable, Joel said. Or the vet said, anyway. And that was it."

"I understand," Longfellow replied. He then looked back at Mary and displayed for the first time what I swore could've been mistaken for consolation. "I'm sorry," he softly offered under his breath.

"Like I told you we would," Longfellow continued, as he began ambling back into the living room, again right between Mary and me, "we contacted the vet."

"Thank you," was all a confused Mary was able to muster.

"We did look into Max's history a bit. Seems he was getting on in years, as you say. But we saw no reports of cancer."

Mary's clueless, blank stare again met mine. We turned back in synchrony toward Longfellow as he continued.

"Seems his death was entered into the vet records as heart failure — slash — organ failure."

Mary looked down at the ground. "Poor guy," she whispered under her breath.

"Yep. Poor guy," Longfellow echoed.

"That's strange," I said, perhaps even saying it *for* Mary.

"Yep. Strange," Longfellow echoed once again. "Also…" he went on, but paused his amble to turn back around and face Mary and me. "Strange timing, too."

We both looked back in utter puzzlement.

"Timing?" Mary prodded.

"Yep. Timing." He paused for a few seconds, then continued, "Wasn't a few weeks ago…certainly not months ago. Definitely not a year."

"Oh no?" I prodded all the same.

"Nope," he continued. "Strangest thing. Vet lists Max's death as heart-slash-organ failure. Not cancer. No cancer ever reported, in fact. And it doesn't fit." One last pause. And then: "Max didn't die several weeks ago. Max died last week."

CHAPTER 16

26 Years Ago

OVERCAST. Chilly. Barren trees and overgrown lawns struggle to maintain life between the spattering of humble homes, some of which dramatically reveal both age and neglect. About every fifth house features at least one boarded-up window; about every tenth house is completely boarded up. Some of the front porches are in a state of crumbling disrepair, while the occasional dwelling desperately needs paint to be scraped off and reapplied to its partial wood facade. A few pearls of restoration and maintenance pop up along the block, advertising both the care and pride of the determined, perhaps defiant, homeowner not ready to surrender to the encroaching blight.

A 1988 Jetta starting to show signs of rust sits idling on the street. A young man sits behind the wheel, eyeing the front door of one of the few such pearls, in front of which his car his parked. He reaches down to the passenger seat, picks up the cellphone, un-flips the bottom to reveal the keypad, and extends the antenna to full attention before typing in a phone number. He raises the phone to his ear upon hitting the green button.

"Hey, Mary. It's Jason...

...

"Joel with you?...

...

"Yeah, I'm here. Waiting for Zig to come out...

...

"Yep, we'll be there. I'm not sure what's keeping him...

...

"I will. Listen, you and Joel decide where we want to go eat beforehand?...

...

"Russell meeting us there?...

...

"I know, I know. I honked already...twice...he'll be out...

...

"What about Comelli's? You guys feel like pizza?...

...

"Okay, Zig and I will meet you guys there. Give us 20 minutes. I'm gonna go see what's keeping him...

...

"Okay, see you soon. Bye."

He flips the phone closed and returns the antenna to its locked, recoiled position, placing it back on the passenger seat. Jason exits the car and uses the key to lock the car door behind him before approaching the house. As he walks, his eyes slowly scan the sympathetic street block.

About 30 feet, now, from the front door, Jason is startled. Muffled screaming from inside the house. A woman's voice rings out, clearly in distress, but the words indiscernible. His eyes widen like saucers. He begins to jog nervously toward the front door.

He ascends the stairs to the front porch, yelling as he does, "Ziggy, you in there?" He knocks abusively on the front door. "Ziggy, let's go! Mary, Joel and Russ are waiting at Comelli's!"

No response.

And then, another scream pierces the heavy air. "Stop it!" is all that can be heard, amid a flurry of tortured beckoning.

"Ziggy!" Jason yells again, as he knocks even harder a second time.

No response.

He moves his hand down toward the front door handle, and frantically gives it a hopeful twist. Success. The handle turns, and he is able to force the door open.

The screaming is discernible now. It's the same woman's voice. "Stop it! Leonard! Get off him! You're gonna kill him!"

He rushes toward the sound of the screams. Through the entryway. Past the living room and beyond the kitchen. Into the den near the rear of the house. He looks down to his right and sees a black woman with a bleeding lip and bruised cheek, crouched into a corner, with clothes disheveled and tears pouring down her face. She screams again. "Leonard!"

His eyes dart quickly toward the apparent target of her wailing. In the opposite corner of the room, a large, older black man with a physically imposing build is crouched over a young man, in what appears from behind to be a choke hold. The victim of the death grip flails his arms and legs in desperate futility.

"Ziggy!" Jason yells toward them, in sudden recognition.

Before the large man has time to turn around, Jason jumps on his back and throws his arm around the perpetrator's neck from behind. He tightens the hold as hard as he can, and wrestles the large man off of Ziggy, dragging him to the floor. The large man resists, and begins to punch backward behind his back, trying to break free of this sudden new death grip, of which he is now the victim.

Tightening his frenetic grasp even more, Jason looks over at the sobbing woman, and quickly back to Ziggy lying on the floor, also bloodied about the face and clothes disheveled. He strengthens the grip yet again, now trying to squeeze the very breath from the large man's neck. He grips a fist with one hand then slams it against the back of the large black man's head. The large man recoils in both pain and shock.

"Jason, don't!" Ziggy pleads.

He tightens the fist again. Another blow to the back of the head. The large man collapses to the floor and tries to shake off the effect of both blows. The woman continues to sob in the opposite corner. Ziggy tries to muster another pleading directive. "Jason," escapes from an exhausted, swollen mouth.

Jason turns the large man's limp and stunned body over onto his back. Another fist. Another striking blow. This time to the face. The large man goes further limp. Another blow to the face.

"Jason! Stop it, man!"

Another blow. And another. Blood begins to flow from the large man's nose and mouth. Another blow. He has gone unconscious.

"Jason! Enough, man! You're gonna kill him!"

Another blow. And another. Another blow, upon a seemingly lifeless victim. Jason's eyes fill with rage. His mouth tightens with determination and vengeance.

"Bro! He ain't worth it!" Ziggy pleads once again.

Jason pauses his fist in the air, mid-punch. He looks over at Ziggy, as he is suddenly woken from his blind rage. He looks back at the bloodied sobbing woman. Then back down at the large unconscious man. He finishes the final punch.

Panting breathlessly now, Jason finally leans back, on both knees and arms at his side. His head tilts back as he lets out a sigh of both relief and exhaustion, then gasps heavily while trying to regain his breath. He slowly turns to Ziggy yet again, then uses his own nearly lifeless arms to dismount the large man.

"What the hell is he doing here?" Jason asks Ziggy.

Ziggy is dazed, but musters an unknowing head shake. "Asshole come back for us. Me and mom."

"What the hell, dude?"

"I dunno, Jays. But if you ain't walk in that door, one or all of us would be dead right now."

He collapses back into a seated position. "Now what, Zig? Call the police?"

They all stare in silence into the blankness of the room. The woman begins to muster the strength to force back the sobbing. Ziggy continues to slowly shake his head *no*. The hero pants heavily. Nobody speaks.

Finally, Ziggy sniffs in some drying blood from the outside of his nostrils. "Jason, brother." Jason looks back at him. Ziggy nods his head in gratitude. "I owe ya one."

CHAPTER 17

THE FIRST SHOE

"I DON'T understand," Mary confessed, as her eyes revealed both distress and despair.

"Neither do we, ma'am." Longfellow's tone wasn't necessarily accusatory, but it wasn't innocent wonderment either. "Doesn't seem to add up, does it?"

I noticed out of the corner of my eye that Murphy had returned to his determined due diligence, scanning the room for clues, dusting and collecting, placing small bits of this or that into ziploc bags. He wore tight rubber gloves, which aptly resembled the trappings of a skilled surgeon.

The examined peer of Longfellow's expression, met with the worried, blank-but-hopeful look on Mary's face, compelled me to step in. It was my mistake, after all...or so it certainly appeared.

"I'm sorry, Detective," I spoke up. "But this may be my fault."

"How's that?" Now the examined peer was directed toward me.

"The timing," I clarified. "I mean, I just assumed."

"Assumed what?"

"About Max. His dog." I was trying to piece it all back together.

"Enlighten us."

"Yeah, Jason," Mary walked toward me, looking for a lifeline of clarity. "Didn't you say Max died a long time ago?"

"I did." If I'm being honest, I was just as befuddled as they were.

But I started to reconstruct it aloud as I thought through it for even my own benefit. "I mean, I guess I just assumed." I collected my breath, and my thoughts. "I talked to Joel about a year ago. He was going on about how Max was on his last legs. Thought he had cancer. Vet said it would be weeks, not months. Unless he was *really* lucky. But best-case scenario was three or four months. Joel was really torn up, too. Felt bad for the guy." I searched my memory for clearer recollection. "I guess I just assumed Max died shortly thereafter."

Maybe my mistake was trying to offer consoling comfort to Mary when we first went to Joel's house that day. Truth is, I *had* assumed Max would've died months ago, based on everything Joel had told me the year prior, so I just offered what little knowledge I had in hopes of providing context and some cold comfort to a distraught woman who was frantically worried about the potential disappearance of her ex-husband.

I gathered my composure. Turning to Longfellow, I asked, "We're sure this dog that died just a few days ago was Max?"

"Pretty sure," he confidently returned. "Seems he was dropped off at emergency about a week or so ago. The owner, or whoever brought him in — we assume it was Mr. Thomas, as that's what the vet told us — checked him in at night."

Mary interrupted, "You assume?"

Longfellow nodded. "Well, we'd have no reason to suspect otherwise. He was the dog's only caretaker, yes?"

"Yes," Mary confirmed.

"The thing is," Longfellow continued, "if it was Mr. Thomas who dropped him off, he didn't wait around to see how it was going to turn out. Emergency vet did her best, but it was too late, apparently."

"Oh God," Mary began to sob.

Longfellow didn't break his stride. "But when she came out to deliver the bad news, Mr. Thomas was gone."

"I'm sorry, Mary," seemed like the thing to offer in the way of condolences. What else was I supposed to say?

"Even stranger," Longfellow went on, not even pausing to acknowledge Mary's mournful sorrow, "this is right around the time you say Mr. Thomas disappeared. Or the last you heard from him. Or when you got the note. Isn't that right?" he finished, now looking directly at Mary.

Mary lifted her head from her hands and looked up back to him, meeting his eyes. She said nothing, but acknowledged with a soft, assenting nod.

"Which keeps bring us back to this package you said you received," Longfellow verbally plodded forward.

"What about it?" I interjected. It was suddenly my business. *Tell Jason*, after all.

"That's another thing that seems strange," he said, now turning that difficult-to-identify glance in my direction. Again, was it accusatory, or simply inquisitive? Longfellow must be one hell of a poker player.

"We couldn't agree more," I said, preferring to swim upstream then against the current during this particular part of the conversation. "What do you make of it?"

"Not much. Yet. But we're still looking."

"Well, if you can figure it out," Mary stepped toward him, "we're all ears. Who sends a box, with only a sticky note inside? Jason and I can't make heads nor tails of it."

"We're looking into it, ma'am."

"Except the possible connection to the safe deposit box, maybe," she continued.

Longfellow's piercing eyes met hers again, then returned to slowly scanning his surroundings. "Yep. Looking into that, too."

To my right, I heard him speak up suddenly, interrupting the flow of our conversation. "Sir?" Murphy was frozen in a genuflection near the kitchen table, an empty ziploc bag in one hand while the other hand was raised into the air holding a cotton swab, which Murphy intently examined against the natural backlight of the kitchen window. "You're going to want to see this."

The three of us, now collected in the adjacent living room, looked back all at once in Murphy's direction. We crept slowly toward him, except Longfellow, who had a brisker pace to his eager gait.

"What'ya got, Murph?" asked Longfellow.

Detective Murphy pivoted just a bit to extend his newly collected evidence back in Longfellow's direction.

"Here." His eyes approvingly and self-satisfactorily scanned the swab. "Blood."

CHAPTER 18

24 Years Ago

FROM THE INSIDE of Manny's, revelers watch the parade go by through the large windows in front of the bar. As one would find at a high school in the fall, the homecoming floats travel slowly down College Drive, underscoring the small-school mentality of a college that keeps alive even high school traditions. The intermittent passing of marching bands is interspersed by flower-covered imitation goal posts that are affixed to a trailer bed covered with green indoor/outdoor carpeting meant to depict a playing field. Then comes the drum line. The flag troop and baton twirlers are close behind. Next up are the cheerleaders, flanked by boys dressed up in imitation football uniforms, pads and helmets. A banner waves: "Beat State."

The sun struggles to fight through the nearly overcast sky, intermittently warming the faces of the bystanding parade fans when it pierces through the thick cloud cover.

Inside, those taking refuge from the breezy chill enjoy coffee, hot chocolate, or beer and other harder beverages according to personal preference. Four alumni are cozily jammed into a small booth, clad head-to-toe in the home-team green.

"Here we are again. Back at the scene of...what...several crimes, right?"

They laugh, and each raises a glass to feign a toast.

"Right you are, Jason," a man across the booth from Jason

concurs. He takes a sip of his beer and playfully rubs shoulders with the brunette seated next to him.

"Together again, dogs. Y'all said *'til death*, right?"

"We did, Zig," Jason confirms to the man seated next to him. "Speaking of which, where's Russ?" He looks over his shoulder. "Should be here by now."

"I'm sure he just wants to make an entrance," Ziggy posits.

"You're so right," the woman concurs.

A round of burgers and fries are delivered to the table by a long-haired young man wearing a flannel shirt and jeans with holes strategically and purposefully ripped into the kneecaps. "Cuds and spuds all around," he remarks, in an overly obvious attempt to coin a phrase that is bound never to catch on. "Anyone need refills on the brews — coffee (looking at her) or otherwise (looking at the men)?"

He takes their order on refills, returns the pen behind his ear and under his frazzled locks, then leaves the table of four to continue their reminiscing.

"Okay, I got one," the man opposite Jason and Ziggy starts. "See if you remember this one. Me, Mary and Jason are in the quad during finals week…"

He holds court as he retells his favorite memory from senior year. They all erupt in hearty laughter at once when he arrives at the hilarious conclusion.

"Totally!" Mary recalls, seated next to him and poking him playfully with an elbow. "Oh my God, Joel…what were we thinking?!"

"Okay, my turn!" Jason announces from across the table.

The four take turns sharing stories, each concluding in eruptive laughter, high fives, elbow pokes, blushing faces thrust into the comfort of a concealing hand or forearm. Ziggy helps himself to the last few fries on Joel's plate, without Joel ever noticing as he intently listens to Jason regaling the group with a memory of his own. Jason delivers the conclusive punch line with aplomb, and they all erupt once again in laughter and hand claps.

"No way!"

"Swear to God!"

They all take another drink.

Abruptly, a well-dressed man wearing oversized sunglasses gallops confidently up to the booth, emerging from the crowd that has now filled the standing room near the bar. "Who's boyfriend do ya gotta sleep with to get a hot toddy around here?!" he blurts out as he strikes a formative pose.

"Russell!" they all exclaim in unison.

Mary forces her way out of the booth over Joel's lap to give Russell a lingering, warm bear hug. "Oh my gosh, mister, you are a sight for sore eyes!"

"You think your *eyes* are sore..." Russell quips, as they slowly separate.

"Gross, Russ," Joel quickly chastises his friend's lewdness.

"C'mon, Joel. You know he ain't into Mary that way," Ziggy says. "...And, just for the record, he ain't into you neither!" They all snicker back at Ziggy in approval.

"Russell," Jason says, as he waves over the long-haired waiter to return to the table. "Let us get you something to drink. You need to catch up. What'll it be?"

"Ooh. Something potent. Let's see," he starts, "how about just a shot for now? Sambvca." Long-hair is dispatched.

"Come, sit with us." Jason motions to Ziggy to slide over in the booth, and he and Russell slide in opposite Mary and Joel. "We were just reliving the wonders that were our days here at Manchester. Don't worry, we saved all the good stories for you."

Russell's eyes widen, and his mouth begins to form a wide smile. "Oooh! Okay, let's go there. Thought I'd wait for my shot, but let's do this." He looks over at Joel. "Did I ever tell you the time I caught Joel throwing up into a lamp at the Delt-Sig house?"

"Oh God, please no," Joel says, bowing his head in embarrassment.

Russell starts in and leans forward. Joel sits back in defeated disapproval. Russell entertains everyone with a gesture-filled, crescendo-building and theatrically voiced tale, interrupted frequently with laughter and pointing. Joel continues to shake his head and looks down at the bottle of Heineken in front of him as Russell holds the floor.

Two hours go by, and the five never fail to find the next story to tell. Branch-off side stories are placed in the queue for someone's "next turn." Manny's slowly empties out, as green-clad rooters exit in groups of four and five to walk down to the stadium for kickoff. The bar is quieter now, and you can finally hear the televisions that now seem to be too loud for the room, featuring talking heads and washed-up has-been jocks clumsily dissecting the "keys to the game."

Once the stories start to slow to a staggered pace, Jason takes the opportunity of a brief momentary silence to reflect. "Guys," he begins. "We simply gotta do this more often. Oh my God, these stories are hilarious. It's like we never left, ya know?"

"True 'nuff," Ziggy concurs.

"You're right, Jays." Mary puts her hair behind her ear and clears her throat with resolve. "We gotta be better about this."

Russell stands up out of the booth. "No argument here." He collects his bag from the booth bench beside him. "But for now, I'm off."

"Aw, Russ. So soon? Where ya headed?"

"I'm meeting someone," he suggestively confesses, with a knowing, pursed-lip grin. "Besides, I have better things to do than to watch a bunch of muscly college men wrestle around with each other in the mud, fighting over some stupid leather ball." He pauses for timing. "Or do I?"

They all laugh. "Okay, fine Russell," Jason acquiesces. "But we're doing this again. Very soon. Okay, everyone?"

"Absolutely!"

"For sure!"

"You got it!"

As he watches Russell walk away, Jason's expression gradually fades from a look of encouraged hope to one of pensive doubt. The TVs have been turned off now, and the overhead speakers play a song he recognizes, which seems to register at the fore of his thoughts. Toad the Wet Sprocket's "Walk on the Ocean" begins to slowly dissemble and finish, and Jason spills himself back into the booth, staring at his empty mason jar of what was once a cold beer, listening to the ending of one his favorite songs.

And half an hour later we packed up our things
We said we'd send letters and all those little things
And they knew we were lying but they smiled just the same
It seemed they'd already forgotten we'd came

CHAPTER 19

SEEMS LIKE OLD TIMES

HEADING back to Mary's house after an ordeal like that seemed both natural and wise, even with the angel on my shoulder advising me to give Mary her space. Had Mary not insisted, I would've taken the perhaps more prudent path of giving us both a night's rest to process what had transpired at Joel's.

It's more exhausting than you might expect to simply *be* somewhere, but also to be the subject to a bunch of questions, none of which you have the answers to. Mary looked like she had been sleepless for days — and maybe she had been. Through the emotional wringer, she was beginning to wear the stress and exhaustion on her face. It was that look — the look of a friend in helpless desperation — that eventually forced me to acquiesce to her invitation.

"Can I get you something to drink?" she asked, as we crossed the threshold to her front door, throwing her car keys carelessly onto the end table just inside the entryway. "I know I could use something."

"I'd take a beer," I obliged her offer.

I could hear her filling a glass with ice in the other room, and the obvious clank of a bottle of something landing abruptly against the lip of a waiting rocks glass. "Well that was a real treat," she sarcastically bemoaned from the other room.

"Yup," I half-heartedly acknowledged.

As she returned to the living room, she took a sip from her dark-

143

liquor-and-rocks concoction as she handed me a bottle of Heineken. Not my brand, but whatever. "I guess we're starting to get our answers," she noted, practically into the mouth of her glass as she went in for another swig.

"Thanks," I replied to the delivery of the beer. And to her comment, "I guess."

"Blood, Jason," she continued in lament. "Blood." Her words both echoed throughout the room and put unwelcome emphasis on what I remember to be the last, self-satisfied utterance that escaped from the mouth of Detective Murphy before they started packing up their discovery kits. *Blood.*

"I know it sounds bad, Mary," I began to comfort her, "but it could be anything." There I go again. The eternal optimist. Why was I always the one who had to try to put on the brave face for Mary and play the part of the voice of reason? True, part of me was convinced that there was some reasonable explanation for blood to appear on Joel's floor: a kitchen carving accident, a squashed bug, Max getting himself into this or that. But the nagging other half of me recognized the blood for what it was: a clue. A damnable, telltale clue that would be but the first in a series of unfortunate revelations, ultimately leading to a story neither me nor Mary wanted to hear. "We still don't even know it was Joel's blood...or how it got there," I offered, helplessly.

"Come on, Jason." Mary wasn't having any of it. "Let's be real here."

"I'm just trying to stay positive, Mary."

"Well, fine. But we'll know soon enough it was Joel's. And if it isn't? Well, I'm not sure that's any better, to be quite fucking honest with you."

I took a hearty swig of my beer, though it was slightly heavier than what I would've preferred. It reminded me of Joel. It was the type of beer he would've liked. It probably was his, left over from when he still lived in the house. I wasn't really sure how to respond, so I used the occasion of my long drag from the bottle to fill the space, hoping Mary would go on.

She did. "And that was a real treat when Longfellow asked us for hair and blood samples, wasn't it?"

"They're just being thorough, Mary."

"What, like we're suspects or something? Why would I call them if I had something to do with all of this?"

I thought Mary was dramatically overreacting, but after the day she'd had, I was willing to let her rant just a bit. It was all very understandable, given the stress she was under. But, again, someone needed to be the voice of reason here. So I tried to re-inject some rationale amid the flurry of speculation.

"Mary, think about it," I started. "They are taking our blood and hair samples to *eliminate* them as factors in the investigation. They already know we were there at Joel's house. They were with us! So our hair would be there, and they know it. It's not like they're trying to find evidence of us being at Joel's. They need to get our DNA so that, when they *do* find something — hair, blood, whatever — they can cross-reference it against our samples and discard the evidence as leads if it matches what we gave them. They're looking for samples that *don't* match ours...not the other way around!"

She processed that for a moment, then took another swig from her drink, now already down to being mostly ice remaining in her glass. "Could be, I guess," she admitted.

"Of course that's it. They know neither of us had anything do with it. Hell, we don't even *understand* it!" I added for effect. "I, for one, am not even entirely convinced there's anything that strange going on."

"Please, Jason." Mary gave me that look...as if to say, *grow up* or *get real.*

"Honestly, Mary," I maintained. "We're still a few days away from what would be the end of Joel's *planned and scheduled* two-week vacation," (I really stressed the words *planned and scheduled*). "I still will bet dollars to donuts that Joel calls one or both of us in a couple of days, wondering what all the fuss was about. Or when he gets back...he'll check back in, and he'll clear this all up."

"Seriously, Jason."

"And he'll have great photos and stories from Spain, or some cruise, or some Alaskan hike through the frozen tundra..."

"I love your optimism, Jason," Mary interrupted, "but I'm not buying it."

"Well, you don't need to *buy* anything. I'm not selling." I took another swig of beer. "All I'm saying is let's be patient and not jump to any conclusions. I'm fine with the police doing their thing. And I'm fine with us both being stressed as hell right now, too. But I'm equally fine with me hoping for the best and expecting what still is, until proven otherwise, the most reasonable explanation for all of this."

"You really think this is reasonable?" Mary shot back in defiance. "No return calls, no return texts...unless you count the one that even the police pointed out doesn't sound like Joel...a dead dog...and now blood found in Joel's kitchen? That all sounds reasonable to you?"

Well. When she put it that way, I realized how fool-hearted my well-reasoned optimism was beginning to sound. "No," I conceded.

"And why would Joel lie about Max?"

"I dunno," I muttered, without explanation of my own.

"Why would he tell you Max was dead so long ago? And why would he not even tell me he was sick, let alone *deceased*!?"

"I don't know, Mary," I practically whispered under my breath.

"And dead fucking rats, Jason! Rats! Poisoned filthy rats!" Mary was beginning to tear up as she got increasingly frazzled. She stormed out of the room. I could hear her fixing her refill at the bar in the other room.

Since she was out of sight, I felt a little braver to respond this time. "We don't know they were poisoned," I called out to her, grimacing in remorse the moment I heard the words come out of my mouth.

"Really?" she aggressively chomped back. "Rats just turn up dead, Jason?"

My next reply was a bit more subdued and contrite. Still reasoned, though, I thought. "Well, they could've just eaten the bad food. The food that maybe was poisoning Max." There's that voice of reason again.

She wasn't quick to reply this time. She simply returned from the other room in silence, sipping her refilled dark-liquor-on-the-rocks with a studied expression across her face, which was now hardening in resolve as she fought back the tears. She lifted her eyes to meet mine, and I could sense the resolve was weakening. A familiar tear began to reform in the corner of her eye. Mary's forehead began to wrinkle, her lip ever-so-slightly quivering. The suggestion of crow's feet began to emerge as her weakening eyes betrayed her prior resolve.

She took a final hearty swig and placed the drink on the end table where her car keys had landed. Before I knew what was happening, she walked briskly toward me, buried her face into my chest and threw her arms around me.

I stood paralyzed for a moment or two, processing this sudden and unexpected turn of events as quickly as possible. What was the right thing to do? What would Joel have wanted me to do? Don't get me wrong, I had no misconceptions about the impetus for this desperate embrace. She was losing it; that much was clear. And she needed a rock. I'm sure Joel would've at least wanted me to be that much, had he been a fly on the wall: the calming rock for Mary to cling to. But I still felt uneasy. As much as I knew this wasn't a "pass" — I'm not a moron — I still felt like I was being watched.

Reluctantly, I slowly and trepidatiously put my arms around her shoulders in a loose, emotionless (but condolent) coddle. She let out a full sob. I very slightly tightened my grasp. "I know," I whispered, with no other words available.

She lifted her head slowly off my chest and looked up at me, her face swelling with fear and dripping with tears. She finally forced the thought across her lips, "It just seems so familiar," she cried, "like it's happening all over again."

"What do you mean?" I innocently queried, despite the fact that I knew exactly what she was referring to.

She sniffed, and pushed herself away from my partial embrace. As she paced the room, she started to slowly regain her composure. But a tear, a sob, a sniff escaped periodically between phrases as she continued. "It's bringing back some very dark memories." Pause. "Painful memories."

"I know," I muttered again, wishing I had something better to offer.

"All of it." Pause. Sniff. "The searching for answers...was there something I could've done..." Sob. "Should I be doing more...how could this be happening...the not knowing...." Pause. A wipe of a tear. "The loss." Sniff. "The sense of crushing, despair, heart-wrenching, bone-crushing loss."

"I know," I repeated.

"The remorse. The anger. All of it just seems so familiar." Pause. "And I fucking hate this feeling."

"I know."

"I shouldn't have to go through this twice in one lifetime. None of us should." She raised her hand to wipe away the tear. "But doesn't this all seem like we're cursed or something? All of us that took the pledge?"

I didn't like where this was going. But there wasn't a voice of reason in the world that would've been able to intercept this runaway freight train of thought.

"'Til Death Do Us Part'? Wasn't that it?" Mary continued, now seemingly on a mission to get the formulating theory out of her head and into the atmosphere of the room. "Seems like a poor choice of words, looking back, doesn't it?" She scoffed ironically a bit as she delivered that observation. "Here we go again. The lack of explanations...the searching for answers...the prematurity of it all...It's not fair. Not again."

"I know." Despite my wishes to the contrary, I knew where she was going. And a lump formed in my throat as she brought the obvious correlation to the fore.

"Doesn't it remind you? The suspicion? The anger?" Mary was about to say it. "Doesn't this remind you of before?"

I knew.

Mary finished. "It's like Russell all over again."

CHAPTER 20

21 Years Ago

DOWNTOWN Calhoune on a bright Autumn afternoon, in a quaint and historically aged small town that hearkens back to a simpler time. Franklin's Pub occupies a small inline space between Carl's Comix and an updated Baskin Robbins that used to play the part of town gathering place for toddlers, teens and grownups alike, now as Ike's Creamery, overlooking the park in Central Square, as it's known.

Inside Franklin's works an older barkeep, perhaps in his late 50s, who cleans the bar top with a white towel before throwing it over his opposite shoulder for safekeeping.

"What'll it be, Mack?" he politely asks of a gentleman in his late 20s, who has just assumed his spot on a barstool.

"Um, light beer. Whatever you have on draft," he responds.

"Keep it open?" asks the bartender, apparently referring to the tab.

The man nods in acknowledgement. "Please," he says in response. "I'm meeting some people."

The barkeep is off to fetch the man's draft.

The man looks around the nearly empty bar. It's not quite dinner time, but well after lunch. "Quiet today," he observes under his breath, to himself.

The barkeep returns with his beer. "It'll pick up," he remarks, overhearing the young man's observation. "Happy hour starts soon."

The first sip is met with a sigh of approval.

The front door opens, casting natural light into the narrow darkness of the pub. Casting a shadow in the doorways stands a black man in his 20s, who recognizes his friend at the bar. "Jason! My man!"

"Ziggy!" Jason responds, leaping up from his barstool to greet the newly arrived acquaintance in the doorway. The two exchange a very masculine hug, pounding one another on the back with a closed fist while grasping each other's handshake with their free hands, pulling one another in, chest-to-chest.

"How ya been, brother?"

"Good, Jays. Good. You?"

"Can't complain. Here," Jason points to the barstool next to his, "take a seat. Let me buy you a beer." Ziggy takes the barstool and rests both elbows on the bar as Barkeep approaches, white towel in hand. "Man, it's so good to see you," Jason continues. "Everything all right?"

"Yeah...yeah. Job's good. Life's good. Love life could always be better, but it's getting there..." he chuckles. "What about you, man?"

Jason is finishing another hearty sip. "Mmm. Good here, too."

"What can I get ya, Mack?" The barkeep asks of Ziggy.

Ziggy looks over at Jason's beer. "Whatever he's having." Barkeep is off to fetch another light draft beer.

Jason pats Ziggy on the back. "So. Everything's good. Awesome." Jason looks up at the television, upon which a football game is airing. He hesitantly continues, "Any more...issues? Ya know...with ...Asshole?

"Dear old dad?" Ziggy mocks. Barkeep places Ziggy's beer in front of him. Ziggy takes it to his mouth and sips. "Nah, man. He still upstate. Let's hope he's staying there this time."

"Here's to it," Jason affirms, raising his beer to meet Ziggy's in a toast.

"Ziggy!" a woman's voice calls out as she enters the bar with her blond male companion. Ziggy twirls his barstool toward the door, as does Jason, and they both spring from their stools.

"Mary!" Ziggy quickly walks over to join her in a lingering hug.

"Joel." Jason follows Ziggy and extends the man his offered handshake.

"Jason! Ziggy! What up, fellas?" Joel returns Jason's handshake, then quickly extends one to Ziggy, which is returned in earnest.

Mary leans over to extend a polite hug to Jason. "Hi, Jays."

"Mary."

"What are you guys drinking? Russell here yet?" Joel asks.

"Come on in, guys. We're at the bar, but let's go grab a table." Jason grabs his beer off the bar, and Ziggy does the same, as the four retreat to the small dining area adjacent to the bar that extends almost the entire length of the back wall of the pub.

"I don't know where Russell is," Jason finally responds. "He'll be here. You know him and entrances."

Almost an hour passes. Two rounds of beers are delivered and consumed, along with a sampler platter of Irish-themed appetizers. They talk quickly and vigorously, as friends do who haven't lost a beat in the years since their last encounter. They take turns making trips to the jukebox to put in a dollar's worth of their favorite surprises. It's Jason's turn, as he grabs four quarters off the table and heads toward the jukebox. Soon, a Barenaked Ladies song is playing through the tavern's sounds system, while Jason considers his remaining selections.

A cellphone rings. Mary raises it to her ear.

"Hello?

...

"Russell, where are you?! You're missing all the fun!

...

"All of us. Me, Joel, Ziggy and Jason. Just missing you. Exactly how long were you going to make us wait for this dramatic entrance of yours, anyway?

…

"Oh. Really? Come on, Russell. We had plans!

…

"Okay...I'll tell them. But they won't like it.

…

"Are you sure?

…

"Fine. Rain check, then. Promise?

…

"Fine. Better be here next time, mister!

…

"Bye."

She flips the phone closed. "He's not coming," she reluctantly makes the expected announcement. Jason is just returning from the jukebox to overhear the bad news.

"Jerk!" Joel is the first to react, with an enmity that is difficult to discern whether it's intended as playful or genuine.

"Aw, man. You can't be buggin' out at the last minute, Russ," laments Ziggy.

"Shit sticks," Jason agrees with Ziggy. "He's not coming? That sucks. I thought we had a deal. No booking over these."

"We did," Mary concurs. "Non-negotiable. It's the pledge."

"What's his excuse?"

"Just said something came up. Didn't specify."

"That's bullshit," Joel chimes in, rather forcefully this time.

"Ugh. Well, to make matters worse," Ziggy steps up from his chair at the table, "I gotta be runnin' too, y'all."

"What? No," Mary pleads.

Jason insists, "Come on, Zig. It hasn't even been an hour. Stay."

Ziggy throws a $20 bill on the table. "Sorry, bros and bras. Date night."

"Date night?" Joel seems surprised.

"Yup. Date night. Going on two months. Traci."

"Whoa," Joel smiles. "Strong work, Zig. But why not just have her meet you here?"

"Sorry, guys. Just me and her. Y'all ain't gonna meet her until I'm damned sure she ain't the runnin'-off type," he jokes.

"Aw, Zig." Mary tugs at his sleeve. "Fine, you're excused. Have fun. But I'll tell you the same thing I just told Russell. Next time it's for longer. *Way longer!* Non-negotiable. Hear me?"

"Right on, Mary." He leans over and gives her a kiss on the cheek. He trades hand-slaps with Jason and extends a more formal handshake to Joel. "Y'all be good."

Mary stands up to give Ziggy a hug, and Jason and Joel both stand to bid Ziggy farewell. As Ziggy walks away toward the door, Joel looks at Jason, then back at Mary, before uttering through a sigh, "Well, maybe we should get going too. Rain checks all around?"

"Don't leave on my account," Jason says.

"No, no...nothing like that," Mary insists. She looks at Joel. "We just have plans later with Joel's folks...across town."

"I guess since everyone else is bailing," Joel picks up where Mary leaves off, "we'll just reschedule. No biggie, Jays."

"Fine...yeah," Jason seems forced to concede, as Joel is already putting his coat on. Mary grabs her coat and purse, then places a gentle and apologetic hand on Jason's upper arm while shooting him a pitying glance. He smiles back at her. "Go ahead guys," Jason forfeits, "I'll get the check."

Mary once again tilts her head sympathetically as she looks back at Jason, then she and Joel follow Ziggy out the door. Jason reaches into his pocket and pulls out enough cash to throw on the table, before grabbing his own jacket. He waves to Barkeep, finishes an ample amount of his remaining beer, then heads toward the door himself.

Halfway toward the door, he stops. A song is recognized beckoning from the jukebox. Jason stops and looks back over his shoulder at the now-empty table. He flips up the collar of his coat and listens to the song as it nears its end.

And half an hour later we packed up our things
We said we'd send letters and all those little things
And they knew we were lying but they smiled just the same
It seemed they'd already forgotten we'd came

CHAPTER 21

A BIT OF INSURANCE

"I KNOW." I said it again. I could hear the repetition in my responses, but I really was at a loss for words. I saw the same correlations Mary was describing. But it was getting late, and I could see a couple steps ahead to where a deeper conversation about Russell would lead. And I just wasn't there, neither mentally nor physically. I suspected, at heart, neither was Mary. Which she confirmed almost immediately, as she attempted to regain her composure.

"It's getting late," Mary said, practically taking the very sentiment out of my head and into her words. "I should get to bed. I'm exhausted." She finished the final remnants of her drink and returned the glass into the kitchen.

"Been a long day," I offered in solace. I reached into my jacket pocket to fumble for my car keys, and downed the rest of my beer.

"You should stay," Mary said softly. I was startled. I looked directly into Mary's eyes, which were still blank with despair. There came that feeling again. Like I was being watched. Before I could formulate a response, Mary completed her thought.

"On the couch."

I hesitated. But I was able to muster an obviation. "Of course." I didn't mean, *Of course, I will*, but rather, *Of course that's what you meant.* "But I can't," I completed my own thought in return. "I should get going."

"Please. Stay, Jason." She walked slowly toward me and placed a comforting hand around my wrist. "It's been a hell of a day. And I'd just feel better knowing someone was in the other room tonight. Call it weird. Make fun if you want." I didn't want. "And it would be nice to not wake up to an empty house tomorrow. A friendly face might make all the difference in the world in the morning." She smiled faintly, like she was finally summoning the strength to pull it together. "If I'll even be able to sleep, which is doubtful."

"I don't know, Mary," I protested.

"Please."

I stared back for a second or two. Then a sense of surrender washed over my body. "Fine. I'll take the couch."

"Thank you, Jason. I'll go grab some pillows and a blanket." Mary left the room, apparently heading to the linen closet to gather my night's bedding. I sighed. Not only did it feel unnatural to be there, I really could've used a good night's sleep in my own bed. But my thoughts returned again to trying to predict what Joel would want me to do, if he was looking over my shoulder. I think he would've wanted me to stay there, to offer comfort and security to Mary. Knowing Joel, he wouldn't have given it a second thought. And if this was all going to blow over and return to some sense of normalcy, he'd thank me for not leaving Mary alone to fend for herself during her time of need like this.

Mary returned with her arms full of bedding and tossed it gently on the couch. "This should do it. Let me know if you need more."

"Thanks. I'll be fine, I'm sure." I could feel her eyes on me as I looked around the room for what to do next. I was exhausted, but I really wasn't ready for bed. Have you ever been so tired that sleeping doesn't even sound good? I needed a distraction. "You got a remote for that TV?" I said as I pointed to the television.

Mary walked over to the coffee table and handed me the remote that controlled the TV. "Help yourself to anything," she offered.

"Another beer, whatever. There's food in the fridge."

"I'll take you up on that beer," I replied. Mary simply extended an arm in the direction of the kitchen, as if to say, *Be my guest.* "Thanks," I returned with a smile.

Mary forced a smile back. And that familiar head tilt. "Good night, Jays."

"Good night, Mary. Try to get some sleep."

And with that, Mary retreated to her bedroom. I turned on the TV and flipped around a bit until I found some meaningless sporting event on TV. Just enough to keep my attention, but not enough to dominate it. It was good passive entertainment. I returned the remote to the coffee table and went into the kitchen to fetch my next beer. Probably not the last.

As I screwed the top off of another Heineken and returned to the living room, my mind began to wander, and my eyes followed suit. If my mind was searching for answers, my eyes were apparently hunting down a distraction. I surely wasn't interested in gawking at the home Mary and Joel had at one time built for themselves, but the photos intruded. They kept reminding me of the entire ordeal, when all I wanted was the distraction. Why did she keep the photos? I mean, keep the photos, yes. But display them on the mantle? Of your ex? I guess I would've done the same. And there was Max, smiling back at me in still-life. Good picture of him, too.

I floated passively like driftwood back to the kitchen table, rifling through the junk mail, magazines and mail-order catalogues that were strewn across the top of it. I don't even think my mind processed anything my eyes encountered. I couldn't even tell you which magazines they were, to be honest. I circled the table, swigging my beer, then decided to retreat back to the living room to watch the game.

I noticed out of the corner of my eye that the car keys that Mary had thrown on the end table just inside the doorway must've slid right off and onto the floor. I walked over to retrieve them, and bent over to pick them up, returning them to the table top. I placed the keys on top of an unpaid water bill. I looked closer at it. It was overdue.

That's when my distracted autopilot mind must've taken control over my aimless bodily actions. Almost reflexively and uncontrollably, my hand opened the top drawer of the end table. It was jammed with papers, pens and all sorts of miscellany. A true junk drawer. I rifled through it all, just as I had done to the pile of junk mail and periodicals on the kitchen table — nothing really registering, and not really looking at or for anything. Just mind doodling.

That's when I saw it. Something that would suddenly awake the conscience. I wrested control from the autopilot in my mind. I focused. Is that what I thought it was? I pulled out a document, probably 15 to 25 pages or so, bound together at the top with a binder clip. It looked like a legal document, with a cover page.

And it was that very cover page that took me aback. I didn't need to peruse the particulars. The very existence of the document itself was enough to give me pause. Mary hadn't mentioned it before — not to me...not to the police. That latter omission was, if nothing else, troubling. This was what I specifically warned her against. A husband (or even an ex-husband) goes missing, and the prime suspect — until proven otherwise — is the spouse or ex-spouse. You'd have to be pretty naive to think that Mary wasn't at least a person of interest in Longfellow's investigation: the primary source of leads and answers, even if she never were to become an actual suspect.

But I was more conflicted than troubled. The document was clearly placed out of view — jammed into the bottom of a junk drawer — but not hidden. If this is something you want to hide from the police, you certainly don't jam it into the end table near the entryway to the home. Hiding something in plain sight only works in detective novels. But the question was, *why not mention it?* Clearly she wasn't *hiding* this. But she wasn't displaying out in the open for all to see, either. In my mind, I knew there was nothing to be suspicious about. Just disappointed. Disappointed at the unwelcomed attention the existence of this document would bring upon Mary. It was all just so avoidable.

But there it was. In black and white. A life insurance policy. The owner of the policy: Joel Thomas. The primary beneficiary: Mary Thomas.

CHAPTER 22

18 Years Ago

OVERLOOKING the bluff at Lake St. Paul sits Willowy Shores, an upscale banquet facility with an expansive, pillared back porch, reminiscent of a colonial plantation mansion. On the back terrace, set back a few feet from the grassy shoreline, are circular tables of 10, covered in white linens and set with china, silver and crystal.

An eight-piece orchestra, clad in matching classic black-on-black tuxedos, plays upbeat Motown classics as dessert and coffee are delivered to the tables. The groomsmen collect on the makeshift dance floor in front of the band, with loosened ties, creeping-up cummerbunds, and un-tucked dress shirts, clumsily attempting to keep time with the beat of the music. "My Girl" is screamed in unison, but not in key. Most are up mingling, as dinner is cleared.

A bride makes her way from table to table, arm-in-arm with the beaming groom, whose tuxedo matches that of his disheveling groomsmen, but with a royal blue bowtie and cummerbund. Those who choose to forego the coffee and dessert infiltrate the dance floor in groupings of three and four, arms raised in celebration and song.

In the adjacent room, two groomsmen stand against the bar service station, waiting for a drink. The bartender hands them each a tall mixed drink, and they retreat to the adjacent lanais, somewhat away from it all. There's a cast-iron park bench strategically placed between two topiaries. They have a seat.

"To the happy couple," he raises his glass to meet his friend's.

"To the happy couple," his friend obliges. They take a sip.

A third friend saunters in confidently. "Thought I'd find you Marys out here!"

"Hey, Russ," one says to greet him and his gibe. "Join us."

"Don't mind if I do, Ziggy." Russell raises a martini effeminately to his lips. He takes a cautious sip, so as not to mire his freshly applied lip gloss, surgically holding aside the olive that's been pierced with a plastic spear. "Speaking of Marys," he chirps, looking around the scene, "where's the blushing bride?"

"Making the rounds, I guess," says the man seated next to Ziggy on the park bench.

Russell looks back at his cavalier response and raises his martini in his direction. "To happy endings, eh, Jason?"

Jason raises his glass back toward Russell. "To happy endings, Russell."

The bride and groom briskly approach, walking hand-in-hand.

"There they are!" Ziggy announces.

"Come! Join us!" Russell mimics yet another toast.

"Ugh," Mary gasps in poorly disguised commentary on the evening's hectic obligations. "We could use a break!"

Russell waves them in. "Come get a drink, we were just toasting you."

A passing waiter has champagne flutes on his tray. The bride and groom each grab one.

"First," Russell starts. "Can we just pause for a moment and gaze upon your dress?" He grabs her by the hand. "You are gorgeous, girl!"

She curtsies mockingly in gratitude.

He continues, "And let's run them down," eyeing her up and down. "Something borrowed: the earrings Jenny gave you when you rushed Gamma Pi. Something blue: Um, can you say garter?" He makes a secretive gesture with the back of his hand at his mouth for effect. "Something old: that's a vintage brooch, I'm guessing your grandmother's. And, finally, something new: that gorge diamond necklace." He takes another sip of his martini. "How'd I do, Mary?"

"Wow, Russell," she chuckles. "That's remarkable. Four out of four."

"It's a gift." Another quick sip, feigning dismissal at her awe.

The band takes a break. Recorded music will fill the interval. First up, *Bust a Move* by Young MC booms over the sound system.

"Ooh!" the groom searches for a place to put down his champagne flute. "This is my jam!" He grabs Mary by the arm. "Come on, babe. Let's bust a move."

She resists. "Hold on, Joel. I still need a break. And to finish this exquisite champagne!" she adds, holding up her glass. "You go on. I'll catch up with you."

Joel looks at the rest of the guys. "What about it, fellas? For old time's sake? Who's with me?"

Russell slams the rest of his martini. "I'm game!" He turns to Jason. "You heard me...*game*," he emphasizes. "Don't get any ideas." They all chuckle at the delivery of another perfectly suggestive quip.

"Jason? Zig?" Joel beckons

Ziggy takes a sip of his drink through a straw and places it on the table next to him. "I'm sure I'm gonna regret this...but what the hell."

"You guys have fun," Jason waives. "I'll be out there when they play some Doors."

Joel, Russell and Ziggy are off to the makeshift dance floor. Mary watches them exit, then turns slowly back to Jason.

"So," Jason breaks the ice.

"So," repeats Mary.

She walks over and takes Ziggy's place on the bench next to Jason. As she sits, Jason raises his glass. "Well," he starts, "'Til death do us part," he mimes a toast clink, which Mary does not return.

She smiles back. "Yup. I heard it myself."

"You were the first of us. You and Joel. Congratulations."

She continues her prior thought. "As soon as the pastor said it, it brought me back to the pledge. Our pledge." She pauses. "Kinda cool, right?" She sips from her champagne.

"Oh yeah," Jason heartily agrees. "Definitely."

"It was cool hearing it again, I thought. This time for me and Joel. I had no idea how the vows were going to go, by the way. Joel worked that out with the pastor. But yeah...'til death do us part. That's us. All of us."

"For sure."

A waiter stops by to offer coffee. They decline. The waiter departs, but there is nothing new to fill the silence. They both study the goings-on across the dance floor. She clears her throat, then offers solemnly, "He forgives you, Jason," she says. "Us. He forgives us."

"I know." Another swig.

"Jesus, you're the best man, for Christ's sake. I think he's moved on," amid a forced chortle.

"I know," he repeats himself. Staring off, he is, surveying the scene so as not to make eye contact.

A long, awkward pause. Mary takes another sip. She fixes her gaze upon her friends dancing on the dance floor, and forces out a chuckle to fill the silence.

"I'm happy for you," he says sternly.

She takes another sip of her champagne.

"Really, I am. So very happy."

"Thank you, Jason."

"All I ever wanted was for my best friends to have their own happily-ever-afters. And for Joel, that's you. And for you, that's Joel." A sip of his tragically diminishing drink. "And for that, I'm happy. You guys deserve it."

"Thank you."

"Absolutely." He now laughs at the scene on the dance floor, Ziggy trying to show his cohorts how to truly bust that move. He then turns more serious for a moment. "So, babies in the future?"

She scoffs in dismissal. "Whoa there, cowboy. One thing at a time. We haven't even had the honeymoon yet!" Her face beaming with a smile. "One thing at a time."

"Fair enough. Fair enough. All things in time."

They both sit in silence, as the remnants of their grins only slightly and very slowly fade. Mary's expression turns pensive. She looks back at Jason.

"You know what? Maybe we'll start with a dog."

CHAPTER 23

BY A HAIR

I WAS wrong, of course. The couple of days went by, and nobody heard anything from Joel. Neither me nor Mary received the return texts or relief-delivering phone call upon Joel's glorious return from vacation. It was foolish of me to try to even get Mary's hopes up that way, when I didn't even truly believe it myself. The end of Joel's vacation was bound to come, and it was only a long shot that we'd get the *What's the big deal?* messages from Joel, even under the rosiest of scenarios. They were not forthcoming. Not even a peep.

Mary confirmed with Pennico that Joel hadn't returned to work Monday morning. And Mr. Pennington personally took Mary's incoming phone call that morning, with as many questions for Mary as she had for him. People were finally starting to share Mary's worry, and there was some comfort in that, she would divulge to me, if nothing else. "I'm not going crazy," she unnecessarily assured me, or perhaps herself.

Mary and I met for lunch that afternoon. We needed to game-plan our next steps. The police investigation was moving far too slowly for either of our likings. A total of two weeks went by since Mary had gotten the mysterious package in the mail, and I had received the phone call from Mary. And here we were, almost two weeks into a rather exhaustive police investigation (not to mention our own amateur sleuthing work), and still not much more to show for it.

We tried to be patient, to let the police do their work. Give them their space. Stay out of the way. But we were growing increasingly impatient. Worry was becoming panic. Hope was turning into despair. What was taking so long?! Occasionally, Mary would try Joel's phone again, with no true hope that it would be answered. An occasional text here and there. She couldn't just do *nothing*. She knew as well as I that there would be no response. But she had to try. The whole ordeal was moving beyond suspicious and well into the *downright creepy* territory.

To make matters worse, the police kept telling us they were "doing all we can." Sorry, we took no solace in that. I'm sure that's how things work in the real world, but we've been conditioned by movies and books and cop shows that things should be moving faster than this. Mary would frequently place a call in to Detectives Murphy and Longfellow, and each was met with the same seemingly careless dismissal. "We will call you, ma'am, as soon as there's anything to report. Until then, please keep yourself available should we have any additional questions for you." That sounded a little foreboding, even for me. Threatening, almost.

Enough was enough. It was time to become active participants in all of this. No more sitting around, waiting to have the bad news delivered to us. And, for Mary's sake if nothing else, I wasn't about to completely forfeit to the notion that Joel was gone. I kept alive the spirit that Joel was somewhere, somehow failing to get back to us, but that somewhere, somebody knew something, and some way somehow this was all going to have a happy ending. But that's me, the eternal optimist. And Mary knew it. Still, I could sense that there was a part of her that wanted to believe it as well. After all, she still had a sense of urgency. A sense that it was a race against time. You don't feel that way if you are one hundred percent convinced that the inevitable has already happened. In that instance, I would guess, you'd rather delay knowing the outcome. No sense in rushing to the conclusion of a tragic ending, right?

"So what are we missing?" Mary asked, as the waiter departed from our table at a street-side cafe downtown.

Good question. I hadn't mentioned the life insurance policy. I figured Mary would tell me when she wanted to. And the last thing I needed to happen was to have Mary's sole ally cast shade upon her.

What was really nagging at the forefront of my psyche was the package. Now that the urgency of contacting Joel immediately was starting to settle down, for better or for worse, the pieces to the puzzle were beginning to present their relevance. More and more, that package and note sent to Mary made less and less sense.

"I don't know. But one thing I keep thinking about is the box," I revealed. "There has to be some sort of connection between what you received in the mail and that safe deposit box Joel mentioned in his last will. I just know it."

"That will got you shaken up, Jason?"

"What do you mean?"

"Well. Weeks have gone by. We have to be realistic about what's happened. You're named in the will." She took a sip of coffee. "Is that what has you focused on the box? Safe deposit or otherwise?"

"Maybe," I confessed. I guess she was onto something. The will made it all about me, in some weird respect, and she was noticing. I thought about that for a moment. The package and safe deposit box weren't, as far as I could tell, leads that the police were chasing down with any noticeable fervor or focus. Perhaps that was ours for the taking.

"Maybe that's it," I continued.

Mary's forehead wrinkled quizzically. "What's it?"

"The safe deposit box."

"That was already a dead end once," Mary reminded me.

"Maybe not," I insisted. "When we went there last time, the bank said we couldn't discuss the details of Joel's safe deposit box…"

"Right…"

"…unless — or until — something happened to Joel."

Mary stared back. I could tell she didn't like where I was going with this. But I persisted, "Aren't we saying that it's looking more and more like something has, in fact, happened to Joel?"

"Yeah, but —"

Before Mary could continue her protest, I forged ahead. "Maybe that's our in."

"Jason."

"We go back to the bank, present the will, tell them the police are conducting an investigation…"

"Jason," Mary interrupted again, this time more forcibly, so as to claim the floor. "We don't know any of that that yet." Now the optimism — or, at very least, the realism — was coming out of Mary's mouth. She was right, of course. The bank was bound to need more process and procedure then us barging in again with reports of Joel's demise, such that it were even true, let alone verifiable.

That's when Mary's cellphone rang. She looked down at the caller ID, then back up at me. "It's Longfellow," she informed me.

"Answer it!" I urged. "Put it on speaker."

Mary held her phone out over the center of our table, and pushed two buttons: one to answer the call, and the other to immediately put the call on speakerphone. "Hello, Detective," she answered in recognition of the phone number on the screen.

"Ms. Thomas. Detective Longfellow," the raspy voice on the other end of the phone confirmed. "You available to chat right now?"

"I am," said Mary. "I'm here at lunch…with Jason Wilhelm."

"Am I on speaker?" Longfellow asked.

Mary confirmed, "Yes, is that okay?"

"At a restaurant, you said?"

"Yes, Detective."

"Well, can I ask you to find a private corner somewhere to chat? Away from anyone who might overhear?"

"Sure," she said, then quickly, "Can Jason listen in? He's right here."

"Sure," Longfellow agreed. "Might want him to hear, too."

"Great," Mary responded, gesturing to me to arise from the table. "Just give us a second to move away. Hold on."

Mary and I got up from the table and pushed our seats in. We walked to the exit of the street-side dining terrace toward the busy street. The road noise was a considerable distraction as we approached the curb, so I pointed Mary toward the side alley of the restaurant, which was indeed enough out of the way to provide both privacy and aural seclusion from the road noise.

As we found our spot against the wall of the restaurant in the alleyway, both Mary and I looked around to make sure nobody was within earshot.

"Okay," Mary informed Longfellow. "We have some privacy now. How can we help you?"

"Well, we have some news," Longfellow started, in his trademark matter-of-fact tone. Slowly and confidently...in no real rush, which I mentally noted at the time, perfectly matched the pace of his dragging investigation.

"Okay..." Mary prodded.

"It's not all good." Longfellow paused.

Mary looked at me, and her face went pale. I gulped, preparing myself for the rest of the update.

He continued, "And some of it...well, we just don't know. That's why we're calling."

"Sure, officer," I piped up. "Happy to help, in any way that we can. What have you found out?"

My sense of Longfellow's pause was that it was his way of expressing his disapproval of me butting in. But maybe I was just being overly sensitive. He began again. "The blood." Mary's eyes closed. Longfellow let the words hang there, and for far too long. And then, finally, the reveal: "It's Joel's."

Mary kept her eyes closed, and her whole body began to shake, as if she were crying, but nothing audible had yet escaped her. Just the shaking.

"I'm sorry to have to tell you this," Longfellow continued in monotone, seemingly with an uncaring detachment to the tragedy of the news he was delivering, "but I suspect you feared that was the case. Still, I know how hard this must be."

There was a long moment of silence, or what seemed like one, as I searched for something to say and Mary visibly mustered every ounce of energy to force back an all-out sob. She covered her mouth with her hand. Longfellow continued.

"And I hate to put it this way, but I should inform you, as someone close to the case. Both of you."

We waited. He paused. Then continued.

"We are reclassifying the case." Mary lost the battle. She could no longer hold back her tears. The sobbing was almost enough to drown out Longfellow's next words. "From a missing person's case," — Mary sobbed again — "to a homicide investigation."

"What?" I don't know why that was the first word out of my mouth. I mean, logically it made sense. And I knew where he was leading. But the shock took over. "Homicide?" I echoed for clarification.

Mary said nothing, but continued to wage the war against her own wailing.

"I'm sorry," Longfellow replied, showing no audible signs of sorrow, nor empathy. "It's been a couple of weeks now. Mr. Thomas hasn't reported to work. He hasn't responded to an ongoing police investigation." He paused again. "It doesn't look good."

"I understand," offering to fill the void, while Mary was still unable to respond.

"But there is one thing you can help us with," Longfellow began anew, this time with a bit more enthusiasm in his voice.

"Of course, officer," Mary was able to whimper out, in compliance.

"The DNA. The rest of it." Longfellow continued his measured, thoughtful pace. Everything in due time. No rush. "The hair samples we collected."

I was quick to reply, "What about them?"

Longfellow didn't miss a beat. "We were able to match most of the samples we retrieved. Joel's, obviously." Mary had stopped sobbing now. We were both intently listening to the words oozing like molasses out of Longfellow's drawl. "Yours, Mary. And yours, Jason." We waited. "Which stands to reason."

"Yes?" Mary prodded.

"Well," Longfellow responded in due course. "There's another couple of samples that don't match Mr. Thomas's...or yours, Ms. Thomas...or even yours, Jason."

"Oh no?" I volleyed back impatiently.

"No," he replied subduedly. "In fact, they don't match any of the other DNA samples we collected. Except for maybe some skin cells we're still running some tests on."

"Oh no?" Mary said, echoing my wonderment.

"No, ma'am," he went on. "We knew pretty early on they wouldn't be a match to any of yours, just by looking at them, but the tests confirmed it."

"Confirmed what, Detective?" My wearing patience was beginning to reveal itself in both the urgency and tone in my voice.

"The hairs, Mr. Wilhelm. They appeared...and have now been confirmed...to be those of a man of African American persuasion."

Mary and I looked from the phone into each other's eyes, each of us searching for solace.

Longfellow had one more question. "Either of you know anyone like that who may have visited Mr. Thomas in the past few weeks? A black fella?"

CHAPTER 24

15 Years Ago

"I THOUGHT you'd never ask," she says, her smoky eyes looking back at him as she finishes the last sip of wine out of a lipstick-glazed wine glass. He extends a bottle of red, and she presents her glass for a refill. "Don't be shy," she chuckles.

"A woman after my own heart," he laughs back. They each take a sip in synch, their eyes remaining affixed on one another's over the top of their own wine glass.

The flicker of a natural fire provides both the sonic ambience and much of the room's lighting, aided by strategically placed candles around the room, and accented audibly by the hint of soft music playing in the background, almost too quiet to be heard.

"So tell me more," she says, practically whispering, as she folds her legs on the couch, readjusting to get closer to him.

He smiles back, with a sheepish grin. "Not a whole lot to tell. You now know most of the good stuff by now."

Her grin widens. "Now I wanna know all of the bad stuff!" She playfully pushes at his shoulder.

"So soon?" he laughs.

Silence takes over. A mutual stare. A seduction. She finally leans over for a kiss. He leans in to oblige and places a hand warmly on her cheek, caressing her blonde hair softly behind her ears. The kiss begins timidly at first, then becomes more intent. The pace heightens.

The breathing, heavier now. They unlock, but only to emphasize the passion of the moment. She looks deep into his eyes, and he into hers.

The silence is broken. "What?" she whispers.

"Nothing," he whispers back. Then a smile forms. "But I have to pee."

She lets out a deep, tension-relieving laugh, and pushes herself away, standing up from the couch. "Not to a kill a moment or anything..."

"Sorry, Stace," he laughs back. "I'll be right back."

He gets up awkwardly off the couch and walks briskly toward the bathroom, almost with a limp. She stands up and steps back a bit. "Hurry up, mister. We were just getting to the good part."

"Be right back," he repeats, as he closes the bathroom door behind him.

She walks toward the stereo. She tilts her torso back and toward the bathroom, calling back to him, "Mind if I put something else on, Jason?"

"Be my guest," returns, muffled through the bathroom door.

She pushes a few buttons on the console, then turns the music louder, turning around to appreciate the perfect romance of the setting.

He emerges from the bathroom. "Sorry about that."

"Come here." She extends her arms. "Where were we?"

He returns to her, welcoming her embrace. The passion resumes. Without ever loosening neither their grasp nor the lock of their kiss, they awkwardly stumble back as one toward the couch. They plop down together, with her atop him. Roaming hands search for the appropriate next move.

The music begins to crescendo with the elevation of the passion. It becomes louder, more pronounced. Miles Davis provides the increasingly chaotic sound track. Horns blare, and the muted trumpet squeals the melody. The rhythm section matches the pace of their thrusts. Rhythmic, but disjointed. Hurried, yet patient.

The music continues to build. But, gradually, then suddenly, something has slowed down on the couch. The hands are no longer roaming. The breathing is no longer a pant, but rather a slow exhale. She pauses the kiss, then lifts her head, looking upon his still-closed eyes.

"What's wrong, Jason?"

"Nothing," he protests. "What do you mean?"

"Something wrong? You stopped."

"No I didn't. You did."

"Jason."

"Stacey, what?"

"I'm not an idiot."

"What?"

She takes her hand and places it between his legs. "I know when it's not happening."

He looks back in silence.

She kneels back off of him. "And this ain't happening."

"Honestly, Stace —"

"It's fine," she interrupts. "It happens." She readjusts her disheveled blouse and skirt and stands up from the couch. "It's late. We're tired. We both had a lot of wine…"

"Stacey —"

"Honestly. It's fine," She interrupts again, quickly looking around the room for something. She finds her purse on a chair opposite the couch and walks over to retrieve it. "I have to work in the morning…"

"Don't go."

"Jason." She looks directly at him and pauses only for a moment. "It's fine. Really." She walks over toward him and leans down to give him a kiss on the cheek. "Maybe next time."

"Come on. Don't go."

"Call me." She throws her purse over her shoulder and heads toward the front door. As she walks away, Jason lies motionless on his back on the couch, propping himself up slightly with his elbows, staring at the ceiling. He hears the door close behind her as she exits. He slowly closes his eyes and lowers his head toward his chest. He exhales.

He whispers to himself, dejectedly yet forcefully. "Fuck."

CHAPTER 25

BLAST FROM THE PAST

THERE'S something about the inside of a police station that just gives you the willies. You'd expect it to be a bustling hub of activity, like on TV, but in reality it's pretty subdued. Eerily quiet, even. Most everyone on duty is out of the office in the field, so the quietude makes sense when you think about it. And the other thing you notice is the monotony. It feels like everything is the same color: the walls, the floor, the cubicles, the ceiling. The only thing that stands out is the blue of the uniforms worn by the unlucky few that are stuck pushing pencils or manning dispatch that day.

Longfellow, of course, wore no such uniform. Though Murphy did, perfectly form-fitting and meticulously kempt. They were both waiting for our arrival, having asked us if we'd cut our lunch short to bring them up to speed.

We did, of course, know of a "black fella" that might've visited Joel, and we had to enter in a bit more detail on Ziggy for their background.

It made sense that Mary hadn't mentioned him when she filed her initial police report. She hadn't seen Ziggy in a long time, and had no reason to believe Joel had either. Then again, she wasn't exactly up to speed on everything going on in Joel's life since the divorce.

After the pleasantries — such that they were — had been exchanged, and coffees provided, Longfellow opened the floor. "So tell us a little bit more about this Ziggy friend of yours."

Mary looked at me, apparently wondering which of us would go first. She started, "College friends. We all met in college." She shook off a mis-recollection. "Well, Joel and Jason knew each other from before. But I met Ziggy in college, after I started dating Joel."

"And they were close?" Longfellow wondered.

"At one point, yes," replied Mary. "I suppose they were close. We all were. But you know how life goes. Things slowed down after college. We drifted. Got busy. Started doing our own things...going our own ways..."

"Did Mr. Thomas and Mr. Walton remain close?"

Mary looked at me for support. I took the floor. "Not that we know of." Longfellow's eyes shifted to me, almost darting, with no head turn. "I mean, we would get together periodically...for old time's sake. Reunions, ya know?" Longfellow nodded only slightly, but let me continue. "But, like Mary said, we all kinda had our own stuff over time, ya know?"

"You mentioned 'all of us,'" Murphy's boyish voice chimed in. "This being everyone? The four of you?"

Mary replied, "From college, you mean?"

Murphy both nodded and shrugged his shoulders at once, as if to say, *You tell me.*

"There was a fifth," she said softly. "Russell."

Before Murphy could continue the line of questioning, Longfellow regained control. "We'll come back to him." He looked back at Mary. "Let's focus on Mr. Walton. You said you hadn't seen him in a while."

"That's right," she affirmed.

"Haven't talked to him in a while, either?"

"Oh God," Mary said, her eyes searching the room for context. "I can't tell you the last time we spoke." She looked at me, then. "You, Jason?"

"We lost touch," I said, then lowering my eyes and bowing my head. "We all did."

"But you remained close with Mr. Thomas," Longfellow attempted to clarify with me.

I nodded. "Close-*er*," I stipulated. "We'd talk more frequently than the rest of us, I suppose. Get together every now and again...once in a blue." I paused to reflect. "Joel didn't have a ton of friends beyond us."

"Anyone else we should know about?" Murphy again interrupted. "Besides this Russell, I mean?"

Mary and I looked at each other, both of us shaking our heads *no*.

"You say Mr. Walton and Mr. Thomas weren't close," Longfellow resumed. After a beat, he asked, tellingly, "Were they...*un*-close?"

Mary and I both knew where he was going with this. "Gosh no," Mary was quick to blurt out.

"Not that we know of," I concurred. "You just don't know Ziggy. He's...a rather gentle soul. Especially nowadays."

"We'd like to get to know him," Longfellow said. "Either of you know how we can get ahold of him?"

"I have his phone number," Mary said, fumbling for her phone that was somewhere in her purse. "But I don't know if he's even in the area anymore. Jason?"

"Not sure, to be honest."

"Well, we'd like to know that, too," Longfellow remarked, as he watched Mary thumbing through her phone for Ziggy's contact information. As she did, he made a rather cold, calloused observation, in the cold and calloused way a grizzly old detective can. "Seems Mr. Walton has something of a record."

Neither Mary nor I responded, though it seemed obvious he was looking for a reaction.

Murphy added, "Did a bit of time in juvey."

"That was a long time ago," I stated, for the record, trying to cut him off as quickly as possible.

"Just being thorough," came the raspy voice to Murphy's defense, again coming off as cold and calloused. As Mary continued searching, Longfellow asked another question, "Any reason Mr. Walton would've paid Mr. Thomas a visit anytime recently?"

I waited for Mary to answer, she kept looking at her phone, her thumb occasionally pushing a button, then pausing. Another push, another pause.

"I don't know," I spoke up, to fill the silence as Mary continued her search. "I mean, not that I know of...but what do I know? Who knows, maybe they were closer than I thought. Maybe they got together for some reason. I think they're both single still...you know, middle-aged men, looking for companionship, even if it's just buddy time. Maybe they reconnected."

"But neither of them filled you all in on it? This wasn't another one of these...reunions? Recently?"

"No sir," I confirmed.

"That's really strange," Mary said slowly and quietly, as she looked down at her phone, frozen in thought. We all waited for her to continue. She used her thumb to scroll up and down on whatever screen page she was looking at.

Finally, I prodded. "What's that?"

"Well, it's just odd, that's all."

"What's that, ma'am?"

"Well, here's Ziggy's number. I'll give it to you."

"Thank you, ma'am."

Mary continued, "But you know how you can look at a contact, and it will tell you the last time you called them, or they called you?"

"Yes, ma'am," Murphy quickly volleyed back.

"Well, I was curious...the last time I talked to Ziggy."

I asked, "And?"

"Well, it's the oddest thing. I don't remember this."

"What's that?" asked Longfellow.

"Well," Mary began, slowly piecing together her sentence as though she were slowly piecing together the very timeline in her mind. "Maybe it was all the texting...and phone calls...to Joel...and waiting to hear back...from Joel...that I totally missed it somehow."

"Missed what?" Murphy begged the question.

"A missed call," Mary said, her eyes now lifting off the screen and staring blankly into the room. She looked up at me, before finishing, "From Ziggy. Two weeks ago."

CHAPTER 26

10 Years Ago

"YOU'RE back, Ziggy" the barkeep says to him as he wipes the bar top with a white towel. "You expecting the whole gang today?"

"Think so," Ziggy says, hunched over a tattered hardcover book that lay on the bar under his protective hands.

"Get ya a beer, Mack?" he asks, as he looks down at Ziggy's book. He remarks in recognition of it, "Ah. Good book." Ziggy smiles slightly, at least enough to acknowledge the comment. "The best book, huh?" Ziggy smiles again.

"I'll take a beer, sure."

"Never understood why they call it *The Good Book*. Should be *The Best Book*, am I right?"

Ziggy marks his place with the red ribbon bookmark and places the pocket tome into his coat jacket. "Um. See if you got a Pabst," he says, to send the bartender on his way.

A couple joined by another man walk in behind him. "Hey, Zig!", they say, almost as one. Ziggy turns around and forces a smile.

"There they are," he tries to feign enthusiasm. "Mary, Joel. Good to see you guys." He shakes his hand and gives her a quick, almost cursory, kiss on the cheek. "Jason," he says to the other man, in a drawn-out, welcoming way, as he pulls the man in for a hug.

"The usual table?" Joel points at the table in the adjacent seating area. The bartender returns with Ziggy's Pabst, which Ziggy grabs and heads toward the table.

"We'll start a tab," Jason says to Barkeep with a smile, and motions toward their waiting table.

"Russell gonna make it?" Ziggy asks, as they all take their seats.

Mary remarks, out of the corner of her mouth, "You know Russell."

"How is everyone?" Ziggy starts the conversation.

The bartender arrives at their table with menus in hand, dealing them out as he welcomes them. "Welcome back to Franklin's. Haven't seen you all in a while. I've forgotten what everyone's having." He looks at Jason. "Light beer?"

"Good memory."

"White wine," Mary reminds him. "Anything."

Joel pushes her seat in for her from behind. "Heineken for me."

Ziggy is visibly distracted by whatever — or whatever isn't — coming in through the front door, frequently glancing in that direction as conversation begins. They start the small talk. Jason reaches into his pocket for some quarters, then walks over to the jukebox to get the music going.

"Who's got news?" Joel says, as he claps his hands together. Ziggy looks back at the front door. His face suddenly reveals a slight sense of relief upon seeing the entrant.

"What up, bitches!" The larger-than-life latecomer has thrown the front door open and is now striking a prominent pose in the doorway.

"Russell!"

"Russ!"

"There he is!"

Mary leaps up from her chair and rushes over to give Russell her famous bear hug. Jason follows quickly behind, offering and executing a more masculine grasp of Russell's arm and back. "Russell, bud. Glad you could make it."

"I wish I were," Russell starts, "...making it..." He hesitates just a beat. "...with the busboy that was here last time."

"Easy, tiger." Jason pats him on the back, to lead the way back to their table.

Jason, Mary and Russell return to the table and take their seats as drinks are delivered. Russell raises a hand to the bartender. "Shots. Two. One Jaeger, one Jack Daniels. Step lightly, my good man."

Russell continues, with hands clasped in front of him, looking around the table like a kindergarten teacher reading a classic children's story to the class. "So. I have updates…"

They all listen intently, as Russell regales the gathering with his stories, complete with pantomimed gesturing, voice imitations and plentiful punch lines. Ziggy forces a smile, to join them in the revelry. Then, in a departure from the frivolity, he takes another large swallow of beer.

The laughter dies down. "And with that," Russell says, as he stands up from the table and reaches into his pocket, "Time to get this *same old* music off of this jukebox. Who listens to Barenaked Ladies anymore, anyway? I'll be back!" He rushes off toward the jukebox to make his musical rescue.

"Okay, who's next?" Joel asks, looking around the table. Nobody offers. Joel looks over at Ziggy, who's staring intently at his beer. "What about you, Zig?"

"Naw, I'm good," Ziggy replies, with a half-hearted chuckle.

Mary nudges him, "Come on, Zig. Fill us in!"

"Naw, all good."

Mary persists. "Come on. Start with Traci. On again...off again...are we on again? Off again? What?"

"Naw, it's all good."

Russell returns from the jukebox. Inexplicably, "Monster Mash" starts playing over the sound system.

"Really, Russ?" Jason chastises in jest.

"This is my jam, people!" Russell downs another shot. "Okay, who's up? Zig?"

"He won't go," Mary laments.

"Spill it, bitch!"

Jason takes a more respectful tone. "Come on, Zig. You look bummed. What's up?"

Ziggy, still looking deeply and singularly upon his beer, takes another large swig and finishes it. "Okay. I'll be honest with you."

"Please," Mary says, leaning in to place a hand on Ziggy's arm, with a concerned expression washed across her face — her eyes beginning to tear up, but her mouth smiling hopefully. "What's up, Zig?"

Ziggy sniffs, and nervously wipes an index finger across his upper lip. "Guys," he barely forces out, as his gaze rises up from his beer and to each of his friends at the table, one at a time, stopping at Mary. "Guys," he continues, with a morbidly forced chuckle. "I'm dying."

CHAPTER 27

MESSAGE RECEIVED

"DID HE leave a voicemail?" I demanded, my shock likely both obvious and equal to everyone's in the room.

"Not that I can see," Mary returned, somewhat frantically. "Should I try him back?" she asked, looking first at me, then to Longfellow.

Longfellow responded with a confident head nod, and Mary pressed a button to place the return call. She held the phone to her ear, her eyes darting from me to Longfellow, back to me then to Murphy, and back to me again. She waited patiently for almost ten seconds, then sighed. "Voicemail." She lowered the phone to her lap.

"Well," said Longfellow, seemingly unfazed. "We'll try him again later. We'll take his number, ma'am, thank you."

"Sir?" I began sheepishly to Longfellow, "Is it okay if I try Ziggy? He may respond to me. And it's not that I want to warn him you'll be calling. But if he hears from me what this is all about, he might be more inclined to take your call."

"That's fine," he abruptly assented.

We spent the better part of an hour going over our history, chapter and verse, with Ziggy. I could sense that Longfellow and Murphy were frustrated that neither I nor Mary was able to offer any insights into the more recent timeline as it related to Ziggy, but they seemed somewhat interested in the distant-past background, at least.

We eventually did get back to Russell, but neither Longfellow nor Murphy seemed all that interested, given the circumstances. I was relieved we wouldn't spend much time on it. Mary had been through enough, and she had already shown signs of distress when Russell came up days prior.

When we left the station, I felt both mystified, and in a weird way, energized.

"I'm gonna call Ziggy," I asserted, largely to the open air, and certainly for Mary to react to.

"Me too!" replied Mary. "I can't believe I missed that! What did he want? And why no voicemail? I'm dying to talk to him."

"Me too. I'll let you know when I get him." I changed the subject. "But first, I think there's something you and I should revisit."

"What's that?" Mary queried.

"I think we need to pay another visit…"

"Not to Joel's house," she interrupted.

"No…"

"Don't say the bank again."

"No…" I finally got a chance to finish. "I think we should go back to Joel's office. There's gotta be something there." Mary just looked at me. "And it's the one place the police haven't taped off — literally or figuratively!"

It didn't take much to get Mary to agree, and we were off in my car, back to Pennico. Which was good, because I was going to need her there if I was going to pull this off.

We approached the glass doors to the Pennico lobby and pushed the buzzer. The receptionist lifted the phone to her ear. "Name and business, please."

Mary spoke up, "It's Mary Thomas. Joel's ex-wife. Here to see Mr. Pennington."

"He's not in the office, ma'am."

"Hi, this is Joel's friend, Jason," I called into the speaker. "We were here a couple of weeks ago. Can we speak with someone about Joel?"

Click. Mary tried the door. The receptionist had released the lock, and we were able to enter. We approached the desk, unsure of for whom to ask, now that Pennington was away.

I did the talking when we reached her desk. "Hello, ma'am," I said, introducing myself. "Jason Wilhelm. And Mary Thomas. We were wondering if we could have one last look in Joel's office."

"There's been an investigation," Mary added.

"The police were here," the receptionist knowingly interrupted, not looking up from the work on her desk.

Mary continued, "We were just wondering if we could have one last look around his office."

I added, "See if there's anything...anything that might provide some answers." No response from the receptionist. "Maybe something the police wouldn't recognize as significant."

"But we would," Mary finished. She hesitated, then added, "Please ma'am. I'm his wife. His *ex*-wife," she quickly corrected. But the message got through. The *widow* was asking, and that was going to work better than the friend.

Still not looking up from her desk, the receptionist picked up the phone and coldly acknowledged our request. "I'll have someone show you the way." Then, into the phone, she said, "Pam, will you come to the front? Show Ms. Thomas, and..." she looked up at me.

"Wilhelm," I said.

"...Mr. Wilhelm to Joel's office?" She hung up the phone and returned her eyes and attention to her desk. "Have a seat. Someone will be up to see you."

We did, and soon "Pam" joined us in the lobby to escort us back to Joel's office. Leading the way down the hallway, she stopped at his doorway and waved us in.

"Thank you," Mary said, smiling at her, but also obviously attempting to dismiss her. Pam returned to her station and left us to our own devices.

I hurried to Jason's desk and took a seat at his chair, quickly turning on Joel's computer. As it booted up, it prompted me to enter a password. My first guess worked, as predictable as Joel could be: *M@dM@x08*. Mary stayed near the front door, occasionally poking her head out and motioning back to me periodically that, indeed, the coast was clear — but with a look on her face that would plead, *"Hurry up, Jason!"*

I did. I knew exactly what I was looking for, but I poked around a bit first, looking for clues. Anything that would stand out as conspicuous, or suspicious. Nothing was marked "HERE IT IS, JASON," I sarcastically and subconsciously noted to myself, so I respected the urgency of our limited time and opened up his email program.

Joel's inbox began to flood. I noticed in the upper right corner of the screen, *Downloading, 28 of 932 incoming messages.*

"Crap," I uttered.

Mary looked back. "What?"

"Downloading," was all I returned in response. Mary looked out the doorway again. Then back at me.

I waited. The messages were downloading at a snail's pace, at least in relation to my sense of immediacy. *Downloading, 312 of 932 incoming messages.* "Come on," I urged.

Mary was startled. "Joel! Pam's coming back!" She stood back from the doorway, and started aimlessly examining the bookshelf against the wall opposite Joel's desk, obviously (to me, anyway) faking a search.

Pam stood at the doorway. "Sir," she said to me, in a nasally disapproving tone. "I hope you're not looking at Joel's computer. We have very strict security clearances here."

"No no," I quickly shot back, and opened the top drawer of his desk, joining Mary's faked investigation.

Pam said nothing, but walked away after shooting Mary a very snotty leer.

I looked back at the computer. *Downloading, 916 of 932 incoming messages.* Mary resumed her watch post at the doorway. "Come on!" I pled again, this time in a shouted whisper.

"Hurry up, Jason!" This time Mary verbalized the look on her face, as she gazed back at me with an impatient scowl.

"I am! I am!" I assured her, as desperately helpless as she was, slave to the crawling download of Joel's incoming emails.

I could see out of the corner of my eye, as I stared at the screen, waiting for it — *Downloading, 932 of 932 incoming messages* — Mary suddenly froze.

"She's coming back!" Mary exclaimed, with a similar whispered scream. "And she's bringing somebody. In a suit. Some guy!"

I frantically scanned the contents of Joel's inbox. A full 932 unread messages is a lot to scan with any significant level of detail, especially under the gun of rapidly approaching scrutiny.

"They're coming!" Mary reminded me.

"I know!" My eyes scanned frantically as I forced the mouse up and down until I recognized what I came for. "I'm trying," I assured her.

Finally, there it was. I knew it would be there. And now I had found it...confirmation. I clicked on it to read it. But before I could start it, I heard the approaching nasal voice.

"I told them, Mr. Wayne. But I think he was looking at Joel's computer."

I hit *Forward* on the email and entered my email address as the recipient.

"Jason!" Mary scurried from the doorway and back to the

bookshelf.

I hit *Send*, and the message was sent. I stood up from Joel's desk and reached behind the computer monitor to turn it off, just as Pam and her escort returned to the doorway.

"Sir, we're going to have to ask you to step away from Mr. Thomas's computer," this official-looking Mr. Wayne announced.

I looked back innocently at them, but took one last confirming glance down at the computer screen to make sure it was off. It was. But still emblazoned in my mind's eye was the last thing I saw before I killed the power to the monitor. An email. The one I expected to find, and the one I had safely dispatched to my own account.

To: Joel Thomas
From: Joel Thomas
Re: Goodbye

CHAPTER 28

10 Years Ago

THE BARTENDER returns to retrieve some empty glasses and bottles from the table. The five sit in silence, paralyzed reactions on their faces as they look back at him.

Finally, she speaks. "What are you talking about, Ziggy?"

"Dying?"

"Dying, guys," he looks down at the table. "Dying." He sniffs and stands up from the table. "Man, that sounds strange coming out of your mouth when you say it." The morbid half-chuckle returns. "I don't recommend it."

"What are you talking about, Zig?" Russell probes. "Dying how?"

Ziggy stands up and starts to pace slowly around one side of their table, looking around at the near-empty Franklin's pub. "Not sure myself, exactly," he releases whisperingly. "Something. Doctors got a fancy name for it. Something attacking my insides...my organs. And my body can't form no white blood cells to fight it off."

Joel asks, "Autoimmune?"

"Like AIDS?" Russell appends.

"Some fancy name for something like that."

"Ziggy," Jason says, standing up to take a position at Ziggy's side. "What's the fancy name?"

He looks back at Jason for a moment. "I don't even know, Jays. I could find out, if you care that much...but does it matter?" He sits back down at the table. "Truth is, I didn't hear much mumbo jumbo after I heard the word *dying*, so..."

"Maybe there's something they can do," Mary hopefully interjects. "What did they say?"

"They don't know, really," Ziggy responds. "They said I could have years, with treatment. Could lead a pretty normal life, maybe. Who knows...maybe months, if my body don't react to the medicine. They just don't know."

"This is great!"

Everyone looks coldly back at Joel as he makes the proclamation. Joel pushes aside a dirty plate in front of him. "No, guys...not *great* great. But great that Ziggy knows somebody." He reaches into a breast pocket to pull out a pen, then reaches across the table for a cocktail napkin.

"What are you talking about, Joel?" Jason replies, with perhaps a hint of hopeful enthusiasm.

"This is what we do!" Everyone waits for him to continue. "At Pennico!" More anticipatory silence. "Clinicals."

"What?" demands Russell.

"Clinical trials. For new drugs. Experiments on new cures and stuff."

"What's that?" Ziggy asks, but with a dismissive tone.

Joel gets up from his seat and walks around the table to take the seat next to Ziggy that Jason has vacated. He pushes his chair in and continues, looking directly at Ziggy. He starts with a quiet, comforting tone of voice. "It's like a test," he begins. "For new diseases...and new cures to old diseases. Like cancer. People who can't get other treatment...or who want to volunteer for some new groundbreaking cure or medicine...they sign up for these tests, and they take the medicine while being closely observed. They even get paid." He then looks up at the others. "It's part of the process you need to go through to get FDA approval. We do it everyday. And I can get Ziggy in for one of these."

"That's right!" Mary affirms.

"I dunno, man."

"Come on, Zig. We have all sorts of clinicals going for AIDS. If what you have is autoimmune, maybe you qualify. I mean, I'd have to know more, obviously...but I'm pretty sure I could get you in!"

"I ain't no lab rat."

Mary reaches across the table to grab Ziggy's hand with both of hers. "Ziggy, what are you saying? This could be life and death...literally!"

"Yeah, Zig," Jason walks around the table to face Ziggy. "You gotta look into this," he urges.

"Ziggy, honestly," Joel continues. "It's no big deal. Sometimes they can't even recruit enough people." He pauses. "I can get you in."

"I dunno."

"Really. Let's look into it. Let's get your file from your doctor. I'll have you into the office on Monday. I'll talk to Mr. Pennington himself. If he can't get you in, nobody can."

Russell finally speaks up while they all wait for Ziggy to react. "Ziggy, what the hell's your problem? Say yes!"

Ziggy reaches into his pocket and pulls out a tattered hardcover book and places it on the table. *Holy Bible.* "I dunno." He sniffs again and stares down at the book. He releases his other hand from Mary's grasp and places it on the Bible. "Maybe this is His plan. Maybe this is how it's supposed to go."

CHAPTER 29

CLOSE BUT NO CIGAR

MARY and I scurried down the stairs of the high-rise entranceway to Pennico's building and down to the sidewalk.

"Did you get what you were looking for?" she asked, practically under her breath.

"I think so," I said. "It was there. Like I knew it would be."

Mary looked at me, as we walked briskly toward my car, parked curbside at metered parking. "Now can you tell me what it was we were looking for?"

I stopped at my car. "Get in," I said. "I'll show you."

As we took our seats, I reached into my coat pocket to pull out my cellphone. I quickly opened my mail app. There it was. "Here," I said. "I just had a feeling."

"A feeling about what?"

"An uneasy feeling."

"About what?"

"There's too much to this," I tried to cryptically explain. "I'd say that nothing adds up...but it *all* adds up."

"What do you mean?" she pressed.

"Whatever is happening. It all just seems so...*orchestrated.*"

Mary solemnly replied, "I was thinking the same thing."

"It feels planned, in some weird way. Which got me to thinking."

"Thinking what?" Mary demanded, her tone growing in

frustration.

"Maybe…" I paused to think about how I wanted to say this. "Maybe, it *is* planned." I paused again. *Say it right, Jason.* "By Joel."

She processed that for a bit, then asked, "Planned? By Joel? How? Why?"

I cleared my throat and adjusted myself in my car seat. "I just had an inkling. It felt eerily familiar. Like you said...like Russell. Or like...well, you read a lot about these things in the news, and what have you."

"Spit it out, Jason."

"A note," I quickly returned. "There's always a note."

"Jason, what the hell are you talking about?"

"I just thought — and don't hate me for this — but I just thought...if it *were* planned...well, there would be a note."

"What kind of note?" she demanded to know.

"Like this." I handed her my phone, after quickly glancing to make sure I had pulled up the right email. It was the right one.

To: Joel Thomas
From: Joel Thomas
Re: Goodbye

"What is this?" she asked, with a look of both shock and wonderment on her face as she took my phone in her hand.

"Read it."

Mary started to read it to herself silently, and I could see her lips trembling as they mouthed the words. She paused, then started over, this time reading it aloud, while trying to force down a reaction.

To whomever reads this… (And I hope it will be found by someone who loves me.) Let me just start by saying, I'm sorry. You're the unlucky one. If you're reading this, then my first apology is to you. If I get back, maybe you won't read this at all.

I'm going away. I don't know if I'll be back. I need to start over. Or not at all. Please don't search for answers or places to put blame. I just need to get away for a while. To reflect. To figure out what's worth coming back to. To figure out if there's anything worth coming back to at all. Please don't hate me. And don't hate yourselves.

Maybe no one will read this. And no one will care. And maybe that's the point.

Goodbye. I'm sorry.

We both stared at the windshield in silence. Finally, Mary spoke up. "What is this, Jason? A suicide note? Or someone looking to disappear?"

"My first thought was...both, actually," I joined her in ponderment. "But I don't know. Did he leave? And never want to come back? Or did he *really* not what to come back? Like, *ever?*"

Mary lowered the phone and continued to stare straight ahead. She quietly observed, if only to herself, "This doesn't sound like him."

"I know," I said, to console and confirm.

"No, Jason," she said, more forcefully now, and looking back at me. "Like the text message. From before. This doesn't sound like him."

"What do you mean?" I asked.

"He would never do this."

"You know Joel," I interrupted.

"No...I mean, yes. Joel would plan for something like this. If he were going to do something like this, it would all be perfectly planned out. I grant you that." I waited as she formulated her next words in her head. "But he would never leave Max."

"What? Max is dead," I reminded her.

"Yes, but he didn't know that," Mary insisted. "Not when he supposedly wrote this. This was supposedly written before Joel left, right?" she begged of me. "Obviously?"

"Right…"

"Well, first off, he would never just leave Max behind. He would've taken him. Max was still alive when Joel left, remember? The police figured that out. This note makes it sound like he's leaving and has nothing left to live for."

"Right…"

"But he still had Max. It doesn't add up."

The screen on my phone went blank for a half a second, then began to ring. I recognized the area code, but not the phone number. "I should get that," I said, as I took the phone from Mary's hand. I answered the call, "Hello?"

"Who is it?" Mary whispered.

The voice on the other end of the phone had a familiar rasp. "Hi, Mr. Wilhelm. It's Detective Longfellow. Mary with you?"

"Yes, we're both here," I replied. I placed my hand over the microphone and mouthed to Mary, "It's Longfellow."

"Great," he said back. "We were hoping you and Ms. Thomas would meet us over at the residence of Mr. Thomas one more time. There's just a couple more things we could use your help with."

"Hold on," I replied. I lowered the phone and again placed my hand over the microphone. "They want us to meet them over at Joel's." Mary nodded cautiously. "Sure, Detective. When?"

"Now good?"

I relayed to Mary, "Now good?" She nodded again. I confirmed for Longfellow. "Sure. We can be there in about a half-hour."

"See you then."

I ended the call and looked at Mary. I thought aloud, "Wonder what that's all about."

"Me too. Do we tell them about the email?"

I thought about that for a moment. "Not yet."

"I kinda agree," Mary sheepishly responded. "I mean, not until we can make more sense of it."

"Eventually," I offered.

"For sure. I just want to think about this some more. Something's not adding up."

"Agreed."

We took one of Joel's preferred routes from his office to his house and made excellent time, having beaten Murphy and Longfellow. As we waited in my car in the driveway, Mary was still trying to piece it all together.

"This just keeps getting stranger," she noted. "But I'm starting to see what you mean."

"About what?" I asked for clarification.

"About this all having some sort of coordination." Just as she said that, Longfellow's car pulled up in the driveway behind us.

He and Murphy got out of the car and approached the house, so Mary and I joined them. We all paused on the front porch, when Longfellow began talking. He had his hands on his hips as he looked up at the porch overhang, examining something or other. Without so much as a greeting or exchanged pleasantry, he started right in. "Your husband a paranoid man, Ms. Thomas?"

"Ex-husband," Mary corrected. "And not really. Why?"

"You have an alarm system at your house?" Longfellow pressed on. "The one you and Mr. Thomas shared?"

"No," Mary replied, in both defiance and curiosity. "Why?"

"No surveillance system?"

"No. Why?"

I butted in. "What's this all about, Detective?"

Longfellow nodded his head in the direction of the ceiling, if you will, of the porch overhang. I wasn't exactly sure what we were supposed to be seeing.

I prodded him, "What?"

"Nails," was Longfellow's one-word response. "And holes," he eventually added.

"Nails?" Mary asked. "And holes?"

"Holes, Ms. Thomas," replied Longfellow, his eyes quickly turning to hers.

"What kind of holes?" she asked.

Murphy decided to cut to the chase. "For wiring." He stepped forward, as if into the spotlight. "And nails. For brackets."

Mary scoffed, "Am I supposed to be following?"

Murphy continued, "The kind you'd need if you had a surveillance system installed."

"Surveillance system?" Mary asked, seemingly in a bit of disbelief.

"Cameras," I clarified for her. "Like at a store...to prevent shoplifting."

"That's right," Longfellow confirmed. "Except these ones have been removed."

"By whom?" Mary wondered.

"Don't know," Longfellow answered. "But we're looking into it." He began looking around the rest of the front porch, up and down. "Detective Murphy noticed this last time we were here," he noted. "Some inside, too."

"Inside?" I asked.

"Yep," Murphy smugly fired back. "The whole residence was practically wired. But all of it...removed. Like it was never there."

"The whole house," I responded, again.

Longfellow simply looked at Mary. "Now you see why I'm asking." He paused, then repeated. "Your *ex*-husband a paranoid man?"

"Gosh no," Mary said, dismissively. "Not that I know of."

"Seems odd," responded Longfellow.

"Odd?" I begged. "To have security cameras?"

"To have them removed," Longfellow said.

Murphy added, "And to have them *inside* the domicile." He shot a glance at Mary. "Unless, of course, you're paranoid. Which Ms. Thomas says he isn't. So, yes...odd."

"Speaking of inside," Longfellow went on, seemingly taking his cue perfectly from Murphy, "there's something else we want to show you inside the residence, too."

Longfellow opened the front door and pushed aside the yellow police tape that was visibly barring entrance to the presumed crime scene. "Head on in," he invited us, "head down to the basement."

The basement. The very words brought back that uneasy feeling. Nothing good ever gets found in the basement. And the last time I was there, I heard Mary yelling for me. It was a jarring reminder of just how long this had been going on — and, at the same time, how little had been cleared up since Mary's and my first visit to Joel's. Nonetheless, I led the way, and turned on the basement light while I waited for everyone to follow. Longfellow was last to join us, and I could see his eyes were looking up at the ceiling again.

"More cameras?" I asked.

Longfellow shot me a knowing glance. "Not this time." He walked over to the corner of the basement, just below the exposed rafters. "Here," he said as he stepped up on a folding chair that, seemingly, had already been strategically placed against the wall.

"What is it?" Mary asked.

"This," Longfellow said, as he loosened a small cinderblock from the top of the wall. As he pulled it out with one hand, it was obvious that the block was cut perhaps in half, leaving only the inward-looking facade of the block that was painted in "basement white," while the back of it had apparently been cut off or crudely removed somehow. It was crumbling a bit as he fully removed it, leaving a small cavernous opening in the wall.

Mary piped up again, "What's in there?"

As he descended from his stoop upon the folding chair, Longfellow responded, "That's what we were hoping you would tell us."

Mary didn't respond. She simply walked slowly toward the opening, her eyes never losing their lock on it. She peered in, as best she could without stepping up onto the chair. She slowly turned back at me, looking past Longfellow and ignoring Murphy's presence altogether. Her voice carried as much hesitance as it did discovery. She simply said two words, which were enough to reveal to me what her theory was.

"Cigar box."

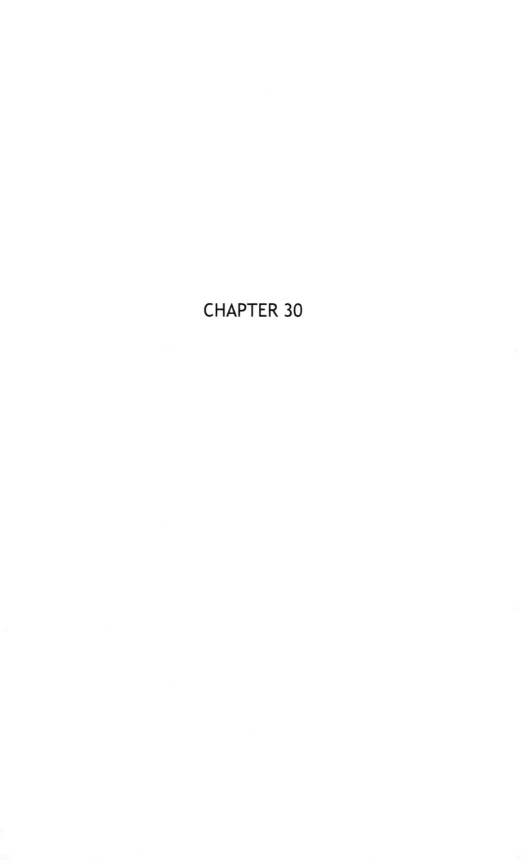

CHAPTER 30

Eight Years Ago

STERILE white walls and floors. Muted conversations flicker in the distance like a dying campfire across the lake. The aroma of air sanitizer fills the atmosphere, providing both a reassuring cleanliness and an off-putting medicinal aura that reminds the visitors where they are. The quickly passing nurses and doctors seem used to it, but the anxious faces of guests and visitors belie those staffers' rote ennui.

Holding a bouquet of flowers in one hand, he approaches a nurse's desk to check in. "Russell Reeves," he says quietly, as he leans over her desk.

"Down the hall, room 301," she directs him, aided by an extended arm and pointed finger.

He moves quickly in that direction, slowing as he nears room 301. He collects his breath just outside the doorway, then peers his head in to see his friend. There he is, in a hospital bed, hooked to tubes and IVs, with an ashen complexion and dark circles under his eyes. The man in the doorway forces a smile, wiping away any telltale signs of distress.

"Russell," he says almost cheerfully, as he approaches his bedside, placing the bouquet of flowers on the nightstand next to his bed. He leans over and kisses him on the top of his head. "How are ya, buddy?"

"Thanks for coming, Jays," the exhausted patient is able to force out.

Jason looks at the patient's fellow visitors, a black man and white woman at his bedside, and another man seated at a chair in the corner.

"How is he, guys?" Jason asks.

"I'm fine."

"No, you're not, mister," she deflects.

"Mary, I'm fine."

"Jason, you gotta talk to him, dog."

"I will, Zig. I will." He looks at the man seated in the corner. "Joel. Good to see you."

"Jason, talk to him," Joel replies, fidgeting just a bit in his chair.

Ziggy places a firm grasp around Russell's wrist, which lay lifeless atop a blanket on his lap. "Look, man. I gotta run. You be good, hear?"

"Thanks for coming, Ziggy."

"We should be going, too," Joel says, as he stands up from his chair in the corner. "Mary, you ready?"

She looks down at Russell. "Yep. I'm coming." She caresses Russell's hair. "See you tomorrow?"

He nods in the affirmative, saving his words and energy. Mary leans over and kisses him on the cheek. She collects her purse and coat, then extends a half-smile to Jason as she passes him, walking toward the door to follow Joel out. As she passes Jason, she whispers, "Help him." Jason watches her, Joel and Ziggy out the door.

Jason looks over at Russell, who forces out a half-hearted smile. Jason extends a hand to fetch a rolling chair, and pulls it close to Russell's bedside to have a seat.

"I came as soon as I heard."

Russell acknowledges this with a slowed blink of his eyes.

"You okay, Russ?"

He nods.

"What the hell happened?"

He shrugs.

"Russell," he says quietly but patiently. "I need you to be straight with me."

"Jason..."

"Russ. Let me finish." He clears his throat and pulls his chair in closer. "Tell me...tell me...that this...was an accident."

"It was!" Russell is able to muster the strength to voice something of an objection.

"They found alcohol. And vicodin."

"For my back!"

"Russ. It was a lot," Jason persists. "Of both."

"I don't remember," Russell whispers back in defense.

"And GHB," Jason continues. "The date rape drug, Russell. GH fucking B."

Russell turns his gaze out the window, so as to avoid eye contact.

"Russell. Who were you with last night?"

Silence. No response.

"Russell. Let me help you."

He looks back quickly at Jason, responding, "It was an accident."

"Tell me, Russ. Tell me you weren't doing this to yourself."

"Jason, I swear. It was an accident."

"Which part?"

"Huh?"

"Which part was the accident?"

"All of it!"

"Come on, Russ. I see the way you drink. We all do. We know that was no accident. And no one *accidentally* takes GHB."

"I don't remember."

"Fine. Okay," says Jason, standing up and patting him firmly on his wrist. "Another time." Jason begins to head toward the door, but Russell grabs him by the arm.

"Don't go." Jason looks down at him. "Just stay for a bit. Sit next to me." He sits back down. Russell continues, "I honestly don't know what happened. Yes. I was having a bit to drink. And yes, I had taken a vicodin — *one!* — for my back...which is a real thing, by the way. But that's it. I don't remember the rest."

Jason stares back, seemingly unsure of which parts to buy and which parts to rebuke. He simply responds, "Okay, Russ. Let's get you some rest. We can talk more when you wake up. I think you're still a little woozy. I'll stay. I'll wait outside, and when you wake up, I'll be here and we can talk some more. All right?"

"That sounds nice," he says, as his eyelids begin to get heavy.

"Hang in there, buddy." Another firm pat on the wrist, and another return towards the door.

"Jason." Russell stops his visitor's exit once again, his speech a bit slurred, and slowly delivered. "Be careful with Mary."

Jason pauses and looks back at Russell, whose gaze is now remarkably coherently fixed upon Jason's eyes. Russell takes a deep breath, and adds, "I notice the way she looks at you. We all do."

CHAPTER 31

SWITCHING GEARS

THERE was a lot to digest when we got back to Mary's house to drop her back home. I saw her in and was perfectly content heading home to try to clear my head. But Mary wanted company.

"Want a drink?" she offered.

"Thanks, but I should get going," I declined. "Long day."

"Please, Jason. Stay. One drink," she repeated. "We gotta work through this a bit. Together." She headed back toward the bar, adding, "I know I won't be able to sleep tonight."

"Fine," I surrendered. "One drink."

While she was out of the room, my eyes naturally moved over to the junk drawer where I had found the somewhat obscured life insurance policy buried under the rest of the junk. I thought better of bringing that up, still. We had plenty more to dissect, after all.

Mary returned with two glasses of something-dark-on-the-rocks and handed me one. "We're out of beer, I think."

I welcomed it. Something stiffer than beer was certainly called for. "Thanks." I smelled it. Bourbon. Yikes.

She sat down on the couch as she took her first swig. "So. Cigar box," she randomly threw out to open the conversation. "Seems to be a recurring theme."

"Seems like it," I concurred. "But we don't know for sure. There was nothing in there," I reminded her. "We're just speculating that's what would've fit in that hole in Joel's basement."

"True," she replied. "But come on. It all fits, doesn't it?"

"Suppose so," I said. "So, that empty box that Joel sent you just happens to be roughly the same size as the safe deposit box that he oddly leaves to me in a hastily written will, and also matches — roughly — the size of some crudely engineered hiding place in Joel's basement." I paused for a moment, then threw out the counter-argument, if only to play devil's advocate. "Coincidence?"

"You still believe in coincidences?" she coldly countered. Mary pulled her cellphone out of her front pants pocket and dialed a number before holding it to her ear.

"Who are you calling?"

Mary said nothing; just waited for someone to answer. Apparently nobody did, so she ended the call.

"Voicemail again," she informed me.

"Ziggy again?"

"Yep. He's not answering."

I offered a little support. "He's not taking my calls either."

"So weird."

"Definitely."

"Wonder if the cops ever got ahold of him," Mary pondered.

"If they did," I responded, "they didn't mention it."

Mary took another sip, staring blankly into the open room. "And the cameras."

"Yep," I replied, to fill the space, as she apparently was formulating a follow-up thought. "Cameras. How bizarre."

"Bizarre that he had them, or that they've been stripped out of there?" Mary tried to clarify.

"Both!"

Mary stood up and began to pace the room. I wasn't sure what to say or what to do, so I just watched her circle. I could almost hear the gears turning in her head. She stopped, and took a large gulp out of her drink. I had barely started mine, and here she was nearly finishing hers. Finally, she looked at me with an exhausted look, as if she was about to give up for the night. "You should stay," she said, more as a directive than an invitation, I thought.

"What?" I contested.

"You should stay," she reiterated. "We got a lot of work to do."

"Work?"

"Yes. Work. Despite the fact that we're not professionals — clearly — we're going to have way more luck piecing this all together than the police would. We just know more. About Joel. About everything. It's like institutional knowledge, ya know? We can't possibly download our entire histories to the police. But, inside of us, we have it all...on instant recall. We might not know what's important and what isn't, but if something triggers something, we'll know it, right? The police won't, as good as they are with blood and hairs and fingerprints and stuff. So, yeah...we've got work to do, my friend."

"Now?" I replied, in subtle protest.

"You feel like waiting?" she sarcastically retorted.

"No. It's just...it's getting late, and —"

"On the couch," she interrupted. "You'll be taking the couch again."

I simply stared back, searching for the best argument against her insistence. She could tell it wasn't coming. She smelled blood, and pounced. "I'm sure I still have some of Joel's old clothes somewhere. Maybe up in the attic. You can put that on in the morning."

"Excuse me?" First of all, I couldn't quite get my head around the fact that Mary would still have Joel's clothes lying around the house, despite the fact that his pictures still adorned the mantle and the hallway leading to the master suite. They'd been divorced for more than two years. That felt creepy. But not nearly as creepy as me *wearing his clothes!* It's one thing to feel like you're being watched by the ghost of your best friend — whether deceased or simply the fly-on-the-wall variety — as you share drinks and overnights with his ex-wife. It's quite another to make a habit of those overnights, then literally assume his wardrobe the next morning. Talk about walking in another man's shoes. (And not in the virtuous way, either.) No thanks.

"I mean," she continued, "if you want a fresh change of clothes. You might not get a chance to stop home first."

"Stop home?" I begged. What was she talking about?

"Yeah, before we go," she cryptically added.

"Go where?" I begged some more.

Mary, much to my frustration, kept it vague in her response. "Chasing down a theory."

I looked into my glass and took a hearty swig. Out of the corner of my eye, I could see that Mary had retreated to the other room for a refill of hers. I thought maybe I'd try to catch up. Suddenly, I needed the drink.

"What theory?" I called to the other room. I heard nothing back until she returned with her freshened cocktail. I repeated, "What theory would that be?"

She had a rather convincing expression on her face. It was a blend of clarity and self-satisfaction. Her pursed lips gripping the rim of her glass added a tinge of determination. Finally, she began. But with a question.

"What's the common denominator?"

"Common denominator?" I echoed. "What do you mean? The box?" I wasn't following.

"Bigger," she pressed. "Beyond that."

"I'm not getting it," I said, clearly expressing my confusion.

Mary walked back over to the couch and sat down. She began again, with another eager sip, the intensity of which matched the confidence in her voice. "Think about it, Jason. We're all connected. All of us."

"All of us?"

"All of us. Max. Joel. Russell. Ziggy." She hesitated a second, before adding, "Me. You."

"Yeah?" I goaded.

"Think of the common denominators."

I was starting to get it, or so I thought. So I took a stab in the dark. "Are you talking about the pledge again?"

"No," she denied me. "Well, not entirely." She thought some more, before going on, "Max...Russell...Ziggy. And now, well, we don't know about Joel. But look at the others."

"What about them?"

"It's all internal."

"What is?" What did she mean by *internal*?

"What happened to all of them...it's all internal. Max: organ failure. Ziggy: chemical. Russell." She took another sip. "And now maybe Joel."

"What are you saying?" I pleaded.

"You're not seeing a connection?" Mary said, with a tone of disappointment in my lack of understanding or appreciation for her powers of deduction. "You think this is all some big coincidence?"

"What are you talking about?"

"All of us. We're all connected. We all love each other."

"Go on," I urged.

"And slowly but surely, we all start..." I could tell she didn't even want to finish that sentence. I knew what she meant. Max was gone. Joel, who knows? Russell...and Ziggy. It was either a rash of really bad fortune, or Mary was obviously beginning to expect something more sinister.

All I could muster in response was, "Mary."

"Seriously, Jason. If you ask me, Max was poisoned. And now Joel is gone missing, but no sign of a break-in at his place. And Russ and Zig...You'd have to be a fool to think this was all just dumb luck."

"Well, what exactly are you saying, Mary?"

"Do I have to spell it out for you, Jason?" She stood again, with a more offensive posture now. "What's happened to all of us, from Max on down, I wouldn't wish on my worst enemy."

"I agree, but —"

She cut me off. "But maybe," she paused, and the confidence began to fade from her voice. She finished the sentence more softly, more quietly, less self-assured. "Maybe, our worst enemy would wish it upon us."

I stood in silence as I began to mentally formulate some specifics around what she was vaguely but pointedly suggesting.

"Enemy?" I begged for clarification.

"Sound like anyone you know?" she asked, more leading the witness than asking for theories.

I wasn't sure I was following. "Mary, what are you saying? Who are you talking about?"

She finished her second drink before responding. Her resolve had returned, along with an icy tone of voice. "I think it's time you pay another visit to an old friend of yours."

"Me?" I objected. "Who?"

"This *black fella* that Longfellow mentioned today on the phone. You know, the one whose hair they found at Joel's place?"

I'm sure she could sense my confusion, as I could tell I was wearing it all over my face. "Ziggy?" I asked. "But he's not responding to our calls and texts."

"No, not Ziggy," she replied. "The other African American we know. The one who hates all of us. Or, at least hates any*thing* and any*one* having to do with Ziggy. Someone who has a bit of a thing for vengeance. Someone with a score to settle. And someone who really does have a record that would be of interest to Longfellow and Murphy."

She lowered her glass to her side and headed back to the bar for her third. She stopped midway and looked back at me, finishing her thought. "I think it's time you pay another visit to Asshole. Leonard Walton. Ziggy's dad."

CHAPTER 32

Six Years Ago

"STATE your name and business," the voice calls back through the intercom.

A black man in his late 30s or early 40s waits on the other side of the glass doors. He leans in to move his mouth closer to the intercom speaker. "Ziggy Walton, ma'am. Here to see Joel Thomas." He looks back at her through the glass, as she talks into the phone to someone, but not in response to him.

Click.

Ziggy jumps to open the freshly unlocked door and walks through it into the lobby. "Mr. Thomas will be with you shortly," she says, never lifting her head from the work upon her desk. He walks over to a chair in the lobby and has a seat, grabbing from the coffee table an outdated *Sports Illustrated* to leaf through while he waits.

Before long, a man in a white shirt and tie, with doffed suit coat, enters to greet him. "Ziggy!" he calls to him, in recognition. Ziggy stands up and tosses the magazine back on the table.

"Joel," he cordially returns, as he walks over to extend a businessman-like handshake.

"Come on back," Joel enthusiastically says to welcome him, extending an arm down the hall. "Head down to my office. Second door on the left."

As they enter his office, Joel takes a seat behind the computer at his desk and offers, "Can I get you something? Water? Coffee?"

Ziggy simply shakes the offer off with a head nod.

"Good to see you, Zig," Joel says. "How ya been?"

"All right," Ziggy responds quietly and timidly. "Been all right."

"How are things? How's Traci?"

"Things are good. Nice office here, dog," Ziggy comments as an aside, as his eyes take their tour of the room.

"Great," replies Joel. "So. Tell me. To what do I owe this pleasure?" Ziggy shifts uncomfortably in the chair at Joel's desk, opposite his. Joel looks at his watch, then continues, "I mean, I'm not trying to hurry this along, but I do have a meeting in about 10."

"Yeah. Cool, man. Cool."

"What brings you by?"

"Well," Ziggy begins, cautiously. "About that thing I got."

"Yeah, how ya been feeling?"

"Not bad. Most days," Ziggy stipulates.

"It's a process," Joel says.

"Yeah," Ziggy concedes. "About that."

"How can I help you, Ziggy?"

"About that clinical trial."

"Yeah?" Joel asks, for clarity.

"I'm ready," Ziggy continues. "To be in it, I mean."

A dejected frown consumes Joel's face. "Oh, Ziggy."

Ziggy summons a bit more courage to press forward. "I mean, I know I was the jerk when you first offered. Maybe I was just scared. Afraid it wouldn't work. Or maybe I left too much power in His hands," he says, as his eyes look up toward the ceiling. "But I been thinking a lot about it lately, and well…"

"Oh, Ziggy."

"…Well, to be honest with you, things ain't all that great most days." His pace is slowing now. "Some days ain't great at all. The pain, ya know? And the energy. I ain't got no energy like I used to."

"Zig."

"I just felt like...you know...if the offer still stands..."

"Oh, Ziggy," Joel repeats. "I'm afraid it doesn't work that way."

Ziggy simply stares back in silence. The look on his face begs for a lifeline. *Please, Joel*, it would plead...*give me some hope*.

"That trial is closed," Joel continues. "That drug is in final approval with the FDA now. Post-marketing. I wish I could help. Honestly. But we're not running any clinical trials currently for autoimmune disorders."

"But—" Ziggy starts.

"There's nothing I can do," Joel interrupts, obviating the compassion in his voice. "The drug is out. I'm sorry."

"Joel, man."

"This is why I was so desperate to get you in four years ago!"

"Joel. C'mon, man."

Joel looks back at him as if he's about to cry, like a crestfallen father sharing his daughter's first heartbreak. "Do you have good insurance?" he asks, to break the lingering, somber silence.

Ziggy bows his head, declining to answer.

"You can probably get the drug we developed. It's out there. But it's expensive at this stage of the game. Not all insurances will even cover it yet."

"I get it, bro."

"It's showing tremendous promise, though. The clinicals went extremely well. Terrific promise. Just terrific. Most people will lead perfectly normal, healthy lives, they say."

"Good for them." Ziggy hangs his head, as he leans forward in his chair, his elbows being propped up by his knees. Joel waits, giving Ziggy ample opportunity to fill the silence. Ziggy doesn't take it.

Finally, Joel speaks up again. "I'm sorry, Ziggy. I don't know what else to say. Just hang in there. Be patient. If your insurance will cover it, great. If not, it'll be nothing more than a high co-pay in a few months to a year or so. For now, just keep doing what you're doing. The doctors gotta have you on something, right? Something to manage the discomfort? Delay the onset?"

"Yeah."

"I'm sorry, Ziggy," he repeats. "I don't know what you want me to say."

"I don't know either, bro." Ziggy stands up and pushes the chair back in under Joel's desk. "I don't know either."

And Joel watches Ziggy walk out of his office without another word from either of them.

CHAPTER 33

AN AXE TO GRIND

OF COURSE, "paying a visit" to Ziggy's dad was a bit more complicated than that. And Mary knew it. Leonard Walton was still serving his sentence — or sentences — upstate in a maximum-security prison for the assaults on Ziggy and his mom, along with God-knows-what-else. He wasn't in for life, necessarily, but he was a "lifer," nonetheless.

The next morning, Mary and I (wearing my own re-used clothes from the night prior, and not Joel's old work clothes, thank you very much) took my car upstate to Jefferson State Penitentiary. On the drive up, Mary had called ahead to arrange a visit through the warden's office, claiming she was an attorney offering *pro bono* legal services to wrongly convicted inmates doing time for crimes they didn't commit, and that, having recently read about Leonard Walton in the newspaper, wanted to "conduct outreach" on his behalf. I have to say, it all sounded rather convincing...even to me, who knew it was Grade-A bullshit.

The drive leading into the prison grounds was about as foreboding as you'd expect. The tall, barbed-wire-covered wall that guarded the perimeter was a prominent reminder as to which side of the wall you wanted to remain on. The practically windowless exterior (save for some small "porthole"-sized openings in the grayish thick concrete) projected despair and forfeiture. A few inmates were lifting weights during their designated yard time, but beyond that, the grounds were as desolate as a graveyard on a cold rainy day. It was a place you'd never want to be, unless someone was forcing you to be there. And, despite the reality of who deserved to be where, you'd feel nothing but pity and remorse for the unlucky suckers who found themselves trapped inside.

Mary and I were officially escorted into the visitors' station, a long narrow room with wooden chairs lined up against a thin countertop affixed to a wall that was covered almost entirely in plexiglass. On the other side of the glass, a holding room, where prisoners were escorted in by uniformed and armed guardsmen to meet their guests, one by one. Today, only one other prisoner was entertaining, as he sat on one end of the holding area talking into a phone-like headset, on the other end of which was apparently his significant other, seated on our side of the plexiglass and talking into the headset, back at the inmate.

We waited in our chairs on the other end of the visitors' room, doing our best not to make eye contact with the other prisoner, or his visitor, and making sure we showed no signs of eavesdropping. It's difficult enough trying to make yourself "comfortable" in a place like this. Even harder to "act natural," so as not to incur the wrath of someone doing hard time, armed guards and plexiglass notwithstanding.

Finally, we saw the door in the holding room crack open. It was him. Leonard Walton, certainly older and more haggard than when I saw him last, was entering the room in handcuffs, escorted by the guard who extended a hand in the direction of a chair stationed opposite ours. He looked at Mary first, then at me, seemingly making the instant recollection of my face.

"Aw, hell no," he uttered, as he lowered his shoulders, hung his head, and attempted to turn back around to exit. He was restrained only slightly by the guard.

"Wait, Leonard!" Mary hollered, before he could make his exit. "We just want to talk!"

Leonard paused, turned back around, then looked directly at me. Then back to Mary. He waited for a few seconds, then begrudgingly walked toward the chair. Asshole plopped down, as the guard released his grasp on his forearm. Leonard's hand moved slowly to the headset on his side of the glass, and he drew it cautiously to his ear.

Mary picked up our share of the corresponding headset and placed it to her ear. "Thank you," she said softly. "It's about Ziggy."

Leonard closed his eyes and scoffed, slamming the headset back down on its holster, as if to hang it up.

"No!" Mary yelled. "Okay, sorry! Forget Ziggy," she pleaded. "Please, Mr. Walton. We only want to ask you a few questions."

He stared back at her with a scowl on his face — a scowl that only tightened as his eyes wandered over to meet mine. He slowly returned his grip to the headset, and placed it back by his ear.

Mary repeated, "Thank you." She looked over at me, then back to him. "Jason is here to apologize. I know you had your run-ins with him. One time in particular. It's time to bury the hatchet."

Leonard said nothing, but just stared back at me. I struggled to maintain eye contact. "I'm sorry," was all I could muster. I should've stopped there. Having not thought through it sufficiently, I stupidly added, "No hard feelings."

Leonard shrugged that off with a dismissive facial tick, then looked back at Mary, who continued. "We need your help. I know you have no reason to help us, but we wanted to ask you..." she hesitated, before going on, "My husband, Joel. He's missing. We wondered...maybe there's something you would —"

I jumped in. "Anything you can tell us would help. Look," I was done with Mary's beating around the bush. "We know you had an axe to grind. With Ziggy. His mom." I gulped. Was I actually going to remind him?! Indeed, I finished, "With me."

He just stared at me.

"But, so help me God," I strengthened my voice and leaned forward, "Joel and Max had nothing to do with you." I sat back in my chair. "And neither does Mary."

He just continued to stare, but now the expression on his face went from determined and intimidating scowl to one of blank disinterest.

I went on. "So if you're trying to settle some sick score...stop. Just stop."

Still, nothing. No reaction. I wasn't sure, suddenly it dawned on me, exactly what I was expecting him to do or say. A confession? Hah. An admission? Hardly. Help? Never. I thought about something Mary said on the drive up. She was able to confirm with the warden's office that Leonard Walton had had no visitors in the past few weeks, and he certainly was not privy to any release furloughs. Asshole hadn't gone anywhere; and nobody had been there to see him. So, either he was a master escape artist, in Mary's mind, or he had someone working for him on the outside. But who? And with no in-person coordination? It wasn't jibing. At a loss for words, I ceded the floor to Mary.

"Mr. Walton," she jumped in, mercifully, "if there's something you know about my husband, please...I beg of you. He has nothing against you, and you have nothing against him. Please. And certainly Max had nothing to do with this."

Finally, he spoke. His first words. He actually showed a hint of interest in the conversation for the very first time. "Who's Max?"

Mary leaned forward, as if to say *Oh, good. You're willing to cooperate.* "Our dog," she said, enthusiastically. "Max is our dog." She waited for him to reply. None was forthcoming. "Please, Mr. Walton. Anything you know. Anything at all."

I jumped back in, as the counterpunctual bad cop. "We're not fucking around, Asshole." He shot me back a look that felt like a proverbial shot over the bow. I backed off, both metaphorically and physically in my chair. That trademark scowl was now skewed in Mary's direction, as she looked back in desperation.

Leonard slowly placed his headset back on the holder. He stood up, and pushed in a button on the side of the thin countertop that matched the one on our side of the plexiglass. A buzzer sounded over a loudspeaker, and soon the door to the holding room unlocked and opened, entered by the guard.

"Let's go, Walton," the guard called out, and Leonard backed up toward him, never taking his squinted eyes off of Mary.

"Please, Leonard!" she pleaded one last time.

And with that, Leonard Walton, the Asshole, exited the room, and the door slammed behind him.

CHAPTER 34

Five Years Ago

OVERCAST skies hang over Central Square in the heart of Calhoune, refusing to give way to the hopeful bloom of spring. Winter's chill remains, and although the snow is mostly melted now, it has only done so to reveal the ugly clutter of Autumn's un-raked leaves being blown about the park alongside the debris of uncollected litter. The trees have not yet begun to bloom, staying stiff in the air as the skeletal monuments to last summer's brilliant foliage, refusing the wind's influence in cold, dark defiance.

He sits alone on a bench near the fountain in the center of the park, reading intently a tattered hardcover book, out of which hangs a dangling red ribbon blowing gently in the breeze. He closes the book, after using the ribbon to mark his place. He looks up to the sky, his lips mouthing the words, as he closes his eyes and tilts his head back.

With his eyes still closed, he doesn't notice the other man approaching, wearing a long dark overcoat and sunglasses, unnecessary as they might be. Standing above him, he greets him, warmly and compassionately. "Hey, Zig," he says softly.

The man opens his eyes and looks up at him. "Jason. Thanks for meeting me, bro."

"Anytime, man," Jason says, as he takes a seat on the park bench beside him. "Anytime." He places a hand warmly on his knee and gives it a gentle shake. "How ya hangin' in?"

"Um." He chuckles. "Aw, shit. You know, man. I been all right, ya know?"

"How's your health?"

"Hey," Ziggy smiles. "Cutting right to the chase, huh, Jason?"

"Well, Zig. I'm worried, that's all. Wanna make sure you're still taking your meds. Eating right."

"Getting by, brother."

"Good."

Ziggy looks out over the scenery, espying the lonely desolation of a park whose latent guests have abandoned it for the season. "Getting by," he repeats.

"How are the meds working?"

"Well..." That's it. Nothing further to finish the thought.

Jason fills the void, "Anything new with Joel's company?"

"Not yet," he responds. "I told ya about the clinicals. That's a dead end. For me, anyway. Now they trying to get insurance to cover it."

"Yeah? And? Will your insurance cover it? Have you looked into that?"

Ziggy bows his head. "Yeah. About that..."

"Aw, Zig."

"This thing...it's making it so I can't work no more." Ziggy lifts his head to make eye contact with Jason. "Just so damned weak, ya know?"

"Aw, Zig. I'm sorry man." He puts his hand on Ziggy's shoulder now, offering another gentle, comfort-imparting shake. "What about disability? You got disability?"

"I got something. And there's always Medicare. But they won't cover it yet. I looked into that."

"Aw, Zig. Man...I'm so sorry." Ziggy says nothing, but continues to stare back at Jason with a vanquished frown upon his face. "What can I do?"

Ziggy struggles to get up from the park bench, and lets out a groan as he makes it to his feet. He takes a few steps away from the bench, so as to position Jason behind his back as he continues to survey the desertion of Central Square. "Jason," he says, with a crack in his voice. "Brother. I would never ask this, if I didn't absolutely, positively run out of options." Jason waits for him to go on. Ziggy exhales, then continues, "And I think I'm running out of options."

"What, Ziggy?"

"I need your help. I'm sorry. I just don't know who else I can go to."

"What is it, Zig?"

Ziggy turns back around, forcing himself to regain eye contact with Jason. "I need some money. For the drugs. I can't afford it." His eyes move off of Jason, back to the park. "But I can't afford *not* to take them, either."

"What about Traci? She have a good job? Or family to help?"

"Jason, there ain't no Traci no more."

"Sorry to hear that, man." Jason quickly stands up, visibly attempting to wrest control over the hopelessness of the careening conversation. He speaks quicker, more confidently now. "Of course, Zig. Yes, of course, I'll help. How much do you need?"

Ziggy coughs, perhaps feignedly and nervously. He musters the courage to respond, tentatively, "Five."

"Hundred?" Jason replies, revealing obvious surprise in his delivery.

"Thousand," Ziggy answers matter-of-factly. Jason looks at him in stunned silence. "A month," Ziggy adds.

"Five? Thousand? A month?"

"Jason, I wouldn't ask if it wasn't…"

"Ziggy, I don't have that kind of money."

"I ain't asking you to pay for it, brother. I just need…I just need…well, help. And I ain't asking a whole bunch of folks." He scoffs, "Hell, I don't even know a whole bunch of folks to ask, to be honest with you. But I need help. And I don't know where else to go."

Jason searches for the words to say, matching Ziggy's look of desperation with a sullen, sunken expression of his own. He walks over to Ziggy and throws his arms around him, bringing him in close for a comforting embrace. "We'll find a way, Ziggy. We'll find a way."

CHAPTER 35

HAT'S OFF

AS WE were being shown out of the visitors' station, the guard showed us a bit of sarcastic empathy.

"Better luck next time, eh?" he said to Mary.

Mary returned a half-hearted smile, in part to acknowledge his poor attempt at humor, but partially, perhaps, to curry his favor. She was about to ask him for one — a favor — and one that I hadn't seen coming.

"I suppose so," she responded, still maintaining the smile.

"Not sure what else we were expecting," I interjected.

As we walked back down the hallway to be seen out, Mary slowed up, then stopped in her tracks. She turned to the guard. "Say," she politely began, "maybe you can help with that."

"Help with what, ma'am?" he asked.

"The next time."

"I beg your pardon, ma'am?"

"Well," she said, reaching into her purse. "We never got a chance to deliver this." Mary fumbled around a bit in her bag and eventually pulled out a knit winter cap. I recognized it right away as bearing our familiar alma mater's logo: Manchester College. Green, with a white pom on top of it. "It's his son's," Mary continued. "He wanted us to deliver it to his dad today. A little peace offering. Something to remember him by." Mary's voice lowered. "His father gave it to him for his birthday, when Ziggy got the scholarship to Manchester. Would you deliver it to him?"

She handed it to the skeptical-looking guard. He took it from her hand and examined it with a careful eye, patting it down thoroughly and squishing it in his grip to make sure, I suppose, there was no file or anything in it. "We'd have to examine it first," he pointed out.

Mary replied, "Of course." As he continued to inspect it, she asked again, "Would you, sir? It would mean a lot to Ziggy."

I hadn't expected this, and Mary hadn't mentioned it. What was she up to? I should've kept my mouth shut, but reflex took over. "Mary, where did you get that?" I pressed.

Mary ignored my inquiry completely. "Please, sir. Won't you try?" she begged of the guard, with that smile I've seen a million times before when Mary wants something...and knows how to melt your heart in order to get it.

The guard looked at her. With reluctance, he gave in. "I'll try. But if it doesn't pass inspection — or he won't accept it — you're walking out of here with it."

"Understood," replied Mary.

"Wait here." The guard left us in what I guess could best be described as a lobby. In reality, it was nothing designed nor decorated for waiting guests. The room was as cold and harsh as the facility's unwelcoming exterior. Gray concrete cinder blocks, dim lighting, chipping paint, a dirty brown floor, and an unmanned desk that probably used to be some unlucky stiff's workstation, before layoffs eliminated the position to make budget cuts.

I shot Mary an inquisitive and almost accusatory glance, which she returned with nothing more than a self-satisfied raise of an eyebrow.

We waited there, in silence, pacing around the room anxiously for what seemed like 10 minutes or more, until finally the door opened and the guard re-entered the room. He was carrying the hat, a sure sign that it either failed inspection for some reason, or that Leonard had declined to accept it.

"Sorry, ma'am," the guard spoke right up.

"No luck?" I asked.

"Passed inspection just fine," he answered. "But Inmate Walton won't take it."

Mary asked, "Oh no?"

"Nope. Once he found out it was from his son, he had no interest. I told him you were delivering it as a peace offering, but he didn't seem to care."

"I see," Mary replied, dejectedly.

"Besides," the guard went on, "he said *the stupid-ass thing don't even fit.*" He cleared his throat quickly. "His words, ma'am...not mine."

"I see," she repeated. "Well, thank you for trying." She reached out to retrieve the hat from the guard, who politely relinquished it back in Mary's care.

"Sorry I couldn't be of more help, ma'am. I really did try."

"I understand," Mary humbly replied. "Thanks again, officer."

She bowed her head in defeat and led the way out of the State Pen — finally. And I followed right behind her.

On the car drive out, I wasted no time in commencing the inquisition. We were barely exiting the creepy drive of Jefferson State Penitentiary when I started in on her. "What was that?"

Mary played dumb. Or she really didn't understand what I was asking. "Not sure what I was hoping for," she innocently offered. "He really is an asshole. He was never going to help us."

"True," I acknowledged out of obligation. "But what was with the hat?" I asked, turning to the matter I found much more interesting, unplanned as it was. "Where did that come from?"

"Well," said Mary, "I guess I knew he wasn't going to help us get to the bottom of this." She paused. "Especially if he's somehow involved."

"Then why did we cart our asses up here?" My waning patience was beginning to become apparent, I'm sure.

"A long shot," Mary said coyly.

"Fifty-three miles and a rhetorical prostate exam for a long shot?"

"Well, as you acknowledged, he wasn't just going to come right out and help us."

"Yeah..."

"So I decided to help myself."

"What?"

Mary reached into her bag and pulled out the hat that the guard had graciously returned. She held it in one hand and smiled back at me like the proverbial cat beginning to digest a big fat canary. With her other hand, she reached into her purse and pulled out a large empty ziploc bag. She finished her train of thought, "Help myself," she repeated, "...to some DNA."

"Some what?!" I took my eyes off the road to look back at her, startled as I was. There she was, in frozen tableau, holding the hat in one hand and the ziploc in the other, grinning ear-to-ear.

She simply and subtly replied, "He said it didn't fit. Leonard did. If it didn't fit, maybe that means he tried it on. I thought he might."

"Why?" I was asking that one-word question to represent a whole bunch of complicated queries that were swirling around my head. Why did she think he would try it on? Why would that be a good thing? Why did she bring the hat to begin with? Why did Ziggy give it to her? *When* did Ziggy give it to her? *Did* Ziggy *even* give it to her? Not least of which: Why didn't Mary tell me what she was planning all this time?

She answered, "Because he'd want to wear a piece of Ziggy...either out of sentimentality, or out of spite. Sick, demented conquest, maybe. I knew he'd be curious about Ziggy's peace offering.

And I had a gut instinct that that asshole would try to put on Ziggy's hat."

"Ziggy asked you to do this?"

"Of course not, silly," she retorted with a chuckle. "It's not even Ziggy's hat."

"Whose is it then?"

"Joel's," she replied. "From the attic."

"And what's it doing here?"

"Collecting evidence," Mary said. "A hair," she continued. "You know...the kind of hair a *black fella* might leave at Joel's house if he was there? Now we have Asshole's hair...and DNA." She thought about that for a moment, and smiled some more. "And now...Longfellow will have us to thank for giving him another lead."

CHAPTER 36

Four Years Ago

"ZIGGY coming this year?" Barkeep asks, openly to the table of four. "He's usually the first one here."

The bartender makes his way around the table. "Here we go...the usuals all around." One by one, he places drinks in front of his patrons. "Light draft...white wine for the lady...a Heineken..." Last, he places a soda in front of the gentleman wearing a casual but trendy blazer, pressed slacks and polished loafers, a scarf strategically adorning his shoulders. "Except for you, sir. A Diet Coke. That's a new one."

"Attaboy, Russ."

"Don't think I can't spike it, Jason," Russell quips.

"Don't you dare," she scowls at him.

"Relax, Mary, Quite Contrary" he replies. "I would never do that..." a pause, and then the conclusion, "...in front of you."

A hesitant, uncomfortable chuckle is shared by all.

Finally, Jason clears his throat, before forcing down a sip of his light draft. "I don't think Ziggy is going to make it, guys," he begins, standing up from his chair as he ventures to speak.

"You talk to him, Jason?" Mary asks him.

Jason pushes his chair back under the table. "He's not feeling well. Said he wasn't up to it."

"That's a bummer," the third friend says, seated next to Mary with his arm resting on the back of her chair. "I thought this was non-negotiable. Didn't we make that rule?"

"Joel," Mary scolds him, "Jason said he's not up to it. Show some compassion."

"Sorry."

"That's all right, Joel," Jason says, brushing the front of his shirt down as he grabs for his beer on the table. A familiar Barenaked Ladies song plays over the sound system, harkening from the nearby jukebox — one of their more melancholy selections, which accentuates the more somber tone this year's version of the reunion ritual has taken on.

"Toast time?" Russell suggests.

"Uh, no."

"Not another pledge."

"No, Joel. Not another pledge." He pauses. "A plea, perhaps."

She begs for clarification, "A plea?"

Jason holds up his hand symbolically to stave off additional questioning, and gets right to the point. "Listen, gang. I have some news. It's not great." he pauses. "It's about Ziggy."

"What is it?"

"Is he okay?"

"Jason, tell us."

"He's fine...he's fine. Well, he's about as fine as can be expected, all things considered." He takes a swig of beer. "But you know how it goes. Joel, you of all people. These drugs do their best to manage the pain, or whatever. But they're not always attacking the root cause. He doesn't look great, I can tell you that. But this isn't really about Ziggy's health."

"No?"

"Well, not directly. I mean...obviously, it has *something* to do with Ziggy's health. But...it's more about...helping Ziggy deal with it."

"I wish he would've taken that clinical when I offered it to him!"

Joel says, crossing his arms as he sits back in his chair.

"We know, we know, Joel," Russell mocks. "You could've been the hero!"

"All right, Russ." Jason continues, turning to Joel, "I know...I wish he would've taken you up on that, myself. But hindsight is twenty-twenty, and all of that. Can't re-wage that war."

"The drug is out now!"

"Yes, Joel," Jason extends a hand again, this time as if to suggest that Joel back off a bit. "We know the drug is out. But you know as well as I how expensive it is right now."

"Isn't his insurance picking it up?"

"That's just it. He's in too much pain to work. He's got some sort of disability plan, I guess, but it's not enough to cover the cost of the medication. He can't afford the COBRA health coverage, and he certainly can't afford to pay retail price for the drug."

"How much is it?" Mary interrupts.

"You don't want to know," he continues. "He needs help, guys. From us."

"How much?" Russell reiterates Mary's question.

He clears his throat, if only symbolically. "Five. Thousand. ...A month."

"What?!"

"It's twelve-fifty a dose," Jason clarifies. "He takes one shot a week."

"Sounds about right," Joel confirms.

"Whoa," Russell says. "That's a lot of cake."

"That damn clinical trial!" Joel repeats. "Maybe he'd have it covered for him by now."

"Enough, Joel," Mary stops him, shooting him a glare.

Jason regains the floor. "So, guys. Ziggy has no idea I've called you all here. He'd probably kill me if he knew I was doing this. I've been helping him out for a few months, but I can't keep up, to be honest. I wouldn't ask, but I just don't know how much longer I can keep at this."

Joel interjects, talking down to the table, if not to anyone in particular. "He came by a while back...to the office. Wanted back in the trial. There was nothing I could do. It was over. I wanted to help...really, I did."

The rest sit silent, staring back at Jason. Russell speaks first. "Don't look at me, Jays. I'm broke. And therapy ain't exactly free, ya know."

"I get it, Russell. I had a feeling. No worries...but any little bit would help. Let me know…"

"I'd love to!" Russell shoots back. "I just don't have it! Honestly."

Jason looks at Joel, who shoots Mary a quick look of despair, before looking back at Jason, finally opening, "This is just a really bad time, guys. We just bought the house...and we were thinking of starting a family. I still haven't gotten that promotion…"

"Joel," Mary interrupts. "We can find something." She turns a sympathetic eye in Jason's direction. "I just don't know how much. I'm sorry."

"Anything, guys," Jason repeats. "Any little bit would help. I'm not asking for me, obviously...I'm asking for Zig."

"We'd love to help. Really, it's just."

"Just what?!" Jason snaps back, to the startled shock of all of them, who look back at him, both taken by surprise at his sudden outburst, and perhaps disturbed by his change in tone. "Just what, guys?"

"Jason, calm down."

"Lower your voice."

"Lower my *voice*?! Maybe I should lower my expectations." He turns around, as if he is about to storm out, then quickly turns around to face them again, his hands now placed squarely on his hips. "'Til death do us part? What was all that shit? The pledge, right? 'Til death?

That mean nothing to any of you?" He looks them all in the face for emphasis, one by one...slowly, so that each has their turn in the unfortunate spotlight of Jason's disapproving glare. "'Cause this is real life and death, guys. And here we are all. With an opportunity to mean it. And what do I get? *We'll see...I'm sorry...it's not a good time...*"

"Jason."

"Mary, please!" he snaps back. "We made a pledge. All of us. I didn't think it meant, *Until we all have better things going with our lives.* Or, *Until one of us really, truly needs help.* That's not what I meant by it. Maybe you did!"

"Jason."

"No. No...forget it," Jason takes a hand and firmly rubs it against his forehead, then his palm into a closed eye. "Forget it. I'm sorry I asked."

"Jason," Mary pleads. "We said we'd chip in."

"We just don't know how much," Joel reminds, finishing her thought.

"Geez, we're sorry, Jason," Russell mocks. "Not all of us run our own big fancy computer company, ya know."

"So that puts me on the hook for this? I thought we were all in this together." Jason picks up his mug of beer and downs the remaining half in three large swigs. He tosses the mug carelessly on the table, and reaches for his jacket, hanging on the back of his pushed-in chair. "You know what? Forget it." He throws his coat on. "Sorry, I asked." He heads toward the exit.

"Jason," Mary calls to him. "Where are you going? Come back."

"What are you going to tell him?" Joel yells across the room.

Jason turns around and looks at him, then at Russell, and finally at Mary. "I don't know, Joel. I don't know." He turns back around and continues toward the door. "Certainly not that all of his best friends said *no*." He slams the door open with an open palm, storms out, and lets the heavy bar door slam behind him.

CHAPTER 37

THE LONG RIDE BACK, PART ONE

"SO WHAT now? I asked, keeping my eyes fixed on Country Road 72 leading back to Calhoune. "Where to?"

We had almost an hour's drive back to our side of town — ample time to plan our next move. But Mary didn't seem to need it.

"Back to the police station," she spoke up. "To see Longfellow. We have to take him this hat...and see if Asshole was kind enough to leave a hair in it."

"You really think he has something to do with this?" I asked, my eyes now alternating between the road and Mary's face, which looked deep in speculative thought.

"You don't?" she challenged me.

"Seems like a stretch."

"Does it?" She didn't seem to want an answer, only to shut me down. She dismissively reached into her purse to pull out her phone, and proceeded to dial a number then raise the phone to her ear.

I asked casually, "Calling Longfellow?"

Before she could even answer, she began speaking into the phone. "Hi, Ziggy. It's Mary. Listen, I saw that you called the other day. Sorry I haven't been able to get ahold of you. You didn't leave a message...so...call me back. Let me know what's up. Okay? Miss you. Bye."

"Still no answer, obviously?" I innocently asked the apparent.

"Nope. Have you had any luck getting ahold of him?"

"None," I said. "Wonder if the police have talked to him."

After a brief, pensive silence, Mary challenged me again. "So you really think there's no way Leonard could've had something to do with Joel's disappearance?"

"Not really," I said matter-of-factly. "Why would I?"

"Oh, I don't know," Mary sarcastically responded. "A man with a track record of abuse — and probably worse — just happens to be getting the perfect revenge on all of us...all of us who he clearly hates...and you just think it's a coincidence?"

"Seems really far-fetched. You talked to the warden yourself. He hasn't been out. How could he have had something to do with this?"

"That we know of!" she abruptly shot back. "I mean, he got out once, didn't he? When he came back to beat the shit out of Ziggy's mom? I'm sure you remember saving Ziggy's life...beating Asshole within an inch of his? Good job, by the way," she digressed. "Although, you should've finished the job."

"Trust me," I acknowledged, "it's crossed my mind." I returned to the working theory, which really wasn't working for me at all. "But, how could Leonard's hair have gotten inside Joel's house? The warden said he's not eligible for furlough, so it's not like he paid him a weekend visit...he hasn't had anyone come see him in jail..."

"That we know of," Mary interjected again.

"He certainly hasn't broken out."

"That we know of," again.

"Mary, I think the warden would have mentioned that. When you were asking all those questions...as Ziggy's *lawyer*?"

"Maybe," she said dismissively. "Maybe. Or maybe a warden doesn't like to brag about prison breaks, if they haven't made the news already. Not exactly résumé-building material there."

"Mary," I said, perhaps too condescendingly, "you're really reaching here."

Mary ignored the condescension completely. "Or maybe he's got someone working for him. And maybe that someone had been to see Leonard. And maybe that someone visited Joel's, and inadvertently transported one of Leonard's hairs along the way."

"You said yourself the warden told us he hadn't had any other visitors for weeks, until we came along."

She ignored me again. "Or maybe..."

I interrupted her again, this time absent of condescension, but with a bit of scolding and reality-checking thrown in for good measure. "Mary, listen to yourself."

She raised her voice considerably and shot me back an icy stare. "Or maybe I just want to show Goddamned Longfellow that there's a million and one ways any number of hairs could've found their way into Joel's house! Maybe show him there's more than one fucking *black fella* (she would mock Longfellow's voice with disdain every time she repeated those words) in the world! Did you ever think of that?"

Her point was taken. It finally made sense. This wasn't a new lead for Longfellow. It was a misdirection. It was a scent to throw...off of one of our best friends...who apparently was the police's newfound primary person of interest. I could finally see how much that was bugging Mary, and that she'd do anything in her power to move the shade off of a friend. It was a sudden reminder of everything I've ever known to be true about Mary. There was a certain warmness that flowed through my body because of it.

I waited a second for the metaphorical smoke to clear, then offered a bit of acquiescence. "You're right."

I thought that was enough to establish the validity of her line of reasoning, and we could change the subject to something other than Leonard Walton's hair sample. I was wrong. My concession to Mary's motivations was not enough to completely quash her formulations. She began speaking again, after about ten seconds of silence. "Still," she said, now lowering her voice...almost too much for my liking.

"Think about it."

I knew I was going to regret entertaining this train of thought, but I played along nonetheless. "Think about what?"

"Let's say that someone really did want to hurt us. All of us." She paused, perhaps almost thinking better of continuing. But she didn't think better of it. She finished her thought. She took her eyes off the road before us and turned to me for a reaction. "If Leonard Walton or anyone else is, in fact, on some long-tailed vengeance tour...are we next?"

CHAPTER 38

Four Years Ago

"SUCH a shame."

"So sad."

Whispered conjecture floats through the room like stock tips passed in a smoke-filled martini bar.

"Has anyone heard why?"

"Or how?"

"He's still so, so young."

"I heard he OD-ed once already. A few years back."

People dressed in dark suits cram into a viewing room at Vermaden Funeral Home to pay their respects. They gather in small pods of sorrowful conversation, greeting newcomers with a sympathetic, forced smile...or others, a tearful, sobbing embrace.

"Was he ill?"

"Anyone know the cause?"

"What do you think?"

A small line forms at the guest registry. One by one, a visitor kneels beside the casket and says a silent prayer. From one corner of the room floats a chuckle, "That was certainly his way." From the other, a woman collects herself, trying to forestall an all-out sob. "It's just so damned tragic."

"Thank you for coming."

"How's his family holding up?'

"When's the last time you talked to him?"

"It's good to see you. Wish the circumstances were different."

"Are they saying what happened?"

In the back corner of the room stands a middle-aged couple. She wears sunglasses to conceal the smudging of her eye makeup, and holds a tissue to her nose as she quietly but quickly sniffs in. He stands beside her with an arm around her shoulder, occasionally drawing it into his chest to comfort her. They both turn toward the room's entrance as two men walk in: a skinny black man in his early 40s and a white man, of similar age, wearing a long, dark overcoat. The men spot the couple in the corner from across the room and hasten toward them with a nod of their heads.

She reaches for him as he nears, then lunges her head into his chest, her arms thrown around him. "Oh, Jason," she sobs, as her battle to hold back the tears is lost. "Jason." The sobbing continues. "He loved you so much." Jason hesitantly wraps his arms loosely around her shoulder blades.

"I'm so sorry, Mary," he mutters.

She eventually pushes herself back a half a step and looks over at the man's friend. "Ziggy. He loved you, too. You know how much." She throws her arms around Ziggy, struggling all the more to fight back the tears.

"He loved you too, Mary."

Mary lifts her head off Ziggy's shoulder to look him in the eye. She is able to force a sentimental smile, then her eyes turn pensive as the hug she is giving him evolves into a mild grope. "My God, Ziggy," she whispers, as she looks at his abdomen, where her hands grasp for flesh to hold onto. "Are you eating?"

Ziggy reaches down to grab her wrists, then takes both of her hands into his and holds them waist-high between them. He returns the sentimental smile, and gives each of her hands a gentle squeeze.

"This sucks," her companion finally butts in, from a couple feet away. He steps forward just a bit, and shakes Jason's hand. "This really sucks."

"Hey, Joel," Jason responds, returning the handshake. "Yes...yes, it does." He then looks over to the half-opened casket, the traffic around which has cleared for the moment. To all of them, he nods in that direction and asks hesitantly, "Should we head over?"

Mary begins to cry again, as she nods her head in the reluctant affirmative, returning the tissue to her mouth and nose.

They slowly move in the direction of the casket. When they arrive, they look down at the deceased, his eyes closed and hair perfectly styled, he clad in a bright-colored linen suit with an ill-matching patterned tie. Mary's tears turn more vocal; a sob returns. She kneels down beside him, collapsing clumsily onto the kneeler and forcing her forehead firmly into the tissue-laden hand. Her whole body trembles, and Joel puts his hand on her shoulder nearest to himself. He kneels down beside her. Jason puts a hand on her other shoulder, remaining standing by her side. Ziggy leans over from behind her to deliver a soft kiss on her head.

Eventually, Mary is able to take the tissue and wipe her lower eyelids from beneath the sunglasses. She takes them off and forces them carelessly into the purse that hangs at her side. She searches the tissue for a clean, dry spot and uses it to clear the drippings escaping her nose.

Ziggy reaches into his coat pocket and removes a tattered hardcover book. He takes the red ribbon between his thumb and index finger and uses it to assist in opening the tome to the designated page. He does the sign of the cross, and raises his closed eyes to the ceiling, mouthing the words he has apparently memorized from the text. The rest of them stare down at him in silence.

Finally, Joel breaks the silence. "What do we say?"

Jason turns to him. "Whatever you want," he whispers. "Whatever's in your heart."

"Pray for him," Ziggy says under his breath, now looking down at him.

"I'm so sorry, Russell," Mary whispers, shaking her head slowly as she forces herself to look at his face. "We should've been there. We should've known." A sound resembling a cough escapes her mouth, turning into a cry as its tail follows quickly behind. "We should've done something," she forces through the tears.

Joel puts his arm around her and draws her closer to him. "We can't, Mary."

"Joel's right," Ziggy says. "We can't blame ourselves."

They continue to stare down in silence for several seconds. Jason's upper teeth grasp firmly his lower lip. A tear forms in his eye. He sniffs as he slightly leans over above him. He takes his hand and places it over the man's folded hands, clasping a rosary. He leans a bit closer to him, and turns his gaze to the deceased man's face.

He whispers, "Goodbye, Russell. We will never forget you."

CHAPTER 39

THE LONG RIDE BACK, PART TWO

"LET'S say that someone really did want to hurt us. All of us." She paused, perhaps almost thinking better of continuing. But she didn't think better of it. She finished her thought. She took her eyes off the road before us and turned to me for a reaction. "If Leonard Walton or anyone else is, in fact, on some long-tailed vengeance tour...are we next?"

"This again?"

"Seriously, Jason. Think about it. Let's say someone had something against us. *Specifically* us. How could things have turned out much worse for us? Starting with Russell."

I thought about administering another dose of reality-check, but considering how quickly I had triggered Mary's temper just moments prior, I thought better of it. Besides, a passing highway sign had indicated we still had 42 miles back to Calhoune, so I had plenty of time to let Mary get this off of her chest.

"I tried to describe it last night," Mary resumed. "*Internal*, is how I said it. I don't really know how else to put it. But, between Russell, Max and Ziggy, everyone has either died — or is dying — from the inside. Like, from the inside out."

"Mary," I was obliged to remind her. "Russell did that to himself."

"Did he?"

"There was a note! You read it!" She probably didn't want to remember reading the note Russell had left behind. But we were all there. We all read it. "And I don't think that was the first time he tried it, either."

"Notes can be faked, Jason!"

"By whom?"

"By whomever wants this all to happen, Jason!"

"Oh, come on." My condescension had returned, but I couldn't help it. And I'm sure Mary could feel it. But she persisted, heedless to my objections.

"And Max, okay?" she went on. "Poisoned, if you ask me." She turned her head to look out the window, the back of her head now turned toward me. "I know you don't think so, but whatever." She continued, "And Ziggy."

"Mary, Ziggy's being treated by doctors. I think they would know if there was anything suspicious going on. You've heard Ziggy describe it. It's a real, bona-fide illness. With a treatment plan and everything."

"Do some Googling, Jason," Mary reprimanded me. "Do a search for *fatal drugs mimicking autoimmune disorders*. Oh wait...you don't have to. Because I have."

"And?" I felt like a judge, saying "I'll allow it" to an objecting defense attorney.

"All kinds of shit turns up. Including a case about five years ago. A woman who had taken out a handsome life insurance policy on her husband started lacing his morning orange juice with a small, untraceable and undetectable amount of bleach."

"For real?" I looked over at her again. Now she was looking back at me, with an eager confidence flushed across her face.

"Her husband turned really ill, over the course of several weeks. Months, maybe. Sure enough, he started getting treatment for everything under the sun. Like Ziggy. The doctors had no clue what they were even treating! The diagnosis was deferred, but they thought his own body had begun turning on itself." She looked down and lowered her voice a bit. "Turns out, it was trying to fight off the contaminant...the bleach...and his organs were shutting down one by one. Eventually, it got him."

"No shit," I said, with obvious macabre shock and disgust.

"The wife eventually copped to it, but the doctors would've never known. Police found her search history on her computer. She was looking for a way to do exactly that." She cleared her throat. "And she found one."

"Holy shit."

"Yep," Mary replied, putting on a bit of an air, as if the tide in the battle of the wills was turning in her favor. "So...call it far-fetched all you want. But this shit happens, Jason. All the time. In real life."

"I suppose so," I humbly acknowledged, hopefully with enough of an apologetic reticence to get the message across to Mary. I owed her that.

She looked back up at the road in front of us. "Which brings us back to Max. Sure, maybe he was eating that bad food from China. Or maybe someone needed him out of the way...no longer guarding the house...so they could get to Joel. Without raising a huge ruckus for the neighbors to hear...or to avoid getting attacked by a faithful, loving guard dog."

As crazy as this was all sounding, I had to admit, if only to myself, that Mary had thought through this way more than I had been giving her credit for.

"And maybe," she continued, reminiscent of Sherlock Holmes or Detective Columbo, "whatever did in Max, and whatever's doing in Ziggy, and God forbid, whatever may have gotten to Joel...is the same thing that happened to Russell."

Sure, she had thought through it. But did it add up? I chose to challenge her, just a bit. "But Mary, we're talking about three or four years apart. Do you think that, if someone was trying to do us all in, they'd do it this slowly? This strategically? This patiently? I don't know…"

"I don't know either," she was willing to concede. "But I do know this." She paused just for a moment or two, apparently collecting her thoughts. "If someone is executing some sick master plan to exact some sort of revenge against all of us…one thing is for sure…either you or I is next."

"Mary," I scolded. That was frankly too much to consider right then and there. Tracking all of this stuff down and finding out about Joel was enough. Thinking about someone hunting down Mary and I was quite another.

"What?" Mary protested. "Think about it. You acknowledged yourself that crazy stuff like this happens all the time…in real life. Or were you just patronizing me?"

I could sense the growing resentment in her voice with that suggestion. "No, no. You *were* right. Stuff like that does happen all the time. But I'm not sure that that's what's going on here. Over the course of four years? I just don't know, Mary."

"I know you don't, Jason. I know you don't. And I don't blame you. But think about this. One more piece. Think about this…let's say you were going to single us out for some sick plan like this. Just put yourself in this sick fuck's mind for just one minute."

"Yeah," I reluctantly encouraged.

"Who would you want out of the way first?"

"Huh?" I asked, legitimately not following.

"Who would you take down first?" she repeated.

"First?"

"Yeah. First. Who would you want out of the way?"

"What are you talking about?" I contested. What was she getting at? I was getting it, but not entirely. Following the timeline of events in my head, I asked, "Russell? Why would he be the initial target? I'm not following. Everyone loved Russell. Someone like Leonard Asshole Walton would certainly have no grudge to bear against Russell. And Russell loved everyone."

"Yes, yes he did," Mary said, like a prosecuting attorney who was just about to turn the witness's own words against him in cross examination. "He loved everyone...and everything." Her tone softened just a bit, momentarily. "Including himself, I might add. Which makes what happened all the more suspicious," she threw in, almost as an aside.

"Mary," I admonished once again.

"He loved everything," she reiterated, then paused for a moment, and thought carefully about her next words. "He also *noticed* everything, remember?"

"What?"

"Everything. The tree where Joel was hiding when we went camping at Tomahawk in college. Remember? The one with the moss scuffed off of the trunk? Who else would see that? The gay boy who would be waiting for him in the concourse at Ziggy's basketball game...the one who was overdressed and not paying attention to the game? That was the guy he could introduce himself to. Or, every last detail of what I was wearing the night I married Joel...and where it all came from!" I took my eyes off the road to look over at her once again. She was staring right at me, still with that eager confidence. "Jason...he noticed *everything!*"

"And?"

"Well," Mary finished, "if I was coming back after all of us, I know who I'd want to get out of the way first." She looked back at the road and delivered the final piece of her morbid theory. "I'd start with the one person who notices everything."

CHAPTER 40

Three Years Ago

SHE RETURNS from the kitchen to deliver a bowl full of salad to the dinner table. He waits patiently in his chair for her to fetch the remaining preparations, including a bottle of wine to refill their glasses. Lastly, she brings a serving dish with spaghetti and meatballs, and sets it on the table before taking her seat opposite him.

"Dig in," she says.

"Everything looks great, Mary."

"Thank you," she says, with a half-smile, as she begins to serve herself some salad. He grabs for the pasta dish, and determinedly forks a large helping onto his plate. "How was your day?" she asks politely, setting the salad bowl back on the table.

"Not bad, I guess. Had my meeting with Pennington." He starts in on his dinner. "He said he thinks it'll only be another few months before Smitty retires. Then, supposedly, the job is mine."

"That's great," is her monotone reply.

"Yep," he mumbles with his mouth full. "We'll see." He takes another forkful. "How was your day?"

"Um. Not bad," she says softly, then takes a nibble of lettuce. She reaches for the wine and tops off her glass, immediately grabbing for it upon returning the bottle of the wine to the table. She takes a hearty swig.

"I gotta tell you, though," he continues. "Pennington's turning into something of a dickhead, if you ask me." Mary looks down at her plate in silence, as he continues to ramble. "I don't even know if I belong there anymore. There's probably a reason Smitty is retiring at 60. Probably wants the hell out of there. Wouldn't blame him. Got me asking myself: Do I really want his job? Drove him to an early retirement...hell, maybe an early grave." He continues to fork spaghetti into his mouth while he talks, barely pausing to chew or swallow. "I mean, yeah...sure. The money would be nice. And the title is nice. But I keep wondering. Maybe I should get while the gettin' is good. Or, do I simply take the promotion for what it'll do for my résumé? Then leave. But, if I stay, and take the raise, we might be able to finally get that bigger cabin up north." He looks up from the twirled-up spaghetti that hangs from his fork to look over at Mary. "What do you think, babe?"

She is staring back at him, her hands on her lap, with a look of apprehension on her face. Her eyes begin to well up. She doesn't answer, so he shakes his spaghetti-laden fork just slightly, as if to prod her, *Well?*

She tilts her head slightly, with a look of sympathy in her eyes. "Joel," she says softly. "We need to talk."

Joel sits frozen, looking back at her, his fork still hanging in still-life above his plate. "What do you mean?" he asks. "Talk? About what?"

Mary folds the napkin on her lap, then places it purposefully on the table. She takes another sip of wine. "I'm sorry," she finally says.

He forks the spaghetti into his mouth. "Sorry? About what? What is it, Mary?"

She lowers her eyes to her untouched salad. "Us, Joel. We need to talk...about us."

"What about, Mary? C'mon, babe. You're scaring me." He chuckles nervously.

"I'm sorry," she repeats.

"About what, Mary? Sorry about what? C'mon...out with it. Let's talk. I'm all ears." His pace is heightening now, as he sets his fork down on the table. He grabs his wine and washes down what will for now be his last mouthful of pasta. "Don't leave me hanging here."

"Joel," she starts. "You know I love you."

"I did," he forces another chortle. "Until about 20 seconds ago."

"Joel. I do. You know that." She pauses, apparently gathering the courage to continue. "It's just...I'm not *in*..."

"Stop," Joel interrupts. "Don't." He gets up from the table abruptly and throws his napkin down on the table. "Don't finish that sentence."

"What?"

"The whole, *I love you, but I'm not* in *love with you* routine. Save it."

"Joel."

"Mary, what is going on? What is this, all of a sudden?"

"It's not all of a sudden, Joel."

"Well, it's the first I'm hearing of it!" he snaps back.

"Joel, listen to me," she quietly tries to calm him.

"Cut to the chase, Mary," he snaps again. "What are you trying to say? Spit it out."

"I don't know, Joel." She begins to cry. "I don't know."

He sits back down and places a closed fist in front of his tightened lips. He looks at her, as she empathetically peers into his eyes.

"You're my best friend," she forces through the tears.

"Really?" he asks. "This is how you treat a best friend?"

"Joel, please try to understand."

"Try to understand?! Understand what?! I don't even know what we're talking about!"

She tries to calm herself. And pace herself. And control herself. "It's just been a long year. Things are different. It hasn't felt the same in a long, long time, Joel. You can't tell me you haven't noticed."

"Noticed what?"

"All of it. The intimacy. The togetherness. The passion. Can you really say nothing has changed between us?"

"Not for me, it hasn't!"

"You're lying."

Joel grabs for his wine and finishes what little is left in his glass. He stares at it as he places it on the table, his hand still affixed to its stem. He speaks more measuredly now. "Bottom line, Mary. What are we talking about right now?"

A tear finally escapes from the corner of Mary's eye. "Joel, I'm sorry." She gathers herself, and readies herself for the finally delivery. "I want a divorce."

Joel shakes his head with a sarcastic and vanquished forced grin, then looks over at the floor. Lying at his feet is a dog, looking up at him with an eager smile across his face. The mastiff's tongue hangs lazily as he pants, patiently waiting for table scraps to be awarded. Joel reaches down to pet him on the side of his large, fur-covered body. Without looking up, and keeping his eyes fixed upon the dog's smiling face, he makes a singular announcement, seemingly openly, into the room at large. It is message of acceptance, and one of measured calculation. "I want the dog."

CHAPTER 41

SINGLED OUT

MARY walked quickly and eagerly up to the police station doors, her purse stuffed with the specimen: a large ziploc bag carrying the knit Manchester College cap that Leonard Walton had been so gracious to unwittingly try on. I followed quickly behind, trying to keep up with her. I managed to beat her to the door, and held it open for her as she rushed inside.

"Detective Longfellow," she blurted out to the officer manning the front desk, before she even walked up to it.

"Can I ask what this is regarding, ma'am?" the officer asked.

"Tell him it's Mary Thomas and Jason Wilhelm. We have something he's going to want to see."

"I'll let him know," the officer said, as she left her station to notify Longfellow of our arrival.

Mary paced the front lobby with a nervous anxiety that matched in deed what my psyche was enduring mentally. Before long, Longfellow was joined by Murphy and entered the lobby. "Ms. Thomas. Mr. Wilhelm. Welcome back," he rasped. "To what do we owe the pleasure?"

"We'd like to show you something," Mary replied. "In private."

Longfellow shot Murphy a glance, then extended an arm. "Please," he obliged. "Be our guest." Mary followed the extended, welcoming arm back to the interrogation room we had endured the day before. I apprehensively followed her, fearful of the skepticism with which Mary's evidence and theories would be met by Detectives Longfellow and Murphy.

When we got into the room, Murphy rearranged some chairs around a table so we'd all have a place to sit. One by one, we took our seats, and Mary opened her purse. She pulled out the ziploc bag and placed it on the center of the table. "There," she said smugly, "we want you to have a look at that."

Murphy grabbed for it, and began to study the hat through the clear plastic bag. Longfellow inquired dryly, "What is it?"

"A hat," I answered. "Worn by Leonard Walton."

"Who?" Longfellow asked.

"Leonard Walton," Mary jumped in. "Ziggy Walton's dad."

"Oh?"

"Yes, sir," she continued. "We think it may contain a hair sample."

"A hair sample?" Murphy begged.

"Yes, sir," Mary repeated. "Leonard Walton's hair sample." She scooted in her chair just a bit. "We thought you could cross-reference the sample against the hair you found at Joel's house. You know the one...the one from an African American?"

Longfellow's and Murphy's eyes quickly met, obviously sharing both cynicism and curiosity, as Longfellow took the bag from Murphy and opened it. He gently removed the hat and gave it a careful examination with his squinted eyes, careful not to manhandle the evidence too much. He placed it back in the bag and returned it to Murphy's care.

Mary spoke up, "We thought maybe there's a chance that it was Leonard who had paid Joel a visit that night. Not Ziggy. Leonard's dad — Asshole, as we like to call him — has a bit of colorful past. And he had a grudge against us." She looked over at me, then sat back in her chair. "All of us. Ziggy included."

Longfellow looked at her and inquired with what seemed like a genuine interest. "Grudge?" he prompted.

"Yes, sir. A bad one," Mary said.

"Against all of you," he said, to confirm.

"Yes, sir."

Murphy joined in, "All of you...being Joel, yourselves, and Ziggy Walton?"

"You might say that," I chimed in. "He and I had a very physical altercation years ago. He ended up back in jail as a result."

"And you?" Murphy asked of me.

"Self defense," I said, with just a hint of obstinate pretension.

"This Leonard Walton character," Longfellow regained the floor, "where is he now?"

Mary sheepishly looked down at her lap. "In prison, sir. Jefferson State."

"Prison, huh?" he asked, like a father listening to his daughter tell him about the time she saw the Tooth Fairy sneak into her bedroom at night. Longfellow wasn't buying this any more than I had. "And you think he somehow got out of prison...and paid Mr. Thomas a visit? That it?"

"I don't know," Mary conceded. "But I do know that he had a motive. And he had a history of things like this. I just thought it might be possible...that...whoever...did whatever...to Joel...maybe he could be added to the suspect list. I mean, it couldn't hurt, right? If you look into his past, you'll see he got out of jail once and immediately went to settle a score with Ziggy's mom. Went directly to her house to beat the shit out of her. Didn't care who knew or saw...broad daylight and everything." The look she extended back to Longfellow now practically begged for affirmation. She shot Murphy a similarly beckoning glance, then back to Longfellow. "I know it sounds crazy right now," Mary continued, "but I think there's a chance, however slight, that Leonard Walton has been orchestrating a vengeful scheme against all of us...one by one...Joel included." She paused there for a reaction from Longfellow, and one I knew wouldn't be forthcoming.

Longfellow shot Murphy another skeptical look ."We'll look into it, Ms. Thomas," he finally said. "Murphy, take this back to forensics, will you?" Murphy gave him a head nod then got up from his chair and exited the room with the hat in tow. Longfellow looked back at Mary. "Anything else we can help you with today?"

Mary let out a deflated sigh. "No, sir. Not today."

"Good," he replied. "I'm glad you came back today, though, to be honest." He stood up from his chair, and began to walk slowly around the table, his hands on his hips as he looked around the room. "Look, sorry to be taking up so much of your time lately." He looked at Mary. "We're just trying like hell to find your husband. I'm sure you understand." Mary nodded back, without correcting him— no adding the *ex* this time. "But, we were going to call you back anyway." He smiled, only slightly. "Saved us a dime."

"What can we do for you, Detective?" I was first to ask.

"Well," he replied gruffly, "We're making a bit of headway over here."

"Oh yeah?" Mary asked, with a suggestion of hope in her voice. She leaned forward again in her chair.

"Well, we think so. And we want to run some of it by you."

"By all means," she answered.

"Great." He continued to subtly pace the room, circling the table ever-so-slowly. "First thing is, the text message."

"The text message?" I asked.

"Yes," he confirmed. "The one supposedly from Joel. *Call off the dogs, I'm fine?*" he recited for clarity.

"Of course," I returned.

"I think we were right to suspect that it wasn't coming from Joel."

"Oh no?" Mary's eager anticipation began to wash into troubled concern.

"No, ma'am. You see, we were able to triangulate the location of Joel's cellphone, with a little help from our friends at the phone company. We knew whose phone had sent the text, and now we're able to determine its whereabouts. And then there was the matter of the text itself. We were able to determine that it wasn't coming from overseas. There was never any international roaming ever turned on for that device with the phone company. So, it appears that Joel never left for vacation...a cruise, or trip to Europe or something." He quickly added, "Or if he did, he didn't take his cellphone with him. And even if he did, he didn't activate the data roaming, so there's no way he could've sent that text from abroad."

"Whoa," I uttered in shock, feeling the need to interject, perhaps, or perhaps just allowing the sentiment to involuntarily escape my mouth.

"So where was it sent from?" Mary pressed, with the concern now dripping from both her face and voice.

"Well, it was definitely Joel's phone. We were able to cross-reference the data logs, and sure enough, it was sent from his phone. Not spoofed, in other words...that is, faked or something."

"And?" she pressed again.

"We were able to use GPS to determine the location of the phone, like I said. At least where it is now."

Me, this time, "And?"

"The ping came from a house in Denton. Not too far from here." Mary's expression went blank. She slunk down a bit in her chair, maybe only noticeable to me. But I've seen that slink before. She was just coming to terms with the horror of Longfellow's theory. "Either of you know anyone in Denton?" Longfellow asked, looking down now at both us, back and forth.

"Ziggy," Mary whispered, the utter defeat now splashed across her eyes, as she stared down at her hands, fidgeting on her lap.

Something akin to a breath escaped my lungs, as I too realized where Longfellow's investigation had led. Mary's utterance, *Ziggy*, was a hit to the gut — one I both saw coming and never expected, all at once.

"Mr. Walton," Longfellow confirmed, lacking any semblance of empathy or remorse. It was all business. Perhaps he lacked the gene that compels most of us humans to deliver bad news with some degree of decorum, reticence and grace. Or perhaps he didn't care.

"You're sure?" I asked.

"Pretty sure," replied Longfellow. "Able to track it down to Mr. Walton's current residence."

"Well," I inquired, "What's he say? Have you spoken with him? He won't return any of our calls. Neither one of us."

"That's just it," Longfellow said, as he resumed his slow pacing, "We paid him a visit. No answer at the door. Made a few calls to that number you provided us...nothing."

"Us neither," Mary said. "I'm starting to worry about him. He called...like I said, that one time...but he didn't leave a message...and nothing since."

"Peculiar," Longfellow noted. Just then, the door opened, and Murphy rejoined the meeting. "There's more," Longfellow ominously continued. He watched Murphy get resituated, taking a determined stance beside the table, hands placed firmly on his beltline.

"More?" I prompted.

"Yes, sir. Detective Murphy and I went back to visit the veterinary hospital where Max — is it? — where Max was dropped off for emergency care. Had another conversation with the on-duty admission nurse. Murphy here asked her to describe Mr. Thomas...you know, the man who dropped off his dog, but didn't wait around to hear the results of the exam?"

"Yeah..." I prompted again.

Murphy took over. "She described him, all right."

"And?" This time, it was Mary who was cajoling the rest of the story out of them.

Murphy continued. "Six-foot...maybe more. Skinny. Mid-forties." He paused for a moment and shot Longfellow a knowing glance. Then he looked back at Mary, with a peering glare, before finishing the description the nurse had provided them. "Black."

Silence.

"That sound like Mr. Thomas to you?" Longfellow sarcastically asked, to break the silence.

"Of course not," Mary softly confessed, practically under her breath.

"Hadn't dawned on us to ask for a description of the man bringing Max to the hospital," Longfellow noted. "Checked in as Joel Thomas...identified himself as Max's owner...though, there was no collar or dog tags to identify the poor pup. Vet records matched Max, so we're pretty sure it was him. But the more we thought about it, and the more evidence we collected, the more we thought it might make sense to double check on the patient's owner. Sure enough, the man the nurse described as Joel Thomas — Max's owner, at least on that night — was a black fella. Skinny. Mid-forties."

"This doesn't make any sense," I abruptly observed. "You guys can't possibly think Ziggy is behind all of this."

"Just following every lead, sir," Murphy shot back, the peering glare now affixed on me.

"It can't be," Mary insisted. "There's just no way."

"We're looking into it," Longfellow echoed his own earlier comment. "All of it," he added.

Mary composed herself, and stood up with determination. "How can we help?"

I came quickly to her assistance. "Yes, officers. Anything we can do to help, just let us know."

Longfellow answered, "Well, help us track down Mr. Walton. That'd be a good start."

I stood up to join Mary. "We'd be happy to, Detective. But he's not answering our calls, like we said. I could swing by his place, if you'd like."

"That won't be necessary," he replied. Longfellow then pulled out a chair and had a seat at the table. "One other thing we found interesting." There was that feeling again...like I was watching *Columbo*. But this time it wasn't Mary playing the part, but rather the lead investigator working on a real-life case, at the center of which was now one of my oldest, dearest friends. That part near the end of every episode, when Columbo inevitably gets to the reveal, saying *One more thing, ma'am*. That's where it felt like this was headed. And it was. "We talked to the neighbors," he began. "You know...Mr. Thomas's neighbors? All of them were perfectly willing to cooperate, so that was nice."

"Great," I matter-of-factly interjected.

"They all have pretty good memories, it seems," he went on. Murphy took the opportunity to also take a seat at the table next to Longfellow. Mary and I took the obvious cue that we'd be there a while longer, and rejoined them at the table. "Had a couple of real good conversations with the neighbors...next door...both sides...and behind Mr. Thomas's residence."

"And?" Mary prodded again.

"Well, we were looking for impressions, or recollections."

"Of?" I asked.

"The night in question," Murphy answered.

Longfellow took it from there. "Or thereabouts. Few nights before. Few nights after."

"What did they see?" Mary asked.

"Or hear," I added.

"Well, that's just it," Longfellow went on to describe. "Nothing much at all. No screaming, no yelling. No glass breaking. No signs or sounds of a forced entry. No struggle. Certainly no gunshots."

"Well that's a relief," said Mary.

Longfellow processed that for a moment. Then continued. "Yep, no nothing to report. Nothing at all."

"Not even a bark," Murphy chimed in.

"A bark?" I wondered aloud, trying to hasten my way to Columbo's big reveal.

Longfellow hesitated. After glancing over at Murphy, he turned his head to me. "You much of a reader, Mr. Wilhelm?"

"Some."

"What about detective stories...mysteries?"

"Some."

"You a Sherlock Holmes fan?"

There it was. First Columbo, and now Sherlock Holmes. I was having eerily familiar déja vu.

"I read a bit," I reported. "Not an expert...but some."

"What about *The Adventure of Silver Blaze*?" he probed.

"Not familiar with it," I admitted, unclear as to its relevance to Joel and/or Ziggy.

"Interesting story. One of my favorites in the Sherlock Holmes canon," Longfellow said with a respectful, observant grin.

"What's it about?" asked an anxious Mary, obviously sharing my enthusiasm for Detective Longfellow to get the point.

"Well, it's a mystery," he began. "Not so much a missing person, like our Mr. Thomas here. But a missing race horse. Really interesting mystery. A curious one. With a curious clue."

"Curious?" I asked.

"Yes, sir," he replied. "In the story, Holmes makes mention of *the curious incident of the dog in the night-time*. Seems there was a dog guarding the stables where the prize racehorse was moored. And with respect to the night the horse went missing, Detective Holmes was especially curious about one particular incident, relative to the guard dog."

"What was this curious incident?" Mary questioned, practically begging him, now, to get to the point.

Longfellow turned to her now. "That's just what another detective wondered, Ms. Thomas." Now looking back at me, he continued, "Detective Gregory Lestrade of Scotland Yard challenged Mr. Holmes, much in the way you all just challenged me." We waited patiently for him to continue. He went on, now apparently quoting Lestrade, "*The dog did nothing in the night-time,* Lestrade insisted." He paused. "To which Sherlock replies, *That was the curious incident.*"

"I beg your pardon?" I asked.

"It came to be regarded as *The Case of the Dog That Didn't Bark,*" Murphy butted in to point out his familiarity with the lore.

"Detective," Mary chimed in, "what are you getting at? And what does this have to do with Joel?"

Longfellow forged ahead. "Well, Ms. Thomas. After talking to the neighbors, Detective Murphy and I found it of interest that not one neighbor could report a disturbance coming from the residence where Mr. Thomas apparently disappeared. Not so much as a dog barking."

"Meaning?" she queried, her waning patience becoming increasingly apparent.

"Meaning, Ms. Thomas, that whoever had been paying a visit to Mr. Thomas's house that week, and on the night he disappeared, was somebody that the dog recognized. You see, Sherlock Holmes was able to deduce, based on the curious incident of the dog that didn't bark, that whoever had stolen Silver Blaze must've been familiar to the guard dog — hence, the dog that didn't bark. Turns out, it was Silver Blaze's own trainer that had led the horse out of the stable. Mystery solved."

We let those words hang in the air, neither Mary nor I sure of how to react. *Mystery solved.* Finally, I summoned the resolve to speak up. "What are you suggesting, Detective?"

"Simple, Mr. Wilhelm," Longfellow confidently answered.

"Whoever was there to do Mr. Thomas harm — if that was indeed the nature of what happened — whoever it was, the dog recognized him or her. Another dog that didn't bark."

Mary contested, "You can't possibly be suggesting…"

Longfellow cut her off, now standing up again, as if to suggest the meeting was drawing to a close. "We will look into this new piece of evidence, ma'am…the hair sample from Leonard Walton's hat." He pushed in his chair, and Murphy stood up to join him. "But unless you're telling me that this Leonard Walton fella was good friends with your Mr. Thomas, my guess is that it's not a match to the hairs we found at the scene."

"We don't know what to say," Mary slowly forced out, apparently willing to speak for me. Which, of course, was perfectly fine with me. I didn't know what to say any more than Mary did. But I stood up, taking the detectives' obvious hint.

"Like we said, Officer," I finally spoke, finding at least some reasonably appropriate response to offer, "anything we can do to help, just let us know."

Mary slowly and hesitantly stood up, resisting the power of suggestion, but succumbing to it all the same. "Anything at all." She alternated glances between Murphy and Longfellow, before uttering to no one in particular. "I just don't get it. It doesn't make any sense."

"That's what we're hoping to do," Longfellow assured her. "Make sense of it all. We're doing our best."

"We know you are, Detective," I offered in the way of understanding. "It's just a lot to take in. A shock is all. There has to be some reasonable explanation for this. There just has to be."

Mary collected her purse and threw it over her shoulder as she slowly advanced toward the door. I followed close behind her.

"Thank you, officers," she said.

"Thank you," I echoed.

As Mary opened the door and got halfway out, Longfellow

stopped us. "Just one more thing," he said.

There it was. Detective Columbo reincarnate. The *one more thing* and everything.

"Mr. Wilhelm," he rasped. I froze for a second, then turned around to look at him. His face bore a forced and counterfeit welcoming half-grin. "Detective Murphy and I were wondering if we could have one more word with you, Mr. Wilhelm." Longfellow then quickly looked over at Mary, who had turned around in the doorway in curiosity. He then added a stipulation: "In private."

CHAPTER 42

Five Weeks Ago

HE WAITS in a plush leather chair in the lobby, looking up at the Greek columns that extend high into the recesses of the cathedral ceilings. Light flows majestically into the room through the large windows near the front of the lobby, casting its aura onto the polished marble floors of the interior.

She approaches him, holding a manila folder affixed to a clipboard under one arm and a small cardboard box, the size of a jewelry box, in the other. She takes a seat next to him. "Welcome back, Mr. Thomas."

"Hi," he responds.

As she sets the small box on the table, she extends a warm smile. "I trust we are doing everything to satisfactorily secure your financial future," she says, almost in the form of a confirmatory question. He nods in the affirmative, as he watches her open the manila folder and extend the clipboard for him to place on his lap. As he accepts it, she reaches over to the coffee table to open the small box, placing its cover upside down underneath the bottom. She holds the box in the air in front of him. Looking only out of the corner of his eye, he takes a thumb and presses it firmly onto the ink blotter that is situated inside the box. He takes his ink-stained thumb and presses it firmly and forcefully onto the page in front of him. She re-closes the box and then hands the man a moist towelette. He accepts it and wipes his thumb clean, returning the inked wet wipe to her when he's done.

He takes a pen that was resting on the clipboard and signs the page, right next to his fresh thumbprint. He places the pen back down on the clipboard and hands both to the waiting customer service associate beside him. "Thank you, Mr. Thomas," she says. "Allow me to show you the way."

She stands up and walks across the marble floors, the sound of her click-clacking heels echoing through the room as they meet the floor with each brisk pace. He walks behind her, passing the teller windows, to a turnstile that needs to be unlocked with the push of a button under the counter, executed by the nearest teller to it. The woman leading the way holds the turnstile open for him to pass through it, and she follows him into the back room.

As they enter, she draws the floor-length curtain behind them. "Please, have your usual seat at the table, Mr. Thomas." She smiles at him. "You know the drill by now, right?" He smiles back and offers a slight head nod in acknowledgement. She walks deeper into the recesses of the room and takes a key out of the pocket of her pantsuit, then extends a hand back toward him. "Your key, Mr. Thomas?" He reaches into his own pocket and pulls out a small golden key and places it in her expectant palm. "Thank you, sir." She uses her key to unlock a door, then disappears into the adjoining room.

After a half a minute or so, she returns from behind the closed door, holding a long, narrow, four-inch-high-by-12-inch-wide metal box, bearing the number 3473 on the front of it. She places the box on the table in front of him. He looks up at her from his seated position at the table and smiles. "Thank you, Judy."

"My pleasure, Mr. Thomas," she returns warmly. "Anything else I can do for you at the moment?"

He waves the offer off with a head nod, reaching down to pull back the lid of the box. He peers into it, then reaches into his pocket to remove a sharpie pen and a small pad of yellow sticky notes. He writes a short message on the top sheet, then removes it from the pad, affixing it to the underside of the lid of the box.

"That'll be all, Judy. Thank you."

"I'll be just outside," she responds. "Give us a holler when you're all set. You know where the buzzer is."

"Thank you."

She exits the room, pushing aside the curtain as she walks through it, then making sure it's closed as she's behind it. She pushes her way through the turnstile upon hearing the click, and click-clacks her way back to her desk. She immediately begins typing at her computer upon taking her seat.

Five minutes pass, and she hears the soft buzzing emerge from behind the tellers' windows. She rises quickly from her chair to return to the back room, being clicked in by the diligent teller controlling the turnstile. She walks through the curtain to greet him. "All set, Mr. Thomas?"

He closes the box. "I think so. For now." He stands up from the table. "But I'd like to see Mr. Stenson, Judy. Along with the sign-in manifest, if you don't mind."

"Sure," she hesitantly responds, for the first time showing a hint of apprehension in the absence of utter warmth and sycophancy. "I'll let him know." She retrieves box 3473 from the table and returns it to the room behind the locked door, re-emerging after only a short time. She uses her key to re-lock the door behind her. "Right this way, Mr. Thomas. I'll let Mr. Stenson know you wish to see him."

"Thank you."

They walk together through the curtains, past the clicked-open turnstile and back out into the lobby. Over his shoulder are the straps to a small canvas tote bag, the size of a standard purse, with its contents hanging against his side, just above his waist. "Wait here for one moment," she says over her shoulder, near the middle of the lobby, and continues toward a well-kempt desk, behind which sits a bespectacled, balding man wearing a brown suit. They exchange some words, and the banker looks back at him, above the rims of the glasses that rest on the end of his nose. He gives her a nod, and she returns to her desk. He walks slowly to the middle of the lobby to greet the waiting client.

"Mr. Thomas," he says as he approaches, his hand extended for a handshake. "Welcome back, sir."

"Joel," he corrects with his preference, as he returns the obligatory handshake.

"What can we do for you today?"

"I'd like to have a word with you about my safe deposit box, Mr. Stenson. I've asked Judy to bring the signature manifest along as well."

"By all means," he confidently replies, then extends his hand back in the direction of his desk. "Please, Joel. Have a seat."

As they arrive at Mr. Stenson's desk, Joel takes a seat and the banker walks around to his side of the desk, welcoming Judy's return, who hands the clipboard and manila folder to Mr. Stenson. He takes his seat. "Now, what is it that you'd like to discuss, Mr. Thomas? Uh, Joel," he corrects himself this time.

"Well, Mr. Stenson, it's about my safe deposit box."

"Yes, sir."

"Or the contents therein."

"Yes, sir. What can I help you with?"

"I'd like to know what it's still doing here," Joel replies.

"I beg your pardon, Mr. Thomas?"

"The contents. I'd like to know what it's still doing here."

The banker stares back with a look of confusion on his face. He looks up at Judy for clarification, who remains standing beside his desk, and who offers nothing back but a shrugged shoulder. "I'm afraid I don't understand," Mr. Stenson begins hesitantly. "Is there some sort of problem? Is the box no longer to your satisfaction?"

"Open the signature logs," Joel coldly directs him.

Mr. Stenson opens the manila folder and pushes his glasses up closer to the bridge of his nose as he examines the paperwork. "Yes, sir, Mr. Thomas. And what am I looking for, precisely?"

"Yesterday."

"I beg your pardon?"

"Yesterday," Joel repeats. Mr. Stenson looks up at him. Joel continues, "I thought our arrangement was fairly straightforward. Rather explicit instructions, I thought. Our contract."

"I'm afraid I'm not following, Mr. Thomas."

"Look again. At yesterday's date line."

He looks down at the paperwork again, more studiously this time. He freezes for a moment. "I see," Mr. Stenson says, dejectedly, removing the eyeglasses from his face entirely.

"You see? Joel replies, a bit of disdain in his voice. "What's today's date?"

"The fifth."

"And yesterday?"

"The fourth."

"And tell me whose signature you see on the line for the date of the fourth."

Mr. Stenson cautiously returns the glasses to his face. He looks down once again at the paperwork, before humbly responding, "Nobody's."

"Nobody's."

"I'm afraid not, sir."

"You see my problem now."

"Of course, Mr. Thomas. I'm not sure what to say."

"I thought this was fairly simple, Mr. Stenson."

"It is, sir. It is. It's just...and this is certainly no excuse...it's just that...I was out ill yesterday. And there must've been some sort of miscommunication in my absence."

"You're right. That is no excuse. You know the drill, Mr. Stenson. I expected — no, in fact, I insisted — that this procedure be followed by you or any other employee of this bank."

"I don't know what to say."

"If there is ever a day," Joel continues seamlessly, "any day at all, that I don't arrive to execute the procedure, the contingency would kick in. You assured me of that."

"Of course, Mr. Thomas."

"So, I'll ask again. What are the contents of box 3473 still doing here at the bank?"

"There's been a grave mistake, sir. Please accept my personal apology...and that of the entire Main Street Bank & Trust organization."

Joel leans over the desk and places an index finger firmly and demonstratively upon the paperwork in front of Mr. Stenson. "If there is ever a day that I don't get here to personally sign this manifest and provide the proper biometric identification, it automatically executes the plan, is that understood?"

"Understood, Mr. Thomas. We send the contents of box 3473 to the address you provided."

"The very next day, Mr. Stenson. Priority. You agreed to all of this. We went over it, time and again. You gave me your personal guarantee. This would be the plan, no questions asked. Which is why I'm paying the arm and the leg to begin with."

"Please, sir...again..."

"I don't want another apology, Mr. Stenson," Joel interrupts, removing his finger from the table and leaning back in his chair. "I want your assurances."

"You have my word."

"That this plan will be executed as written, by whomever happens to be here, or not, on any given day. No matter what."

"You have my word."

"One-hundred percent compliance."

"Yes, sir."

"Without it...without one-hundred percent compliance, every time, by everybody, this whole arrangement is worthless. And if the arrangement is worthless, so is my business with your bank."

"My personal guarantee, Mr. Thomas. You have my word."

"Now. I need your utmost attention to this, Mr. Stenson." Joel looks around the lobby, then lowers his voice just a bit. "I may, from time to time, make slight modifications to the instructions. And when I do, I will confirm them personally with you, and only you...and as you said, demand your assurances that they be entered into the record of our agreement. I may need to change where you're sending the contents...I may need to change how and when...it doesn't matter. The point is, I need your complete attention to every detail, Mr. Stenson."

"Understood."

"And it has to be *my* signature. *My* fingerprint."

"Of course."

Joel pauses and closely examines the expression on the banker's face. He continues, while tugging on the straps of his canvas tote, "I'll be taking the contents of my box with me this afternoon, but I will be returning them tomorrow when I come to record my attendance, as scheduled. This may happen more frequently in the next few days and weeks, so I need your bank to make record of this each time I leave here with the contents of my safe deposit box. And when I return with them."

"Absolutely, Mr. Thomas. Is there anything else?"

"I think that's it."

"Very well. Again, please accept our apologies. It will not happen again. We take these matters extremely seriously here at Main Street. You have my personal guarantee that nothing like this will ever happen again. I will personally see to it, Mr. Thomas. I will treat it as a matter of life and death."

"Thank you, Mr. Stenson," Joel says, as he arises out of his chair, donning a pair of dark sunglasses. "It just might be."

CHAPTER 43

THE TALE OF THE TAPE

MARY stood frozen in the doorway leading out of the interview room, looking back at me as if she were waiting for me to come to her rescue.

"Sure," I replied to Longfellow's invitation. "That's fine. I'd be happy to help, Officer." I turned to Mary and began fumbling through my front pocket for my keys. "Why don't you take my car home? I'll get a cab back to my place."

"No, I'll wait," Mary refused, as I tried to hand her my keys.

"It's been a long day," Longfellow observed. "Kinda getting late. Why don't you go home, get some rest, Mary. Tomorrow morning, maybe we can all go pay a visit to Ziggy Walton together. Perhaps our united front will come off as less confrontational — more cordial than two police officers showing up unannounced on his front porch."

Mary continued to look at me for the rescue. But I happened to agree with Longfellow at that very moment. Besides, I had no idea why Longfellow wanted me to hang back, or how long it would take. So I concurred, "He's right, Mary. Here. Take my car. Go home. Pour yourself a drink...take a warm bath...get a good night's rest. I'll cab it home, and you can pick me up in the morning on the way over to Ziggy's." I looked at Longfellow, "That okay with you?"

"Absolutely," he replied. "We'll follow each over there together. Ten o'clock work for you both?"

"Works for me," I said, glancing over to Mary for confirmation. She simply acknowledged her agreement with a slight change of her facial expression, and reluctantly took the keys from my hand. "Great," I said, hoping to convey a bit of confidence to comfort Mary's obvious apprehension. "I'll see you in the morning. Pick me up at nine? We'll stop here, Detective Longfellow, before heading to Denton together?"

"That works."

Back to Mary, "Call me if anything comes up. If not...go home...relax...we'll talk in the morning."

She shot me a fabricated smile, then walked out the door, which Murphy pulled shut behind her.

With Mary now on her way, and me left alone with Longfellow and Murphy in the uncomfortable confines of the interrogation room, I wasn't sure exactly what to do or what to say, but Longfellow soon absolved me of options.

"Have a seat, Mr. Wilhelm," came the raspy directive. "Detective Murphy is going to fetch something, and we'll both be right back with you. Can I get you some coffee or something? I'm grabbing one for myself."

"No thanks, Detective," I declined.

They both exited together, leaving me alone in the room for my mind to race uncontrollably. What did they want? Why only me? Why no Mary? What have they been holding out on us? Am I a suspect, all of a sudden? Is this still something to do with Ziggy? Something they couldn't tell Mary? What was Murphy going to fetch? Is this an interrogation? Do I ask to call an attorney? Am I overreacting?

Graciously interrupting my wild, hunting thoughts was the opening of the door. Longfellow was returning with two coffees, even though I had declined, and he placed one in front of me. Some attention to detail, I thought. Some detective.

Entering right behind him, Murphy was wheeling a cart upon

which sat a large television or computer monitor, with some out-of-date electronics equipment on shelves beneath it. I swear I even saw a VCR. I couldn't help but thinking it looked like a high school's old audio-visual cart that the A.V. Club would clank through the halls and classrooms back in the day. The equipment looked like it hailed from that era — back in the day — as well.

As Murphy wheeled the equipment in behind him, pivoting it in the corner of the room to face me, I politely inquired, "What can I do for you gentlemen?"

"We just want to have you look at a few things," Longfellow responded, barely sipping from the steaming styrofoam cup at his lips. "Hope you don't mind us excusing your acquaintance," he said with a short pause, and then, "Acquaintance, is it?"

"Friend," I replied.

"Friend. It's just that, we didn't want to trouble Ms. Thomas any more than we already have," Longfellow continued. "She seems like this is all catching up with her. And I'm not sure she was ready for this."

"Ready?" I asked, the intrigue, I'm sure, apparent in my voice.

"You'll see," Murphy butted in.

Longfellow explained, "It's just a lot...for the widow to take in...or ex-wife, or whatever. Besides, we're just exercising an abundance of caution here."

"Caution?" I asked, again obviating my apprehensive intrigue.

"Well, you see, Mr. Wilhelm, Ms. Thomas said something the other day that we found just a little bit interesting. Especially given what we had found."

"I'm not following," I said.

"At Mr. Thomas's residence," Longfellow clarified. "In the basement."

"The basement?"

"Yes, sir. The basement. When we took you both to examine the loose cinder block in the basement. You know...to get your impressions of it."

"Yeah?"

"Well, Mr. Wilhelm. Something Mary said led us to believe that she may have had an inkling as to what was hiding in that crevice."

"Hiding?"

"Yes, sir."

"What was it that she said?" I asked. "I don't recall."

Murphy stepped forward to deliver the dark punch line. "Cigar box."

I looked over him. "I beg your pardon?"

"Cigar box," he repeated.

"I'm sorry, gentlemen, I'm just not following." In fact, I did remember Mary uttering those words, but I was privy to the context the detectives were lacking. Should I share with them that we had been searching for something the size of a cigar box ourselves from the very beginning? Something that would fit into this mysterious safe deposit box willed to me by Joel, the same size of which would fit into the empty package mailed to Mary? I decided to hold off for now, to see instead where they were going with this.

Murphy reached onto the A.V. cart and removed a black box — sure enough, about the size of a cigar box! — and placed it on the table in front of me.

"Cigar box," he said a third time.

"What is this?" I asked obtusely. Of course, I knew what it was. It looked like an external storage hard drive that would hook up to a computer tower to provide added capacity to a typical personal computer from the late 90s. It was a bit out-of-date, given that most file and document storage was being handled in the cloud nowadays, but some less sophisticated types were still relying on the old tried and true external hard drives. For the tin-foil-hat-wearing crowd, in particular, they provided a secure, unimpeachable alternative to cloud storage. Disconnect the device from the computer, and its contents were entirely impregnable to online hackers or remote access of any kind. It was a relic of an older era, but there were still a great many who preferred manual storage to whatever advancements in technology were offering as better, and actually more reliable, alternatives.

"We thought you might recognize it," Longfellow shot back.

"Me?"

"Don't you own some sort of computer or IT company?" Murphy was quick to point out.

"Well, yes," I acknowledged. "But nobody uses these things anymore. Not my clients, anyway."

"It's a hard drive," Longfellow casually re-established for the room, as if he were entering an evidentiary exhibit in court and wanted to codify it for the official record. Perhaps he was just trying to get us back to the matter at hand. "For a computer," he reasserted the obvious.

I continued to take nothing for granted, glibly asking, "And what's it for? Why is it relevant?"

"We had found it at Mr. Thomas's residence," Longfellow said. "In his car, to be precise."

Murphy jumped in again. "Just sitting there. On the front seat. In an otherwise unremarkable canvas tote bag."

Longfellow added, "We searched the car, Mr. Wilhelm. Joel's car. It's been parked in his driveway ever since he went missing. We found this, and little else of note."

Then Murphy again: "Before we contacted you."

"So you already knew what was in Joel's basement when you had us down there?" I asked.

"That's right," Longfellow affirmed. "Assuming this here cigar-box-shaped object was being hidden in the same cigar-box-shaped opening in Mr. Thomas's basement."

"Then why did you ask us down there? Why did you need us to clear that up, if you'd already found this thing? This is your theory, not ours," I reminded them.

"We wanted to see if you'd recognize it," Murphy confessed. "Get your reaction."

"Well," I scoffed, though innocently, "I've never seen it before. I can assure you of that."

"We believe you," Longfellow confirmed. "And we don't think Ms. Thomas has seen it before, either."

"A relief," I observed. "Then why dismiss her?" I thought about that for a moment, then offered my suspicion. "You want to get our reactions separately? See if you can divide and conquer, is that it?"

"Not exactly, Mr. Wilhelm," Longfellow said, taking another faux sip of steaming-hot coffee.

"What then?"

He shot Murphy another one of his now famous knowing glances, before answering, "Well, like I said. Ms. Thomas seemed to have some sort of knowledge as to what might be in her ex-husband's basement. Hiding out of plain view. Something the size of a cigar box." I chose to maintain my silence about that still. He added, "And then there's the matter of the phone call."

"The phone call?" I asked. "What phone call?"

"The one from Mr. Walton," Longfellow calmly rejoined. "Ziggy."

"The *missed* call?" I objected.

"Yes, sir. The missed call. Your...*friend*...is the only person who's heard anything from Ziggy Walton since we've been trying to track him down. Sure, she says she hasn't spoken with him. But she showed us her phone." He paused. "Sure looks like Mr. Walton was sure as hell trying to get ahold of her."

"I can assure you they haven't spoken," I was quick to point out.

"Nonetheless," he replied, "we're just exercising an abundance of caution, like I said."

I surrendered my objections, if only momentarily. "So, how can I help with all of this?"

Murphy got immediately to work. He grabbed the hard drive from the table and returned it to the cart, stepping behind it to hook it up to the computer that was attached to the large monitor. He booted up the computer and turned on the screen.

As I waited for the screen and drive to boot up, I involuntarily reached for the coffee in front of me and took a sip, almost not even realizing I was doing it. The slight burn on my lip suddenly made me aware of my actions, and I immediately cursed Longfellow in my head. *Some detective*, is right.

"Well," Longfellow began. "Detective Murphy is going to show you a bit of what we've found on this hard drive. After you look at it, we'd like your impressions."

"Sure," I agreed. "Fire away." Though I feigned a casual disinterest, I was breathlessly waiting for the screen to come to life, to reveal what it was they had been sitting on. My hope — against my worst fear — was that it wasn't something so unexpected that I'd immediately regret agreeing to send Mary on her way. Suddenly, the screen went from blank to that of a typical computer's operating system desktop, outdated as it were. I could see Murphy fumbling with a mouse on the table in front of him, as his squinting eyes traced his own mouse movements on the large screen.

The external hard drive, once it mounted and its icon appeared on the aged desktop, was quite uncreatively labeled "Removable Hard Drive." Don't people personalize anymore? Murphy clicked on it. Inside the hard drive's main directory was one single file folder. Equally unimaginative was the title of this folder. "Files." Murphy double clicked on it. The new window filled with file folders, probably 15 or more of them. I quickly scanned to see their titles, no longer judging on creativity, but rather trying to study them all quickly before Murphy opened another window, in order to learn as much as possible — as quickly as possible. I only caught a few, but what I did see was enough to raise the hairs on my arms just a bit. There were others I could've recalled immediately after, but there were three in particular that would stick out among them.

THEORIES
LAST WILL AND TESTAMENT
SURVEILLANCE VIDEO

The only other item in the list, that wasn't a file folder, was a video file — a ".mov" file, to be exact. I watched the pointer, controlled by the mouse in Murphy's hand, moving slowly toward it. The file was named "WatchMe.mov." I gulped, not knowing what to expect, but intrepid enough to be spooked by what was about to come.

As the file loaded, and the media player launched, Murphy maximized the window so it would take up the entirety of the screen.

"You ready?" he asked, looking over his shoulder back at me.

"I'm ready," was all I could muster in response.

"Take a look at this," Longfellow said. "Tell us if you can make any sense of this."

To my utter shock and horror, shortly before Murphy hit *Play* and the video started rolling, there he was. It was him, staring back at me. A face I hadn't seen in weeks...maybe months. Joel Thomas, in the flesh, freeze-framed on the screen in front of my very eyes!

Murphy hit the *Play* button and the video rolled. Joel's image disappeared, as the video's thumbnail went away and the video cued to the beginning. An empty room, at first, then a man was entering from behind the camera to take his seat in a chair that looked like one I'd noticed in Joel's living room. There he was once again, larger than life on the screen, now facing the camera. Joel Thomas, the long lost, looking perfectly hale and hearty, was peering back at me, getting ready to deliver a message of some kind. He straightened his hair, and then looked down to the right corner of the screen, before speaking.

"Is it on?" he giggled nervously. "I think so. I think it's on." He readjusted in his chair before continuing.

"Um, hi." A nervous wave to the camera. "Um...if you're watching this — God, that sounds weird — but, if you're watching this, I guess that means...well, not good, I guess. Um, it likely means you've received the hard drive. And I'm hoping you don't! Honestly, I'm hoping you don't. I hope I tell you about all of this in person one day, and you can make fun of my paranoia. Hell, maybe it's a topic for Franklin's next year, who knows?

"Anyway, if you're watching this, it means my paranoia was at least just a little bit justified. You're going to think I'm crazy. Well, maybe you won't. After all, you're watching this, right?"

He cleared his throat, again displaying obvious nerves. Aside from my utter shock and dismay at what I was watching, I was struck by how unplanned this all was. The video, I mean. But at the same time, based on the files and folders, and the hard drive, and the video, it was all perfectly planned, I supposed...vintage Joel. But the video itself was rambling and disorderly. It was a bizarre paradox to watch, on top of all of the other anxiety it was inducing.

Out of the corner of my eye, I could sense Longfellow's eyes fixed more upon me than the video screen, and it made it all the more uncomfortable. Murphy, for his part, was perfectly content watching the screen full-time, with a smug confidence built into every knowing chomp of his hardening chewing gum.

Joel continued.

"So, when I tell you all of this...I mean, if you don't watch this, and I'm just telling it to you later, you'd better not laugh. I admit it sounds crazy. But just in case it's not...just in case I'm not crazy, well, I've planned for this. As crazy as that sounds now coming out of my mouth. I had a plan.

"You see, I'm getting a little nervous. Things aren't adding up lately, and it has me a little...well, a little paranoid. For starters, I woke up one morning several days ago and noticed that my bathroom window was half open. Now, does that sound like me? Leaving the bathroom window open in February? And before you say it does, let me just point out what else I noticed. Footprints. On the floor. Large, dirty footprints. They must've been size 12. Anyway, I know I didn't leave the window open, and I sure as hell didn't leave size-12 footprints on my own bathroom floor, so I was scared as hell. I looked all over the house. I carried a baseball bat around with me and everything. No sign of a break-in. Nothing was gone...nothing was broken. No other sign of an intruder. Nothing. Truly bizarre.

"I was willing to forget it all, as the day wore on. But then something else weird started happening. Max started barfing that night, and wouldn't eat. Again, I was willing to think nothing of it, but it went on for a few days. More barfing, no eating...for days. I took him to the vet, and they told me to change his food...something about a food recall from China or something. But it went on for a few more days. Again, call me paranoid, but the fact that it happened the exact day as the opened window, and I started getting all crazy, I guess.

"To top it all off, I was outside, checking the lawn and stuff outside the bathroom window one day, and Ed, my neighbor, stopped by. Said he didn't want to alarm me, but he saw a black guy — his words, not mine...so don't think I'm profiling or anything — a black guy come to the door and knock for several minutes the other night when I was out. When I didn't answer, he started walking around the back of the house and peeking into windows and stuff. Now, you know I'm no racist...and I don't care if the guy was black or white or brown or purple...someone goes lurking around my yard and peeking into windows, and I'm gonna get even more than a little paranoid, ya know? Anyways, it just reminded me of that time Ziggy's dad came in and busted the door down at his mom's and...well, call me crazy, I think my imagination got the better of me. It was just too much all at once...too many coincidences.

"Anyway, if you haven't turned this off by now — and who would blame you? — you're probably already saying 'Joel's lost his shit' by now. But if you haven't turned this off, I just wanted you to know what's up. As paranoid as this all may sound to you, I decided to do a few no-brainer things.

"First off, I'm installing a surveillance system in the house. Cameras. All around. I got a really good deal. And it's not crazy to have a security system in place, right? Can't hurt. So, I'll periodically look at the tapes. If I do see anything suspicious — and I hope I'm way overreacting here — I'll download copies of the video and start a folder on this hard drive for safe keeping. I'll have it...you can see it...you can show it to...whoever, I guess. If you need to, I mean. Better safe than sorry. So check out the drive for that video.

"Next, and don't call me macabre, but I've started to get my affairs in order. I never had a will before, so I figured it might make sense. I'm not getting any younger, right? And, I don't even have next-of-kin. The probate courts would have a hell of a time tracking anyone down to give my shit to. So, I decided I might as well get that all ironed out with an attorney. There's a copy of that on this drive as well. I'm leaving most everything to you, Mary. Who else is there?

"Lastly, like I said, I'm changing Max's food. Too many coincidences at once has my mind racing. And I'm all fucked up right now...about Russ...about Zig...about all of it. Too much death and illness in my life these past several years. So, forgive me for freaking out, but you know me...I'm a planner!"

He laughed to himself as he delivered that last self-deprecating observation.

"Oh, a final thought. If you do get this, will you show it to Jason? You and he are the only ones I know that I could even trust to get this to the police. Should it come to that. Again...drama queen, I know.

But, regardless. I think Jason would help. He loved us.

"So, if I'm wrong, I'm wrong. And this all ends with a happily ever after. And I'll be happy to take whatever shit you all want to give me at Franklin's over a beer next time. But if someone tried to break into the house, and so help me God, if he comes back, and I'm not ready for it, I want someone to know. And I'd want someone to do something about it.

"Thank you, Mary. I hope you're well."

Joel got up from his chair and walked toward the screen, eventually past it. Soon, the movie stopped, and both Longfellow and Murphy reclined back a bit in their chairs to turn toward me.

"So?" was all Longfellow asked.

"So?" I aped.

"Any reactions?" he prompted, suggestively.

I looked at them both. "Reactions? No. Sounds like he was losing his fucking mind, if you ask me!"

"This not typical for Mr. Thomas?" Murphy asked.

"Not at all," I replied. "I mean, a planner, yes. But paranoid? Never."

They looked at each other as if I was no longer in the room. Murphy took Longfellow's silence as his cue to open another file folder on the hard drive.

"We'd like to show you one more thing," Longfellow said, almost too casually.

Murphy's mouse closed the media player, then hovered over the file marked "SURVEILLANCE VIDEO." He double-clicked it, and inside the directory were eight or so video files. He double clicked on one that had no discernible file name — just a series of numbers and letters. The video player re-launched, and again Murphy widened it to full screen. He hit *Play*.

The video was fuzzy, and there was no sound. To make matters worse, it was obviously shot at night, as the only light cast onto the scene was whatever street light or moonlight was entering the windows from outside. It was hard to make anything out, but it appeared to be a shot of the kitchen area in Joel's house. Again, it was hard to tell, but I couldn't see any movement or sign of life on the screen whatsoever.

Finally, I saw Max walk into view. He paused, and stood there, apparently looking at something. His tail began to wag slowly. Slowly but surely, entering the left side of the screen was a dark figure, practically impossible to identify. The video was both grainy and under-lit, and the shadows of the room were cast over the person's face. The grainy figure walked over to pat Max on the head, then walked right past him. The figure moved past the kitchen table and all the way to screen right, near what I recalled was the pantry — the same pantry where Mary had found Max's dog food with the dead rats in it. Sure enough, Max knew the cue, and followed the figure over toward the pantry, probably expecting to be fed. The figure stopped there for a moment, and looked over a shoulder. This shadowy blur slowly opened the pantry door, and slid the large bag of dog food slightly out and opened the top of the bag. The figure loosened its coat and reached into the inside pocket, removing something to be held over the opened bag of dog food. Whatever it was, was shaken, like an oversized pepper shaker, into the bag. The figure re-closed the bag and shoved it back into the pantry, slowly (and apparently quietly) closing the pantry door. The figure patted Max on the head, then slunk off screen-left into obscurity.

As the video froze upon its conclusion, Murphy closed the media player and sat back in his chair.

I stayed speechless, as I actually was, hoping someone else would break the silence.

"There's your dog that didn't bark," Murphy noted, as he crossed his hands with intertwined fingers, resting on his stomach.

I sank bank into my seat, paralyzed in shock, which was, I'm sure, obvious to the two detectives in the room.

"That look like anyone to you?" Longfellow coyly inquired.

"How could I tell?" I rhetorically observed. "It was so dark. So blurry. Could've been anybody."

"Even Ziggy Walton?" Murphy jumped in.

I shot him a look so as to suggest he was jumping to a premature conclusion. "Could've been anybody," I repeated.

"Could've been," Longfellow acknowledged. "Could've been."

"What does the rest of the video show?" I asked. "The rest of the surveillance videos in the folder?"

"More of the same," Longfellow revealed. "Same night. Different angles. Different rooms. All of it just as dark, all of it just as blurry. What we just showed you was the best angle and lighting." He stood up from his chair. "But there'll be more," he pointed out. "We have a warrant in to the security company for the release of the rest of that video. There's gotta be more where that came from," he surmised.

"Until then," Murphy started, joining Longfellow in the standing position, "we'll have to play our hunches...and remember what Sir Arthur Conan Doyle taught us...about the curious incident of the dog in the night-time."

This time, the look I shot Murphy had just a bit more enmity assigned to it. "What are you saying, Detective? That Max didn't bark because he knew whatever intruder may have snuck into Joel's house to do him harm?"

"Not exactly," he snidely shot back at me. "Our theory isn't that Max was quieted by a friendly face — though, that's perhaps what happened in the video you just watched."

"What then?" I demanded.

Longfellow answered for him. "We don't think the dog was comforted by a familiar face on the particular night in question." He paused. "We think he was dead."

CHAPTER 44

Three Weeks Ago

NIGHT has fallen on a humble suburban neighborhood block. It's mostly quiet now, as families and singles alike have retired to their beds in preparation for the next day's arrival. An occasional car drives down the street, but most are parked, either curbside or on the driveways of the mid-century-modern abodes that line the street.

A car is parked on the driveway of an understated bungalow. The headlights illuminate only briefly, then the interior dome light fades on. The locks are disengaged.

Inside the house, a man is still awake. He wears only a t-shirt and boxer shorts, making his way around the house in his slippers, the home lit only by the soft illumination of a desk lamp situated next to a desktop computer in the living room.

He sets his car keys on the desk next to the computer keyboard. He then disconnects a wire from his computer, and places a piece of formerly connected hardware into a white canvas tote bag. He throws the strap of the bag around one shoulder and starts toward the front door.

On the floor in the middle of the living room, a dog lies on its side. The man's canine companion lets out a gentle but extended moan. Otherwise motionless, the dog's tail begins to slowly beat against the floor, in recognition of his passing human. The man leans over and reaches down to caress the dog's side.

"What's the matter, buddy? Still not feeling good?" He pets him some more, and the large mastiff lets out a comforted coo, akin to the purr of a cat. "I know, bud. We'll have you back to normal in no time. Gotta get you to eat something, though. I think you're gonna like dad's new food. Made in America."

He stands up and continues toward the front door, tote still slung over his shoulder. He turns on the porch light and descends the steps, making his way toward the car. He opens the passenger-side door and places the bag on the passenger seat. He locks the doors using the button inside the door, then closes the door firmly. The vehicle's dome lights fade to black.

The man turns back toward the porch, when he is suddenly startled. He pauses. His eyes focus on the left side of his house. His head tilts and his eyes squint to get a clearer picture of the darkness in the distance next to his house. "Hello?" he calls out into the anonymity of the foreboding darkness. He looks, and waits for a response. Silence. He repeats, a little louder this time, "Hello?"

Rather than return toward the porch, he slowly makes his way toward the side of the house. "Someone there?" he calls out again. He moves furtively...cautiously. The dew on the grass starts to soggen his slippers, but he continues his intrepid gait toward the side of the house unabated.

Something suddenly darts out of the darkness next to the man's house. He jumps. "Hey!" he yells, in a whispered breath toward the direction of the motion. The scurrying object runs into the cast of the moonlight — a cat escaping to safety. The man exhales and places a hand over his chest. In an actual whispered voice, he utters, "Get the hell out of here, dumbass."

He returns to the porch, and takes one last look back at the car parked on his driveway. He reaches just inside the house to turn off the porch light, then re-enters his home and locks the door behind him.

He finds the dog still lying on the floor in the center of the room. "Coulda used you out there, Max," he says, "We had an intruder of the feline variety." Max simply lets out a loud snore. He reaches down to give the dog a final pat on the belly, then begins his nightly retreat toward repose, stopping first at the computer to turn off the desk lamp.

In the bathroom, now brushing his teeth, he watches his image in the mirror self-administering a thorough dental cleanse. He looks quickly over at the closed bathroom window to his right, then moves his eyes back to his reflection, as he briskly brushes his rear molars. His eyes suddenly dart off of the mirror when he hears the creak of the home's wooden floors echo from the other room. He calls out to it, "You coming to bed, Max?" He finishes his nightly routine with a gargling rinse, then extinguishes the bathroom light.

He makes a right turn into the adjacent bedroom, turning on the light as he enters and looking down at the empty floor. His head turns back toward the living room. "Max?" he summons. "That you out there? Come on to bed, buddy." He flips off the light, then turns back the bed and sits down on it, placing the bedding over his legs. "Come on, Max." He waits to hear his loyal beast making his way toward the bedroom, but the house remains silent. He lets out a frustrated sigh, then rips the sheets off his lap to stand up.

Walking out of the bedroom, he calls again. "Max." He stumbles in the dark back to the computer desk and turns the desk lamp back on. He looks down to the floor where he last saw his four-legged roommate, and finds the dog still lying there. The dog lets out another extended groan. "Fine," the man says, under his breath. "Sleep out here tonight."

As he's reaching to turn the desk lamp off once again, he is frozen at the sound of another creak escaping from his old home's wooden floors. He stands still, slightly hunched over next to the lamp. His head turns slowly to survey the room. "Hello?" Rather than switching off the lamp, he erects himself and calls out to the emptiness of the house again. "Hello?"

He waits for a response. When none is forthcoming, he steps slowly and cautiously in the direction of the kitchen. He moves toward the sink without turning on any lights as he enters the kitchen. Standing in front of the a sink full of dirty dishes, he reaches up to a cupboard and pulls out a drinking glass. He turns on the water and fills the glass. Once it fills, he turns off the water and moves the glass slowly to his mouth.

Creak.

He abruptly turns around, spilling much of the water on his t-shirt as he does. He clumsily places the glass on the kitchen counter without looking, spilling some more on the counter. His eyes squint to bring focus to his stare, holding his breath as he stands, refrozen and motionless with his back against the sink.

The man exhales, and his whole body relaxes in relief. "Oh. Hey," he utters. "What are you doing here?" He pauses for only a moment, and then, "How did you get in?"

CHAPTER 45

THE FIGURE IN THE DARK

I KNEW, as I exited the cab, that it wouldn't be straight to bed for me. Not by a long shot. Not with the adrenalin still pumping through my blood like that. I handed the cabbie a 20 and stepped out into the pouring rain. Thankfully, it was just a short walk from the curb up to the entrance of my building. I scurried toward it as quickly as I could.

When I got back up to my apartment, I headed straight for the computer to boot it up. It was nice to be back in front of a real set-up for a change. It would only take a few seconds for the system to awaken, but it was enough time for me to mentally relive the day's events, like, as they say, one's life flashes before one's eyes right before one's demise. It was all a quickly paced blur, but I could not get the image of that surveillance video out of my mind. It was the imperfect cap to a whirlwind of a day, and it was the haunting reason I wouldn't be turning in for the night. At least not until I checked something out.

When I was at the police station, something of interest caught my eye. Though my eyes were transfixed on what little action I was able to make out through the blurry, grainy coverage of the surveillance camera video, I did make particular note of a watermark logo that was affixed to the lower left corner of the screen while the video played. "SafeHouse," were the words in the logo. An apt name, I thought, for a home security company, and an admirable play on words, to boot.

The first course of action was to Google "safehouse security, calhoune." Sure enough, the first result was ostensibly exactly what I was looking for. I clicked on the blue link. A quick review of the website confirmed that I was likely in the right place. In the upper-right-hand corner of the screen, I saw more precisely what I was in search of. "LOG IN," the link read. I clicked on it.

The log-in screen popped up. I immediately keyed in Joel's email address into the username field, and the only password that would come to mind: *M@dM@x08*. I hit *Enter*. To my slight surprise and disappointment, I received an error message: *The username or password you've entered does not match our records. Please check your credentials and try again.* I sat back in my chair in pensive disappointment. Did I have the right company? Joel was so damned predictable, there's no way he used a different password for this...for the first time in his life. I tried the username and password again, considering the likelihood that I had entered a typo in my zealous haste. I hit *Enter* once again, and the same error message appeared.

I hit the *Back* button on my browser, hoping to find another SafeHouse Security Company serving the Calhoune area, but none of the other search results appeared to be a match. I went back to my original result. What was I missing? I tried a bunch of other variations on the password, replacing the @ with an actual *a*, removing the case-sensitivity, eliminating the *08*, and so on, but nothing I did granted me access. For a moment, I considered clicking on the *Forgot Password?* link, but that would require hacking into Joel's email account to retrieve the auto-generated password-reset message, and that didn't seem like the wisest course of action at the moment, given everything that was going on at the time. I was stumped, and I sat there for several seconds, staring at the screen for inspiration.

Then it dawned on me. This was a personal matter. Joel would use his personal email address, not the work address he'd typically used as his primary. I quickly typed his personal email address into the username field, then the password — *M@dM@x08* — in the field below, finally hitting *Enter*.

"Welcome back, Joel!" read the message in big bold letters splashed across the screen, as my eyes widened with triumphant wonder. My eagerness was tempered, suddenly, as I looked below the *welcome* line. It read, *"We don't recognize the computer or device you're attempting to log in on. Please answer a few security questions for your own privacy protection in order to proceed to your account."*

No problem. The first: *In what city did you attend high school?* Easy. *Calhoune*, I typed. The second: *What is your mother's maiden name?* Of course. I typed in the answer, *Mannheim*. And finally: *What is the name of your favorite pet?* It took me less than a second to key in the final response, *Max*, before hitting the *Submit* button.

Sure enough, I was granted access! My pulse heightened, and my breath shortened, as I quickly surveyed the screen, looking for direction. Where to click? I scanned through the links as quickly as I could. *My Account... Settings... Support... Update Records... Watch Live...* and, finally, *Video Archive*. There it was. I went right for it.

When I clicked on the Video Archive, a whole slew of folders appeared, each assigned a name bearing a month and year. For Joel's account, there were only two months that appeared to have records in them, indicated by the *(12)* and *(28)* next to the months listed. I clicked on the appropriate one, and opened the folder. A long log of video files appeared, each tagged with a file name that matched the file naming style of the video Murphy and Longfellow had shown me. The naming convention made sense now. Each video file was assigned its title based on the month, year and precise date of its recording. Based on my understanding, now, of the file naming syntax, my eyes scanned the list until I found the date I was looking for. There it was. With both hesitation and anticipation at once, I clicked on the video, and it loaded onto my screen.

I took a deep breath, and hit *Play*. It was the interior of Joel's house — unmistakable, as I had been there so often recently. It appeared to be morning, from what I could tell. I dragged the playhead further along in the video, watching the time lapse of the video file as I forwarded the cue. As I scrubbed, when I could tell the interior of the living room had darkened for the night, I released the playhead and allowed the video to play at normal speed.

The room was mostly dark, but a desk lamp in the upper left corner of the screen cast enough light to make certain figures out — certainly better lighting than the video the detectives had shown me earlier. I could plainly see it was Joel's living room. I could make out the furniture...I could see that his out-of-date personal computer on the desk in the corner was plastered with sticky notes, just like at work...I could make out the kitchen in the background...and, there in the middle of the floor, I could see Max, just lying there on his side.

From the bottom of the screen, I saw a man enter the room from what I remembered to be the front door, based on my recollection of the house's floor plan. He was entering from the front porch. Sure enough, I could make out his build and his familiar gait, as he came onto screen. It was Joel. He was in his skivvies and slippers. He paused for a brief moment to pet Max, then headed toward the upper left of the screen and turned off the desk lamp. The screen went darker, and it was almost impossible, again, to make anything out. I fast-forwarded just a bit.

I could tell from the scrubbing video that the light in the room turned back on. I released the cue, and the video resumed. Joel was standing at the computer desk, his hand reaching under the desk lamp, apparently having just turned it back on. He stood motionless for a bit, hunched over, before finally standing straight up and moving toward the right top of the screen, toward the kitchen. The light was dimmer where Joel was now standing, I believed at the kitchen sink. It looked like he was getting a final drink of water or something, but the lack of light made it difficult to be certain. I could, however, still see Max, lying sound asleep in the middle of the living room floor near the center of the screen.

Joel turned around suddenly and threw the glass down on the counter. He looked startled. Through the poorly lit grain of a blurry video, I could see why. Standing just beside the kitchen table, now facing him, from about 10 feet away was a dark figure! The two of them stood there facing each other, and I couldn't tell if they were exchanging words or not. After what must have been two minutes or more, they sat down at the kitchen table together.

Almost immediately, Joel stood back up and went to the refrigerator. I could see, from the brief and dim illumination that the opened refrigerator provided, that he was pulling out a couple of bottles of beer. He handed one to whoever else was with him there in the room, still seated at the kitchen table, and placed the other bottle of beer on the kitchen table. Joel walked past the seated figure, down the monitor screen, past Max, pausing only briefly to pat the dog on the head, and then back off-screen-left.

I kept my eyes on the figure still seated at the kitchen table. Whoever it was reached across the table and pulled Joel's beer bottle in closer. This figure held it close to its chest for several seconds, but the person's back was to me, so I couldn't see why, or what this person was doing with it. I could see the figure look over its left shoulder, then slide the bottle back across the table to where Joel had left it.

Eventually, Joel re-entered the screen from the left, now wearing pajama pants and with his slippers back on. He rejoined the figure at the kitchen table, and the two of them sat there, apparently talking for several minutes. I couldn't make anything out, and nothing appeared to be happening, so I fast-forwarded the video some more — about 25 minutes or so of actual footage time. Joel was still seated, but I resumed *Play* right at the perfect time, as Joel appeared as though he was about to get up from the table.

The footage was blurry, but I could make out that Joel had placed one hand on the rear of his chair, and the other on the top of the kitchen table, in order to prop himself up. He struggled to stand, stumbling a bit as he got to two feet, nearly falling back down in the chair before regaining his balance. The other figure in the room stood now, and took three steps back toward the camera. Joel was staggering, like a boxer in the 10th round of a prize fight. He leaned on the table and chair to make his way toward the other figure, who took another couple of steps back toward the camera, still a dark and grainy blur. Joel made his way to the near end of the kitchen table and stood there, if you can call it that, looking at the figure in front of him. He was swaying, like a man who had consumed 14 Heinekens, not one.

Slowly, I could see Joel losing his balance again. Mid-sway, his body became lifeless and formless, then suddenly fell backward. I think I saw his head hit the kitchen table on the way down. The figure sort of leapt toward him to break his fall, but didn't try hard enough or react quickly enough to catch Joel's fall. His head bounced off the table and his body lunged to the floor. The figure approached the fallen body and kneeled over it for a bit. The figure then stood up, and walked behind Joel's idle body. The grainy blur bent over and grabbed both of Joel's wrists, hunched over him. This person then took labored steps backward and toward screen-right, dragging Joel's body toward the pantry. The dark figure dragged and dragged, until they were both off-screen, behind the pantry and into a short hallway that I recalled would lead out to Joel's rear mudroom.

Aside from Max's body, the room was otherwise empty for several seconds. Finally, the figure re-emerged from the mudroom, apparently, and approached the area of the kitchen near the table where Joel had hit his head and fallen unconscious. The looming, blurry blob knelt down to examine something on the floor next to the kitchen table, then quickly stood up. The figure began to pace the kitchen, opening cupboards, peering into the pantry, and circling purposefully around the kitchen table in search of something or another.

It then moved into the living room, into better light, causing my pulse to heighten all the more. Would I finally get a look at this mysterious dark character?! The figure stopped when it got to Max, and knelt down on one knee next to him. I was beginning to learn, from the figure's build, clothes and movements, that I was probably watching a man on the screen in Joel's living room. He placed an open hand on Max's chest, then lowered his head and put an ear to Max's mouth. Max didn't react at all; just lied there without so much as a tail wag this time. The figure stood up from his genuflected posture and moved forward in the living room toward the camera.

The desk lamp had remained illuminated, so if there was a chance I was going to see the face of this mysterious dark intruder, this was going to be it! He stood up and examined the room, his head darting back and forth. Finally, he was frozen, as he looked up in the direction of the camera, apparently finally noticing that he was being watched. He stared at the camera dumbfounded, and stood there for three seconds or more, and finally I had my answer.

At long last, I saw the face of the intruder. I was certain now. It was a man. It was a face I certainly recognized, and the image was unmistakable. I hit pause on the video, just to be sure. There was no remaining doubt. Plain as day, and in a room now lit well enough to remove both the shadows and grain from the figure's face. It was definitely a *him*. And it was definitely *the him* I recognized. Longfellow would be proud and vindicated.

It was, after all, the image of a *black fella*. There — staring right back at me, as I tightened a vice grip around the computer mouse in my hand and sat, mouth agape, looking back at the screen — was none other than the perpetrator himself: Ziggy Walton.

CHAPTER 46

Two Weeks, Five Days Ago

AN OLDER, balding man wearing a dark blue suit sits at his orderly desk, talking into the phone as he reviews the paperwork in front of him, through spectacles that rest upon the end of his nose.

A woman approaches his desk, the click of her heels echoing off the marble floors into the cavernous room with tall cathedral ceilings and prominent Greek columns. From his seated position behind the desk, he raises a hand in her oncoming direction to stave off her interruption, continuing his conversation into the phone without so much as extending her a welcoming glance.

"Yes, ma'am," he relays into the phone, "four-point-nine percent. Annual yield. That's right."

She waits at the side of his desk holding a manila folder attached to a clipboard. She taps her toe anxiously but lightly on the floor, waiting for the bespectacled man to conclude his phone call. He gestures toward the chair on the other side of his desk as he looks up at her, practically commanding her to have a seat while she waits. She obliges, abruptly and impatiently.

He continues his conversation. "Absolutely, Mrs. Raymond. Anytime. You can come by anytime you wish to sign the paperwork. My pleasure. Bye now." He hangs up the phone and looks at the woman seated at his desk opposite him. "What is it, Judy?"

"I need to show you something, Mr. Stenson," she replies. "It's important."

"Go ahead," he casually responds, continuing to look down at the paperwork on his desk. "You have my complete and undivided attention."

She clears her throat before beginning. "It's about box 3473, sir," then leans over with a whisper, "Mr. Thomas's box."

Mr. Stenson pauses from his perusal of the paperwork to make eye contact with Judy. He removes the eyeglasses from his face. "What is it?" he anxiously inquires.

She places the clipboard in front of him on his desk, laying it carefully atop the paperwork he was reviewing. She reaches over to open the manila folder for him, then subtly pushes its contents — a piece of paper — toward him to examine. "Look, sir." She pauses. "At the manifest. Yesterday's date."

He returns the eyeglasses to his face and peers down at the paper she references. After a careful review, he looks back up at her, and slowly removes his spectacles once again.

"It's been two days, sir. No signature yesterday."

"I see," he says, slowly and apprehensively.

The man places the end of one of the arms of his eyeglasses into his mouth and bites down on it. He looks blankly past Judy, into the room in general, searching his thoughts. He then re-situates the piece of paper back into the manila folder and closes it, pushing the entire clipboard back toward the woman.

"Judy," he says softly and timidly. "I'm going to need you to bring me box thirty-four seventy-three."

CHAPTER 47

COMING TO TERMS

THE TEXT message from Mary indicated she was on her way. As I had picked up the phone anyway to respond to Mary's text, I decided to put in another call to Ziggy. I hit redial then waited...five rings or more, and still no answer. I ended the call, opting again not to leave a message. He hadn't answered either phone call the night before, and still wasn't picking up this morning. I thought about what message I might leave on his voicemail, but what was there to say that didn't sound completely messed up? I needed to talk to him in person. A voicemail wouldn't do. I sure would've preferred that such a conversation would happen before I show up there with Mary and two Calhoune Police Department detectives, but it didn't look like that was going to happen.

As I showered, I thought about what I was going to tell Mary, if anything. I knew she was still holding out hope that Leonard — or anyone in the world *besides* Ziggy — was behind all of this. I feared what it might do to her to learn about what I watched on that security video the night before. It would kill her inside. And it might totally render our visit to see Ziggy pointless. How would she react? Would she be able to maintain her composure? One thing was certain: I definitely wasn't going to give Ziggy up to the police without giving him the opportunity to clear things up. That was their job...I was just doing it for them, better than them, as it turns out.

So, no. I wouldn't tell Mary much on the way to the police station, if I could get away with it. And I wouldn't tell Longfellow or Murphy about the extra video I'd found until there were no other options. I was fairly certain that confessing to hacking into someone else's private security account was not the type of information you typically offer up freely to the authorities. Besides, this was their case. Work it. Sure, Ziggy was going to have to get himself out of this, but I wasn't going to work the other side, either.

On the drive to the police station, Mary peppered me with a million questions about why Longfellow asked me to hang back. I saw no need to lie to her about this, but Longfellow and Murphy both asked for my discretion in relaying anything to Mary for the time being. To be honest, it felt like they were more than *asking*. My options were limited. I could tell her, and lie to them (which they would no doubt sense); or I could lie to her, and extend my loyalties to Longfellow. I opted to play the middle, and told her — in the strictest of confidence — that they had gotten their hands on some of the surveillance video from Joel's house. She remembered that the police had discovered the existence, and subsequent removal, of surveillance equipment, so it wasn't all that shocking to her. I also took great pains to assure her that the video was too dark, too blurry and too grainy to make much of anything out, so I hinted at the suggestion that it was much ado about nothing, squirming in my chair just a bit, as I recalled what the SafeHouse video logs had actually revealed.

"Figures," she said, offering thinly veiled commentary on my reassurances. "They're just so damned determined to pin this on Ziggy...without any evidence whatsoever."

I squirmed again.

When we got to the police station, Murphy and Longfellow were awaiting our arrival on the front steps. I pulled my car up and used the button to roll down Mary's window. I lowered my head to look out the window to greet them.

"Morning, Officers."

Longfellow approached the car, while Murphy hung back. He leaned down to meet my eye. "We'll pull around," he said. "You can follow us to Mr. Walton's residence," he added, before heading off to retrieve their means of transportation. And soon, we were caravanning to pay our unannounced visit to Ziggy.

Denton is not the best part of town. There are pockets of acceptability, but they represent the rose between many thorns, as opposed to the other way around. Ziggy had continued to live with his mother long after college, even though he had found work and eventually started having a somewhat serious on-again, off-again relationship with Traci, a woman he met at work shortly after graduation. It was probably just as well that he never moved in with Traci, as Ziggy's mom, I'm sure, felt much more comfortable having a man around the house.

Ziggy's house, in particular, was one of the proverbial roses. He and his mom enjoyed working in the yard together, keeping the house well kept, both inside and out, actually. I used to surmise that it must have been cathartic to keep a beautiful home, perhaps in defiant and overt resistance to the ugliness that Asshole had continually tried to interject into their lives.

It felt so surreal, then, to watch Longfellow's car pull into Ziggy's mom's driveway, and not one of the any number of crack houses that almost assuredly littered the block. He pulled fairly far up the driveway, so as to allow room for us to pull in behind him.

Longfellow and Murphy got out of their car, and waited for us to do the same. We met them at the front of their vehicle, and Longfellow stood for a moment with his hands on his hips, staring at the house with a fierce, pained interest. He looked at me, "You ready for this?"

I nodded.

"Let's hope he answers this time," Murphy said.

Mary stepped forward abruptly. "Detective?" she beckoned to Longfellow. "Would you mind if I went to the door first?" She smiled graciously, so as to butter him up just a bit, I thought. "He might answer for me."

Longfellow looked at Murphy for only a second before looking back at Mary. He nodded his approval.

"Thank you, sir," she practically exhaled, then started toward the front door.

The three of us waited near the hood of Longfellow's car, watching Mary step up on the porch and approach the door. She looked back at us for reassurances, perhaps, then gently rapped her knuckles against the door. She waited only a second or two before administering a second round of knocks, adding the second time, "Hey, Ziggy. It's me, Mary. Jason and I are here with some friends. Can we come in?"

She waited some more. Longer this time. She knocked again. "Ziggy? You home?" She stepped back from the door just a bit, and the doorbell caught her eye. She reached over and pressed it a couple times. "Hey, Zig. It's Mary. Come on, open up. I really need to talk to you."

Mary took a few steps to her right and peered into a front window, placing her hands next to either side of her head and against the glass. She tapped gently on the window. "Ziggy?" she repeated, "You in there?"

She looked back at us, both in disappointment and confusion.

I could tell she could use a co-pilot, so I walked up to the door to take her side. I rang the doorbell again, and did my best to help, calling out just a bit louder than Mary was able, "Ziggy? Answer the door. It's me, Jason. Open up, bud. We just want to talk." I waited a few seconds, then knocked on the door, again, louder than Mary was able. "Ziggy, we're here to help. Whatever's going on, we can help you. Just let us help. Open the door, brother." I waited some more. "We can't help you if you don't let us in."

I looked back at Longfellow, both in defeat and surrender. The look on his face said it all. It was his turn. He was just starting to approach the door, his hand slowly moving its way toward the billy club affixed to his belt, when something suddenly caught Murphy's attention to the side of the home.

"We got a runner!" Murphy screamed, as he bolted off running toward the rear of Ziggy's house.

Longfellow immediately ran off behind him, removing the billy club from its holster as he started into a full sprint. "Stop!" he yelled, "Police!"

Mary and I looked at each other with jaws dropped, our eyes wide open. "What the hell?!" Mary blurted out, as I stared back at her.

Reflexively, I jumped off the porch and started running in the same direction the detectives had run off to, and Mary did the same. I looked further up the driveway, to the side of Ziggy's house, and all I could see was the back of Longfellow, lagging in chase behind the younger, more fit Murphy. Longfellow was rounding a corner near the back of the lot, and turning right into the alleyway that lined the rear property line of the lots on Ziggy's block. I picked up my pace to try to keep up, and I could sense Mary was not far behind, doing the same. As we rounded the corner, I could see Longfellow again, about 20 paces behind Murphy, who was running in full sprint. Sure enough, 20 or 30 yards ahead of him was Ziggy, running away at full speed!

As I ran like hell after them, I couldn't help but wonder what was going through Mary's mind right then and there. Surely she was just as able as I to figure out that it was Ziggy we were chasing, and more to the point, that Ziggy was in flight. Even with instinct taking over, that was a lot to process, especially for a racing mind in hot pursuit.

"Ziggy!" I heard her scream from my aft. "Please! Stop!"

From up in the distance, I could hear Murphy make his plea. "Walton! Halt!"

Ziggy ignored both pleas and, rejecting the physical pain he must've been in with his condition, continued to summon his younger inner athlete to make his escape. Despite Ziggy's athletic prowess, history and former pedigree, it appeared that Murphy was closing in on him, even as Longfellow, Mary and I were starting to lag farther and farther behind.

Without him ever breaking pace, I saw something fly out of Ziggy's hand, and into the brush to his left. It looked like an intentional discarding. Longfellow noticed it too, and broke off his chase to retrieve it. Mary and I sped past him, without so much as pausing to see what it was that Longfellow was tracking.

Up ahead, I saw it. Maybe even before Ziggy did, who was probably about 50 yards ahead of me by now, but only perhaps 15 yards ahead of Murphy. It was a chain-link fence, about 10-feet high, that must've marked the end of the neighborhood block. Was it the proverbial dead end, as much as it was the literal one?

Ziggy was forced to slow his escape as he approached the barrier, but he immediately began to scale it without giving it much of a second thought. Up he went, quickly and cat-like, but the slowdown was enough to allow Murphy to close the gap. As Ziggy climbed the fence, Murphy reached up for his ankle, but Ziggy was able to evade his flailing grasp. Undeterred, Murphy began scaling the fence himself, just as Ziggy was atop it, straddling the crossbar with a leg on either side.

Murphy was able to climb the fence skillfully and quickly, approaching the top as fast as Ziggy was able to swing the other leg over, just beyond the reach of a second flailing grasp from the hand of Murphy.

As Ziggy swung the leg, he lost his balance, and went crashing to the ground on the other side of the fence.

"Fuck!" he screamed out in agony. It looked like he turned an ankle on the landing. "Son of a bitch!" he yelled, grabbing for his lower leg. He lay on the ground in obvious pain, looking up in fright at Murphy, who was about to descend from his perch atop the fence.

Murphy alighted like Batman, and masterfully landed just beside his injured and fallen prey, rolling Ziggy into a clumsy tackle as he hit the ground. He threw the front of Ziggy's shoulders onto the ground, as he mounted Ziggy's back like a rodeo roper. Ziggy's face was buried in the gravel, as Murphy grabbed for each wrist and forced them into the handcuffs he removed from his back pocket.

"Ziggy Walton, you are under arrest!" Murphy forced out, through his panting breaths.

Mary and I caught up, now decelerating into a brisk jog from our all-out sprint. We slowed up just on our side of the fence and struggled to catch our breath, as we looked at Murphy atop Ziggy's back on the other side of the chain-link barricade.

Mary screamed, through her own bated breaths and the onslaught wail of a cry, "Ziggy! What the hell is going on?!"

He just looked back at her, tears now forming in his own eyes, with his face still pressed against the cold gray gravel on the ground. He didn't speak, but his eyes told a story of both horror and regret, along with the utter self-loathing that burdens one's soul as he devastates someone who thought so much better of him.

She repeated, "Ziggy!" Then, trying to compose herself, retreated just a bit. Softly and slowly, she begged of him, "Tell me they're wrong. Tell me they're so...very, very wrong!"

Longfellow was just catching up to us, his a slower jog than ours. He was breathing more heavily, and stopped a bit shorter, to put his hands on both knees while trying to collect his breath. In his clutch, he held something in one hand against a knee, hard to make out through his tightly cupped hand.

"What'ya have, sir?" Murphy asked him through the fence. "Find it?"

Longfellow pushed out the response. "Found it." He gasped some more, then held it up. "Seems Mr. Walton didn't mind parting ways with this here." He opened his hand to reveal its contents, primarily toward Ziggy. "Drop something?" he drolly inquired.

It was unmistakable now. A cellphone, for sure...but unmistakable all the more, given the protective case it was sheathed in. It was a dark green plastic enclosure, with bright orange accents, bearing the brand name of the company that must've sold or distributed this particular make of cellphone case to fans and brand loyalists as a clever promotional item: Heineken.

Mary obviously recognized it immediately as well, as the look on her face went from shock, to despair, and ultimately to utter horror, all in the span of about five seconds. I could see the gears grinding in her head as she pieced it all together — not least of which was coming to terms with the sudden obvious reality concerning the counterfeit text from Joel. *I'm fine. Call off the dogs.* It didn't sound like Joel, as a matter of fact. But it did sound like something Ziggy might say.

She turned her head back to Ziggy, who was more tearful now, but otherwise hadn't moved since Mary had last affixed her glare on him. She moved hurriedly over to the fence and kicked at it forcefully with the bottom of her boot in a display of utter helplessness, mixed with white-hot, blind explosive rage.

"How could you!? What the fuck, Ziggy! How could you?!"

Ziggy said nothing. He closed his eyes, seemingly willing to accept his due abuse. Murphy rose to his feet and pulled Ziggy's wrists to his own waist, in order to force Ziggy into a standing position. Ziggy obliged, but kept his head down, refusing to make eye contact with either Mary or me.

"Sorry, ma'am," Longfellow said, delivering his condolences in the same low, raspy, monotone and un-emotive voice we had come to expect ever since our very first encounter with him. "We'll, uh...we'll be taking Mr. Walton down to the station." He gripped Joel's phone and shook it slightly. "Along with this piece of evidence."

She turned back toward our friend, the apprehended perpetrator. "How could you, Ziggy!?" she verbally hurled at him once again. "Say something, you motherfucker!" Spit was involuntarily escaping from her mouth, and snot from her nose, her face red with rage. "How could you?! What did Joel ever do to you?! Nothing!"

Ziggy finally looked up at her. I could sense a resolve forming in the expression on his face now. He was determined to offer something in his own defense, but was either searching for the words or weighing the risk/reward ratio of saying anything at all. Mary continued to berate him. "He loved you, Zig! You know he did!"

Mary fell to her knees and threw her hands up to cover her face, finally forfeiting to the flood of emotions pouring through her body: a combination of mournful sorrow, shock, disgust, anger and spite. She sobbed harder than I've ever seen anyone sob, and I considered for a moment walking over to her to comfort her. Before I could, she cried out once again, but this time, more of a lament than a persecution. It was softer, more defeated, and through considerably more prevalent tears. "He loved you, Ziggy. You didn't need to do this. You didn't." Finally, she summoned the energy and fortitude to scream from the top of her lungs once more, "YOU DIDN'T HAVE TO DO THIS!!!"

Ziggy finally spoke up, offering the first bit of his own defense. "I know, Mary!" he snapped back. "I know. You don't think I know that? Why you telling me all this shit? You ain't gotta tell me all this shit now!"

Then his eyes turned slowly toward me. They were piercing. Cold. Devastated. Resentful. I was uncomfortable maintaining a lock on them, so I looked away just slightly. Finally, Ziggy finished the thought, "Don't tell *me* this shit, Mary...Tell *Jason!*

CHAPTER 48

Two Weeks, Five Days Ago

SHE DRAWS the curtain behind her and hurries toward the locked room near the recess of the nook. She reaches into her pantsuit and finds a small golden key, with which she opens the door and closes it behind her after entering apace. In less than 30 seconds, she comes back out holding a long, narrow metal box marked "3473" on its front, then re-locks the door behind her.

She tosses the box on the nearby table and frantically uses another key to unlock it. She lifts the lid and draws it back to open it. Upon peering inside, she abruptly shuts the cover, picks up the box, and races through the floor-length curtain marking the entry and exit to the nook.

Across the open room she rushes, the box held firmly against her body in her arms. The hurried pace of her high-heeled shoes clicking against the marble floors echoes out with each distressed step.

She approaches a desk, behind which sits a waiting man in a dark blue suit, holding his eyeglasses in one hand as he nervously chews one of their arms. She places the box on his desk and offers an opening salvo, "Sir…"

"Judy," he rudely interrupts. "Fetch the shipping box Mr. Thomas left with us. It has the mailing address already affixed to it."

"But sir," Judy insists.

"Please, Judy," he shoots back. "The shipping package."

Judy walks away from the man's desk as he pulls the lid open slowly to examine the box's contents, returning the spectacles to his face. He closes the top just as slowly as he opened it, then removes his glasses once again, returning the end of one arm into his mouth.

He lifts his head up from his desk to watch Judy returning quickly, holding a cardboard shipping parcel. She places the empty parcel on his desk and attempts again to get his attention. "Mr. Stenson," she begins.

He interrupts her again. "Thank you, Judy," he responds, in a calm, subdued manner. "But, apparently, the box won't be necessary."

"Mr. Stenson," she repeats. "About Mr. Thomas's safe deposit box."

"It's empty," Mr. Stenson interrupts a third time. "There's nothing to send."

"That's just it," Judy says. "It *was* empty…"

"I just don't get it," Mr. Stenson says. "Mr. Thomas was so adamant. So specific. So dogmatic about the procedure."

"It *was* empty," Judy again interrupts, "…except for this." She holds up in her hand a small yellow sticky note with a short message inscribed on it.

"What is that?" Mr. Stenson nervously inquires.

"A note," Judy says.

"What's it say?" asks Mr. Stenson.

Judy doesn't answer, but rather simply hands the yellow note to Mr. Stenson. He eagerly retrieves it from her and returns his eyeglasses to his face in haste. He holds the note in front of him and reads a short, handwritten message in thick sharpie-pen ink, which bears only two words.

Tell Jason.

He looks up at Judy over the top of his glasses, which rest near the end of his nose. "Well, then" he says softly, "I guess we know what to do."

CHAPTER 49

THE CRACKED WINDOW

EVERYBODY knows someone like Joel Thomas.

I once heard someone describe him as the man who was friendly with everyone...but friends with no one. Which isn't exactly true. It's not that he was particularly at odds with any one person, or even that he was standoffish. It's just that, when it came to having meaningful, deep friendships or relationships, there was nobody you could point to and say, "Those two are very close."

And this was a man who was married for 16 years. A man I've known since high school, and someone who was always "one of the gang." There he was...at every party...every night out...every group outing. But you would be hard-pressed to say why, if asked.

Sure, a person like Joel Thomas may have "loved ones" over the course of his or her lifetime. But nobody will be seen wailing at the funeral...just heads bowed in subdued reverence.

That was Joel. Will he be missed? Maybe. Mourned? I guess.

Forgotten? Of course.

He was unspectacular. And, for that, expendable.

Well, maybe *expendable* is a bit harsh. But I search for a better word, and none is forthcoming. I could sugar coat it for you, I suppose. But why bother? Why now? The facts have no bias nor maudlin sentimentality.

After 30 years, you see, I struggle to explain away a feeling I've had ever since the first time I laid my eyes on Mary that brisk Autumn afternoon on the campus of Manchester College: Joel Thomas is in the way. And he always has been.

There was a calculus that ran through my mind every so often these past three decades. If Joel were to disappear, who would go searching? Who would miss him? Would life move on? I believe I got my answer three years ago, when Mary and he finally announced that they would be amicably divorcing. You could say the love had faded, but if you ask me, there was never any real love lost to begin with. From the outside looking in, it smacked of the prototypical loveless marriage. Stay together for the convenience of it all, not the passion. There weren't even any children. Hell, Mary said herself: his only real reaction to her asking for a divorce was, "I want the dog." Does that sound like the tragic ending to a fairy-tale romance to you?

True, Mary did go searching for Joel when he actually disappeared. And so did I. But honestly, would either of us been on that wild goose chase had Mary not received that package in the mail? Somehow, I doubt it.

There's a song that's been irremovable from my hard wiring, ever since I first heard it the week of graduation — the week we all made the 'Til Death Do Us Part pledge, ironically. It's a song by Barenaked Ladies: "The Wrong Man Was Convicted." If you ever want a taste of the torturous pain I've carried with me through these years, you should listen to it. Every time they showed up together. Every time they left together. Their wedding. Their honeymoon. Their...whole life together. The one they built for themselves in the suburbs. That was my life. Joel was just living it for me. This is the song that captures that agony perfectly.

The whole thing will cut you to the core, but for a taste, consider the chorus.

He sings, in part:

The wrong man was convicted
You know I did the deed
I thought that you would wait for me,
Your wants I needn't heed
The wrong man lies beside you
And waits for you to wake
And all because I lacked conviction,
The judgment's my mistake

You really should listen to it. In fact, everyone should. Especially Mary. I did my best to see to it that she would, but I can't be sure that it ever registered with her. Every time we got together — at Manny's, at Franklin's for one of our "reunions," at one of our houses...anywhere — I put that song on. Between that and Toad the Wet Sprocket's "Walk on the Ocean," I put the same two songs on religiously whenever it was my turn at the jukebox or stereo. I wonder if anyone ever noticed. I wonder, especially, if Mary did. I'm sure Russell noticed...he noticed everything. I wonder if he ever divulged it to Mary. Nobody ever mentioned it, so maybe all those quarters were spent in vain.

If "Walk on the Ocean" is the perfect song to capture the loss and regret of what is forfeited when youthful friendships outlive their meaning and relevance, "The Wrong Man Was Convicted" is the ultimate lover's lament. The singer goes on to bemoan:

I changed my mind; you said that I could change it back
I wanted space, and now change has fallen through the cracks
If I'm again beside your body, don't tell me where it's been
It's cruel, unusual punishment to kiss fingerprinted skin

Sound familiar?

Joel's fingerprints were all over my life — the one I never got a chance to lead. But now, the window has cracked open. There's a chance now. A sliver of hope. One that couldn't exist just a few weeks ago.

As forgettable as he was, Joel Thomas was equally ubiquitous. He wasn't simply going to disappear on his own, that much was certain. Despite my enmity and jealousy, though, I couldn't move forward with Mary knowing he'd be there to see every step, every pursuit, every consummation of what waited 30 years too long to get here. Even knowing he was gone, I could still sense his eyes on me whenever I was in his and Mary's house. Friends don't do that to friends. I hated when Joel referred to "The Bro Code," but there was, and is, no more unforgivable violation of the unwritten code between friends than that cold, harsh reality: You don't make it with your buddy's ex. You just don't do it.

Well, if a tree falls in the forest, and the ranger isn't around to catch you chopping it down, does anyone really care?

I'm sorry, but who is going to miss him? Really. Mary, sure...for now. But that will pass. She got over him once already three years ago. Maybe longer ago than that. Russell is gone. And Ziggy and Joel weren't exactly best friends...ever. I'm not sure that the two of them would have ever said more than one obligatory sentence to the other, had they not been involuntarily bound together by the rest of our friendships with one another. And it only got worse as time went on.

He can defend himself all he likes, but Joel could've done more to get Ziggy in that clinical. And Ziggy knew it. He could've done more to find a way to get that experimental medication to Ziggy once it passed through the FDA. And Ziggy knew that too. And he sure as hell could've chipped in when the burden of helping Ziggy afford his medication fell on me and me alone. Ziggy didn't know that, but I'm sure he suspected. All I had to do was confirm the suspicion.

Someone that cold and uncaring was not Mary's destiny. She deserved better. She deserves better. And now she has a chance at true happiness, with her true soul mate. Better late than never.

Now, I'm not suggesting that Ziggy had it out for Joel. Not at all. But once I confided to him what needed to be done, and why, his reluctance seemed only for appearances' sake. Maybe I was too eager to read that into his reaction, but he seemed legitimately on board. Not for revenge, necessarily. For survival.

Ziggy knew, over time, that he had but one ally in this world. At least, one ally with any sort of real agency. His mom doesn't count. I could afford the medication, if it came to that. But I also believe in recompense. He got what he needed; I was going to get what I needed. Balance. Equity. Partnership. And I was of the firm belief that Ziggy was deserving of that medication, regardless of what Joel or Ziggy's insurance company thought of the matter. I'm a big believer that justice must find a way to prevail, despite the universe's best efforts to deny it. Just ask Leonard Fucking Walton, that miserable Asshole. Hope he rots in there.

Ziggy would be the perfect partner. Motivation. Shared spite. Ability. A track record. And the perfect cover, should anyone get suspicious. He has the past. He has the, er...profile (at least in the eyes of the authorities, not my own). He'd have Joel's trust — at least at first. That would be key. He'd have to get into the house, at least a couple of times, without resistance or much in the way of noticeable ado — nothing to raise suspicions or report to the authorities. He was able to pull that off, no problem, despite the utter lack of relationship existing between he and Joel. I knew Joel would be happy to invite Ziggy into his home and life again — he always does. That's just Joel. He always needed people around.

I had Ziggy's assurances, and that was enough for me. If anything went down, he'd keep our deal between us. Hell, he owed me...and he knew it. And not just for paying for his medication all this time. If I hadn't walked in on Asshole beating the shit out of him and his mom that day all those years ago, he wouldn't even be around to need the medication in the first place! So, even if he got caught, he'd be bound by secrecy, and I trusted him implicitly. Anyway, he'd still get his medication, even if he did get caught somehow. If everything went according to plan, the worst-case scenario was a short sentence for conspiracy. They'd never find the body, so first-degree would never be on the table. We saw to that. He'd serve whatever sentence he might get after a speedy trial, and that would be that. He'd still go on to live a long, comfortable, pain-free life. And that's not nothing.

Besides, it would never come to that. Joel may have had the reputation of being the obsessive-compulsive planner, but Ziggy and I left nothing to chance. It was bulletproof. The timing was perfect. Joel's two-week planned vacation was the perfect amount of time to allow the trail to go cold, before anyone was any the wiser. By then, it'd all be done and over. Suspicion would be that he went away, and never came back. Who would blame him? What was left to come back to?

Furthermore, who would care? Who would notice? And, even if they did, well...we planned for that, too. He'd leave a note. (Don't they always leave a note?) It would be in his voice, sent from his email address...*to* his own email address. Anyone can make that happen. Even if strict security protocols were in place to ensure the impregnability of his email account, Joel would obsolete them all by using the same predictable password he used for everything, *M@dM@x08*.

Then, there would be the text message. From none other than Joel himself. Ziggy would hold onto Joel's phone, just in case we needed it. Turns out we did. Had Ziggy typed the message exactly as I had dictated it to him, nobody would've ever suspected it wasn't from Joel. Still, what he wrote was close enough. You'd really have to have a wandering mind to suspect anything nefarious going on. Or, you'd have to work for the police.

There were really only two unexpected eventualities that ever arose. The first: Why had Ziggy called Mary? Was it an innocent but ill-timed, fat-fingered mistake? Or was he getting cold feet? I never did get my answer on that, as Ziggy stopped taking my calls right around the time that unanswered phone call to Mary came through. I suspected it was, in fact, the cold feet, but he wasn't responding to Mary's return calls either, so I talked myself into believing it was all an unfortunately timed misdial. Probably best that we weren't in contact anymore, anyway. That would only raise suspicions about my cooperation in all of this.

The second surprise was the box. Leave it to Joel to plan all of the spontaneity out of everything. And what an elaborate plan it was! Such work to get word to Mary that he was starting to fear for his life. Why not just call her? Or the police? That was so Joel. He was probably too ashamed to be wrong. (That sort of came through in his video.) Or, he was secretly energized by the sudden intrigue in his boring, un-purposeful life. Either way, I should've known that he'd have something planned. But how was I supposed to suspect he'd put the wheels in motion to ignite some overly complicated Rube Goldberg machine the minute he went missing? So Joel. So unexpected, though. Still...I should've seen that coming. Turns out, he over-planned that, too. He takes the key piece of the machinery home with him — the hard drive — on the exact wrong night. But leave it to him to leave behind a sticky note in the safe deposit box. He left those things everywhere. Can't believe I didn't put two and two together from the get go on that one.

No matter. It wasn't enough. In the end, our planning was enough to at least throw the detectives off the scent long enough to execute the plan, imperfect as it may have been. I maintain that Ziggy panicked when he saw the surveillance equipment in Joel's house, but once he decided to tear it out, there was no putting that genie back in the bottle. If there were any mistakes, that was it. And it was Ziggy's. And it led the authorities straight to him.

My only regret is bringing Max into all of this. But that was Joel's fault. He insisted on tearing Mary's only "child" away from her in the divorce. It was his fault Max was in the line of fire. And, like Longfellow had so aptly put it, we would need a dog that didn't bark in order to pull this off. Even having known Ziggy, Max would've torn him limb from limb the moment Ziggy laid a hand on Joel. So, it was a necessary martyrdom for the greater good. He would've wanted Mary to be happy. For once, truly and deeply and passionately happily. May he rest in peace.

I do also feel bad that the worst-case contingency was necessary, but Ziggy knew that risk going in. I won't say that he wholeheartedly accepted it, but he went in wide-eyed. He knew what he was signing up for. And he reaped his reward for doing so. He won't be in long. And *ever after* is longer than whatever comes his way at sentencing. I'll be there for him. He won't be going through that alone.

I really wish Russell were still here to help me help Ziggy through this. He had a softer side to him, despite the harsh, defensive exterior. He was gone way too soon, and that didn't help the unraveling of The Pledge Society, as I always thought of it. Man, the irony in choosing those words to bind us together couldn't be more bitterly inapt. *'Til Death*...how little we knew that afternoon when we shared those words. How naive we were to believe that our bond would remain so unyielding that only death would separate us. Hardly. And how ironic that it would come to pass that way after all...one by one. But Russell? He didn't deserve his premature departure from this universe. We were all worse off for having it. Yet, I fear, it marked the beginning of the end for all of us. Or maybe it was just the end of the beginning. It was difficult to listen to Mary trying to force fit Russell's passing into having some sort of relevance to Joel's disappearance. But that says more about Russell than you'd know. He was a soul that demanded to be relevant, no matter what the scenario. He may be gone, but never forgotten.

As for Mary, this is her second chance, too. An opportunity to right some wrongs. To live the life unfulfilled. No, we can't turn back the clock, no matter how many times I may have wanted to. But now we don't have to. We can simply watch it move forward together — for the first time, together.

I could sense her softening, even before we both came to understand that Joel was gone for good. I dare say, she even welcomed it. How could she not? I know my feelings were not unrequited. She wore it on her face — Russell even said as much. The smiles. The tears. The soft caress on a wrist to comfort an old friend. An old flame, even?

I've played that night back in my head a million times by now. What if Joel hadn't walked in on us? What if he had gone home from school that weekend, like he said he was going to? What if I hadn't gone to him, to apologize to him? What if Mary simply pulled me back down into bed, consequences be damned? How our lives would've changed. How unnecessary this would've all been. How unwasted these twenty-some years would've become. How different Mary's wedding day may have been...for both of us.

Who's breathless now? Who only hyperventilates?
Who'd die for you? Who's dying inside anyway?
Which one of us is sunshine and which one's growing dim?
When two men dream of you at night, do you just dream of him?

In some ways, you might say this whole thing was Joel's own fault. He was always there. Always in the way.

Well, no more.

Mary will come to thank me for that. Maybe not today; maybe not tomorrow. But soon. And then, the cracked window will open completely. And finally, after all these years, there *will* be a happily-ever-after. Ziggy will have his; Mary and I will have ours.

The long lost Joel Thomas will fade into obscurity, returning to the same anonymous void from where he came. My long lost soul mate will return to me. And a life long lost will have its day in the sun once and for all. Because, after all, the wrong man was convicted.

CHAPTER 50

Three Years Later

A RUSTIC yet magnificent cabin finds tranquil seclusion situated in the wooded mountainside near a stream that trickles through the hills to empty into the Tomahawk River in the valley below. The soaring wildlife flits from evergreen to evergreen, collecting supplies to build the perfect spring nest for chirping hatchlings. The sun reflects brightly off of the large windows of the cabin's facade, generating a reflective warmth that cuts through the crispness of the mountain air.

She sits inside on a barstool, cupping a warm cup of coffee as she watches the large-screen television mounted above the stone fireplace. She takes a sip and returns the cup to a saucer, then reaches for the remote control to turn up the volume. She calls into the other room over her shoulder, "Tom, honey. They're talking about that man on the news."

From the direction of the bathroom, beyond the expansive living room and down the hall past two of the residence's guest rooms, returns a muffled voice, echoing against the shower doors. "What's that, Emily?"

"That guy you know," she shouts back, a bit louder this time. "They're talking about him on the news." She twirls her long, curly blonde hair around a finger. With the other hand, she reaches for the remote control and turns up the volume yet again, before placing it on the counter next to her.

The news anchor continues delivering the update from the television...

Parole was denied earlier today for a Calhoune man convicted of conspiracy to commit murder, a story that made headlines locally three years ago this month, and eventually nationally on the popular true crime series, Crimes of Passion. Jason Wilhelm was sentenced to 10 to 15 years in Jefferson State Penitentiary for conspiring to abduct and do great bodily harm to one Joel Thomas, also of Calhoune, a man believed to be Wilhelm's best friend, and the ex-husband of a Hawthorne woman many linked romantically to Wilhelm.

"Tom, honey? You coming? Want me to pause it?" she calls out again, twirled locks in one hand, and her petite coffee cup in the other.

He calls out to her in return, this time without the echo of the shower doors and bathroom tiles. "I'm drying off, hon. Be right there."

Attorneys for Wilhelm pled to the parole board requesting leniency, pointing to time served, exemplary behavior and the fact that the victim's remains were never recovered nor identified. Had Mr. Thomas's body been found and identified, experts believed at the time, Wilhelm would be serving a maximum sentence of 50 years to life for first-degree murder. A third man, from Denton, Aurelius "Ziggy" Walton, was found to be Wilhelm's accomplice. He served two years at Jefferson State Penitentiary, also for conspiracy, but was released late last year, having received the lighter sentence in exchange for turning State's evidence against Wilhelm, in a plea deal worked out with the state's prosecuting attorney. Walton remains under house arrest.

In a bedroom down the hall, a man continues to get dressed, practically shoe-horning himself into trousers that are much too tight.

He grabs his wallet from the dresser and forces it into his rear pocket as he examines himself in the mirror. He reaches down to the dresser and picks up a silver chain necklace. It bears as its charm a weathered old dog ID tag, which looks to have once been affixed to an actual dog collar. A reminiscent smile begins to form in the corners of his mouth, as he rubs a thumb across the engraved inscription: *"Mad Max"*.

The woman watching television in the living room swivels on her stool to look back down the hallway toward the bedroom and sees him approach. "There you are, babe," she says to him as he approaches. "You missed it, Tom. Want me to rewind it?"

Joel enters the living room, tucking the dog-tagged chain into his undershirt with one hand while scratching his scruffy and fully grown beard with the other. He then uses his fingers to brush back his drying curly locks, the roots of which reveal a natural blond that has been dyed over. He struggles to button the top button of a shirt he has obviously outgrown, before turning his attention to the buttons on his cuffs. "That's all right, Em," he responds. "I'm sure they'll show it again tonight at 11."

"How did you know this guy again? Wilhelm something or other?" she asks.

"College buddy is all," Joel responds dismissively. "Turns out I didn't really know him all that well, to be honest."

Joel takes a light jacket off the back of Emily's barstool and puts it on. He leans over to kiss her on the cheek, reaching past her to retrieve a cardboard box from the countertop beyond where she had placed the remote. He hugs her with the other arm. "I'm going out for a bit. I'll be back...not too long, okay?"

She returns the kiss on the cheek. "Sounds good," she says, smiling. "I may be gone when you get home. Heading to meet the girls."

He puts the cardboard box under his arm and heads toward the door. "Have fun," he says, as he jiggles his car keys in the other hand, waving back to her without looking, as he exits the cabin with purpose.

Four Days Later...

In the living room of a well-maintained humble home, in an otherwise dilapidated neighborhood, sits a man deep in thought, seated upright in a 1970s-style armchair. An elbow sits on the armrest, holding up a loose fist that he holds gently against the front of his lips.

A knock at the door disturbs his trance, and he turns his head to see a courier descending from his front porch to return to his waiting van at the curb. The man arises and heads to the front door.

He opens the door, and the storm door behind it, to find a cardboard box leaning upright on the porch against the wooden exterior of the house. He leans over to retrieve it and examines the mailing address: Ziggy Walton, 38472 Acorn Drive, Denton. He brings the package inside and retakes his position in the armchair.

He opens the box, spotting first a typewritten letter that rests atop the box's contents, almost like a cover letter. He picks it up, and begins to read it quietly to himself.

Dear Ziggy,

I hope this package finds you well. Can you believe it's already been another year? Where does the time go?!

Anyway, I hope to connect again with you soon. In the meantime, here it is, as usual. Please let me know if something has changed on your end, and I can make the necessary adjustments over here.

Listen, I know I say this every year, but I have to say it again. I will never forget for a moment what you did for me, and will always be in your debt. I know full well that you had a choice that night, and I pray every night to thank the Good Lord above that you opted for mercy, rather than mercenary.

I will never blame you for what went down...you should know that. Without you, I wouldn't be here today. And I will go to my grave remembering how you saved my life. You didn't have to do that, but I believe God intervened that night — for both of us.

You will never, ever have to explain to me why you agreed to go along with it in the first place. I understand. I've forgiven you. And I hope you have forgiven yourself. Remember, it was you who changed course. It was you that altered the plan. It was you that reneged on the deal. It was you that resuscitated me. That's the Ziggy I keep in my heart. That's the Ziggy Walton I owe my life to. And I will never know any other.

Ziggy lifts his tearful eyes for a moment, to gaze deep in reflection out his front window. He returns to the letter.

Anyway, enclosed is another year's worth.

Ziggy holds the letter aside to examine the box's contents. Inside are 12 individually wrapped syringes bearing the brand name *Markana Pharmaceuticals* on the package.

I hope it's still working as well as you said it was. It may not be the original, but it's a damned good knockoff. As long as I'm here, I'll find a way to get it to you. You deserve it, and we both know why.

Give me a call some time. You have my new number (not many people do). I'd love for you to meet Emily some day, but we both know that's

not possible. I'm sorry that's the way it's gotta be, but that's the deal.
You might like our place up here in the mountains. It's away from it all.
Maybe we can find a way so you can see it some day.

By the way, I still wear Max's dog tag close to my heart each day...it's
painful and comforting at the same time. It's a difficult thing, to thank
you for saving that memento in the heat of the moment (and to thank
you for trying to save him as well). It stirs up a lot of mixed emotions,
but it somehow gets me through the day. It reminds me to forgive, if
nothing else...to live a loyal dog's life.

With that in mind, be well, my friend. I will keep you in my prayers
tonight, as always. Hope you're still doing well.

Until we speak again,

Joel (aka Thomas Aurelius, now)

Ziggy lowers the letter and places it softly upon the box. He returns
the loosely closed fist to the front of his lips and stares again out his
front window, a tear collecting in the corner of his eye, which is just
about to drop and roll down the side of his cheek.

Four Days Earlier....

Joel returns through the front door of the well-appointed yet rustic
luxury home. He throws his keys on the counter and removes his
jacket, hanging it on the back of the barstool. He picks up the remote
control from the counter and turns on the television, muting it the
moment he hears the sound come on.

Returning the remote to the counter, he heads into the kitchen
and fetches a drinking glass out of the cupboard, filling it with ice

from the refrigerator's ice dispenser. He brings the glass of ice with him back into the living room and walks over to a rolling bar cart situated next to the stone fireplace. He reaches down to grab a bottle of dark liquor from the cart, and pours it slowly over the ice.

He leaves the filled drink on the bar cart to mellow, then heads over to the stereo system. Next to a state-of-the-art audio set-up, he looks at a bookshelf filled with vinyl record albums. He scans them with a finger, finally arriving at his selection. He pulls it out, then gently removes the album from the dust cover. He opens the lid of the turntable and carefully places the record into position. He surgically lifts the needle and takes great care to queue it to Side B's second-to-last song. He lowers the needle, and the soft crackle is heard through the system's surround-sound speakers.

A haunting piano trill is heard, against the emptiness of the remaining orchestration that waits its turn to join in. Joel walks over to retrieve his poured drink, and escorts it to a nearby recliner. He takes a seat, oozing into the soft leather cushioning. He reclines the chair and leans back, taking a sip from his drink. As he takes it in, his mouth savors the smoothness of the finish, and he swallows it down.

The song begins to fully assemble now, and Joel stares off blankly into the open room. He listens, and he marvels. The singer begins. Joel reflects. The room is filled with the soothing yet spectral arrangement of an old classic from his younger years. A Barenaked Ladies song: "The Wrong Man Was Convicted."

EPILOGUE

The Wrong Man Was Convicted

Who's lonely now? Which one of us is suffering?
Who's in his cups? Which one of us recovering?
Who likes to look at pictures and cries, but way too late?
Who doesn't want to change a thing, accepting it was fate?

The wrong man was convicted. You know I did the deed.
I thought that you would wait for me,
Your wants I needn't heed.
The wrong man lies beside you, and waits for you to wake.
And all because I lacked conviction,
The judgment's my mistake.

Who's breathless now? Who only hyperventilates?
Who'd die for you? Who's dying inside anyway?
Which one of us is sunshine and which one's growing dim?
When two men dream of you at night, do you just dream of him?

The wrong man was convicted. You know I did the deed.
I thought that you would wait for me,
Your wants I needn't heed.
The wrong man lies beside you, and waits for you to wake.
And all because I lacked conviction,
The judgment's my mistake.

Who's lonely now? Who's reaching out to no one?
Who's lonely now? It takes one to know one.
I changed my mind; you said that I could change it back.
I wanted space, and now change has fallen through the cracks.
If I'm again beside your body, don't tell me where it's been.
It's cruel, unusual punishment to kiss fingerprinted skin.

The wrong man was convicted. You know I did the deed.
I thought that you would wait for me,
Your wants I needn't heed.
The wrong man lies beside you, and waits for you to wake.
And all because I lacked conviction,
The judgment's my mistake.

It's my mistake.

ACKNOWLEDGEMENTS

I would like to thank my wife for her support on this project: her coaching, ear, scrutiny, judgment and — not least of which — her editing prowess.

Thank you also goes to two musical acts (and their associated publishers, music labels, management, et. al.) for granting their respective permissions to use their lyrics in my book: Toad the Wet Sprocket and Barenaked Ladies.

"Walk On The Ocean"
Written by Toad The Wet Sprocket
Copyright © 1991 Wet Sprocket Songs (ASCAP)
Used By Permission

"The Wrong Man Was Convicted"
Words and Music by Stephen Duffy and Steven Page
Copyright © 1994 Sony / ATV Music Publishing UK Ltd. and Fresh Baked Goods, Inc.
All Rights on behalf of Sony / ATV Music Publishing UK Ltd.
Administered by Sony / ATV Music Publishing LLC, 424 Church Street, Suite 1200, Nashville, TN 37219
All Rights on Behalf of Fresh Baked Goods, Inc. Administered by WB Music Corp.
International Copyright Secured
All Rights Reserved
Reprinted by Permission of Hal Leonard LLC and Alfred Music

Special thanks go to Jennifer Baum of Scribe Publishing, for her invaluable guidance, support and advice.

And, of course, thanks to you, a reader of this book. It means so much to me that you took the time to read *The Long Lost,* a novel 20 years in the making. I sincerely hope you enjoyed it. Until next time…

ABOUT THE AUTHOR

Tom Nixon is an author and entrepreneur with writing credits to his name that span artistic genres. He has written multiple novels, two screenplays, several short stories, a children's story, and has five music albums in his catalogue, for which he wrote both music and lyrics. He discovered his passion for writing and reading at an early age, going on to earn a Bachelor of Arts degree in English from the University of Michigan. He resides in Michigan with his wife and children, along with a couple of the canine variety.

74742014R00231

Made in the USA
Lexington, KY
16 December 2017